WELCOME TO THE WILDERNESS

"You know what a roll-cast is?" Cuyler asked.

"Sorry, no," Frazier said.

"I'll show you. Watch me."

Cuyler put his rod together, attached the reel, ran the line through the guides, and bent on a leader. From his hatband he selected a dry-fly that bristled with dark hackle, and affixed that to the tapered end of the leader. Holding the rod horizontally in front of him, he gave its tip a quick flip. The line looped gracefully and rolled out over the water, the fly pausing for a second in mid-air, then fluttering down like a thing alive.

"You got it? Just don't try to backcast."

"I'll see what I can do," Frazier said.

Backing out, Frazier made his way slowly along the shore in search of another opening. Not for some time was he able with any comfort to get through the brush to the water's edge again.

Then when he stood there, readying his rod for a try at imitating Cuyler's roll-cast, he looked down and forgot about fishing. As before, the bank here was undercut, the water several feet deep but so clear he could see every smallest object on the bottom. What he saw was a turtle the size of a dinner plate tugging at something dark that looked like the torn, shredded remains of a man's clothing, through which something even more unexpected, more startling, became partially visible as the turtle continued its efforts.

It was the skeleton of a man.

THE DAWNING

HUGH B. CAVE

LEISURE BOOKS NEW YORK CITY

For Peggy

This novel is also dedicated to the memory of Ken White, Larry Dunn and Lurton Blassingame, who traveled these wilderness trails with me.

A LEISURE BOOK®

July 2000

Published by

Dorchester Publishing Co., Inc.
276 Fifth Avenue
New York, NY 10001

ISBN 0-8439-4739-X

The name "Leisure Books" and the stylized "L" with design are trademarks of Dorchester Publishing Co., Inc.

Printed in the United States of America.

THE DAWNING

Chapter One

He had set the alarm for 7 A.M., knowing he must not be late this morning or he might have no future.

But the alarm was not necessary. The numbing enormity of what he was about to do had created such a turmoil in his mind that sleep was impossible.

Not once had he even dozed off. At two, at three-thirty, again at four-thirty he had left his bed and prowled through the apartment, snatching up things he felt he must take with him, then discarding them with groans of frustration when he realized they had to be left behind.

Left behind for all time. Abandoned. No

longer to be a part of whatever life he might still have.

Then at five-thirty he got up to stay up, and by the glow of a flashlight—because there had been no power in this part of the city for nearly a month now—donned the clothes he had so carefully laid out the day before. And, this time in earnest, he took the empty backpack from the chair beside his bed and proceeded to put things into it. The very few, the heartbreakingly few possessions he was being allowed to take.

It was like dying, he thought as he carried out this final tour of his apartment. In order to go on living, all of them must give up practically everything that made their lives worth living. Each could take only one pack, and it must not weigh more than twenty pounds.

"And that means you *weigh* it," Gene Cuyler had warned yesterday at the professor's place, where they had assembled for a last-minute briefing. "On your bathroom scales, if that's all you have, but *weigh* it. We'll have canoes and other junk to lug over those portages—the guns, too—and we won't be able to take more'n twenty pounds each of personal stuff. And most of that'd better be clothing and at least one pair of extra boots apiece, you hear? Because where we're going there won't be anyplace to buy even a safety pin if we need one." Finding that funny for some reason, Cuyler had voiced the donkey-bray laugh they had come to expect of him. "So be pretty damn sure

8

you make every ounce count, you hear? Don't take anything dumb."

Like books, Don thought, pausing in front of the bookcase that occupied an entire wall of his small living room. We can take guns, but no books. Because, of course, Cuyler owned a gunshop and loved his toys the way other people loved—well, the way Cricket loved animals. Birds, cats, dogs, all kinds of animals. Like the little Italian greyhound she called Rambi because, she would explain, though he looked like a miniature Bambi, he was inclined to be pretty rambunctious. If she had to leave Rambi behind she would not go, she had flatly stated. "His ten pounds can be part of my twenty."

"And whaddaya expect to feed him?" Cuyler had of course challenged. "We're not lugging *dog* food along, for Chrissake!"

In her own way Cricket could be just as firm as the gunshop owner, even if much more quietly so. "Suppose you let me worry about that, Cuyler." None of them, not even his wife, ever called him Gene; it didn't sound right. "If he can't find food for himself—which he'll soon learn to do, I'm sure—then I'll share mine with him."

So Cuyler would have his guns in the days ahead, but teacher Don Neal would have to do without books. Yet, personalities and personal feelings aside, it was really not illogical, was it? Without the guns they might starve before learning other ways to obtain food.

Not due at Cricket's until eight, and with time to kill, Don stood before his books a good while, feeling a need to fix a lasting picture of them in his mind. As a teacher of special kids in junior high, he had used books every working day of his life until the city's schools were shut down. One slender volume on the teaching of English had his own name on it, and next to it on the same shelf were magazines containing short stories he had written and a scrapbook full of features he had done for the Sunday *Examiner*. The magazines were no longer being published. The newspaper—the city's largest—had been out of business for six weeks now.

But, dear God, what would he do in the new life without something to *read* now and then?

Cuyler was right, though. Despite his domineering attitude, the gunshop owner would probably almost always be right in the kind of situations they were likely to encounter from now on. Already in many ways he had usurped from Professor Varga the role of the expedition's leader.

Shaking his head at the thought, Don reluctantly returned to the bedroom.

The clothing and boots he had selected to take along were similar to what he had donned earlier: the kind he would have worn for a hike in winter woods, though today was the first day of June. As he stuffed the duplicate outfit into his backpack, his parents watched him from large, framed photographs hanging side by

10

side above the headboard of his unmade bed. At one point, out of habit, he had actually started to make the bed before realizing he would not again be using it.

Finished, he stood there gazing at the caring man and woman who had made him what he was: Bradford Neal, a cabinetmaker; Della Rodgers Neal, a teacher. Both gone now, though he himself was only twenty-eight years old. Father, a heavy smoker, had died of lung cancer. Mother had been one of the early victims of the violence, stabbed to death in a library parking lot one evening by a person or persons unknown who had merely wanted the few dollars in her handbag. Probably for drugs, though at that time the ghastly drug they called Halleluja had not yet made its fatal appearance.

Planning not to return to the bedroom, he bade his parents a silent farewell and went into the bathroom for a toothbrush, bars of soap, and a handful of the lightweight plastic razors he had been using since the power outage made his electric one useless. He would stay clean-shaven as long as he could, he had promised himself, if only to be different from Cuyler, who from the shoulders up already resembled some kind of black-haired Bigfoot.

Aspirin. Should he take aspirin? He was never troubled with headaches.

He dropped a small bottle of the tablets into the backpack anyway, guessing there might be stressful times ahead. Then he weighed the pack on his bathroom scale.

11

It was just under his allotted twenty pounds.

A book? he thought. One book?

He tried his Bible first, weighing it on a food scale in the apartment's kitchenette. It was too heavy. Returning to the living room, he reached for a paperback volume called *Our Road to Oblivion*, by their own Professor Varga. Prof's predictions were in it. And the formulae for such survival goodies as the concentrated food tablets and new insect repellant he had perfected in his lab at the university. With *Our Road to Oblivion* in the backpack, Don made for the front door.

But he could not walk out that way. Invisible cords held him, forced him to put the bag down and turn back. With his mouth dry, his hands empty at his sides, his heart beating so heavily he could feel the throbbing in his ears, he went slowly through the apartment one more time. Looked once more at his books. Paused before his tape player and realized he would not again hear any of the old Big Band music he had been collecting for years— Tommy Dorsey, Glen Miller, Woody Herman, all the treasured good music that had given way to the strident obscenities of the present. In the bedroom he stood again before the photographs of his parents and this time reached up to touch them.

"Good-bye, Mom. 'Bye, Dad."

So long to everything. Forever.

Oh God.

He could not have said why he so carefully

closed the apartment door behind him and tested it to make sure it had locked itself. Why should he care if anyone broke in to loot the place, as, already, others in the building had been looted? But it would be like having the grave of a loved one desecrated, wouldn't it? Defilement in a cemetery.

The elevator, of course, was not working. He took the stairs, six floors of them, to street level and trudged out to the parking area.

"Hey! What do you think you're doing?"

There were two of them, he thought. Or three. Although the windows of his apartment had turned gray with daylight just before he left it, the morning was heavily overcast and the cars were still in near darkness under their rows of sheltering roofs. The intruders fled when he yelled at them—just kids, probably, or they would have challenged him—and on reaching his car he discovered they had already smashed a window. Glass crunched under his boots. He stumbled on the rock they had used.

It was getting to be a nightly occurrence now, this breaking into cars and stealing them. He didn't understand. Why steal a car when gasoline was so hard to come by? Weeks ago Professor Varga had warned, "Now be sure, all of you, to save enough gas to get here to my place when the time comes."

Anyway, he seemed to have frightened them off before they could smash anything more than the window. After unlocking the car, he tossed his backpack onto the rear seat and slid in behind the wheel.

As usual, the engine groaned in protest like a drunk being poked awake, but at last, grudgingly, it turned over. Thank the Lord he had worked on it last weekend. These days it was next to impossible to get a car serviced in the city. In some of the other big cities you still could, maybe, but not here. Here you were lucky to find even a supermarket open.

Driving through the city now, from his east-side apartment building to Cricket's little cottage on the far west side, was like driving through a nightmare. With no streetlights to probe its ugly depths it might be only an ill-defined nightmare, but you knew it was full of evil nevertheless. Refuse of all kinds over-flowed the sidewalks, some of it the glass from shattered store windows. Cars everywhere stood abandoned, most of them probably stolen and then left where they had run out of gas. And the predators—always now, except in broad daylight, you saw the predators on the prowl, usually in groups or gangs.

He saw them now as he drove through: dim, twisted shapes scuttling in and out of dark alleys and along the littered sidewalks. At times he saw and heard them fighting among them-selves in a kind of nightmarish ballet of sur-vival. The city was, in fact, fast becoming uninhabitable—at least for decent people.

Which, of course, was why Professor Varga

had decided the time had come for their planned departure.

"There have been three killings in my block this week," the professor had said. "Our time has come."

Chapter Two

"Rambi, I think you know how this is our D-day. Our day of departure. Do you, somehow?"

The remark was addressed by Christina Swensen to the little fawn-colored dog who kept running up and down on her bed, sniffing at the items of clothing she was stuffing into her backpack. But even as she spoke, she was remembering the rainy afternoon she and Don had finally *found* their packs—how they had actually hugged each other on seeing some in the window of a little store miles from home, after weeks of combing the city in vain. The others in the group had had the sense to obtain theirs much earlier, before so many of the city's stores had gone out of business.

Wondering where Don was at the moment,

she paused to glance again at the watch on her wrist: an old-fashioned windup one, thank heaven, because no one seemed to be able to find batteries anymore for the more expensive kind. This one had belonged to her mother, Arva, who in her youth, people said, had looked remarkably like Greta Garbo. Mother and Dad were far away in Florida now, Dad still working at least some of the time as an accountant in Miami. Or he had been when they last wrote. But they had also said, in that last letter she had received all of five months ago before the postal service collapsed all across the country, that things in Florida, too, were swiftly falling to pieces. Parts of the state no longer had water fit to drink, and Miami at night, once so full of life, had become a city of ghosts.

Christina—called Cricket by her friends—paused to gaze solemnly at the animal on the bed, who with his long, slender legs looked more like a tiny deer than a member of the dog family. "Are we doing the right thing, Rambi? Don says we are, and I'm sure he's given it a lot of thought, but do we really have any idea of what we're getting into? Are we even sure that some of the others—Cuyler, for instance—are the kind of people we should be doing it *with*?" The pack filled at last, she placed it on the scale she had brought from the bathroom. "M'm. With you weighing eight and a half, I'm a pound and something overweight. Now, what can I take out?"

What, yes? She and the other women had solemnly agreed to forgo cosmetics of any kind—scented creams and perfumes would only attract mosquitoes and other biting insects anyway, the professor warned—so she had packed nothing in that line. Her hairbrush? She *had* to have that! Her reddish-brown hair might be as pretty as Don always said it was, but without a brush to keep it under control it would soon become a hopeless tangle and drive her crazy. The extra pair of boots, then? No, no. Cuyler, throwing in his usual four-letter words, had warned there might come a time when boots could mean the difference between finding the haven they sought and being left behind somewhere in the wilderness. "Unless you want to bone up on how to make footgear the way the Indians did." That was supposed to be funny. Or to put the Indians down somehow. You never could be sure about Cuyler's so-called jokes.

With a reproachful look at the miniature greyhound, she took a long-sleeved woolen shirt out of the pack and weighed it again. "It's your fault, you know, Rambi. You actually gained some weight last week." Then, quickly: "Oh, I know. I know I've been feeding you too much. But I thought you might find it hard at first and ought to have something in reserve. Come here."

She held out her arms. With the fluid grace of a leaping deer, the dog jumped into them.

She hugged him close to her breast as she began a final tour of the house to make certain she had not overlooked anything important.

"Whatever happens to us, Rambi, at least you won't be left behind." She was thinking of the pack of half-wild dogs she had encountered on her way home from the supermarket yesterday—the one market in her neighborhood that was still struggling to stay open despite the shortages and the blatant thieving. Two of the dogs, looking half starved, had actually bared their teeth and rushed at her.

But, of course, she had known how to handle herself in such a situation. From the time of her graduation from high school eight years ago until Dr. Tom Blakey closed his veterinary hospital in May, she had worked for Dr. Tom. In fact, this little house next door to the hospital belonged to him. When he and his wife had bought a new and much bigger one, he had urged her to leave her small apartment in Don's building and live here rent free, in return for checking on animals left at the hospital overnight.

But the pack of dogs . . . yes, she had escaped without being hurt, actually without even being very frightened. But other people hadn't been so fortunate. Too many owners, overwhelmed by what was happening, had simply turned their animals out to fend for themselves. It was awful. Only a few days ago, within a block of here, one of the roaming

19

packs had killed and half eaten a little girl before men using torn-off fence pickets had finally succeeded in beating them off.

As she finished in the living room and stepped into the kitchen, the sound of the front-door chime wiped the frown from her face and replaced it with a smile. She bent to put the dog down. "You wait here now."

Straightening, she ran through the hall to the door, jerked it open, and stepped into Don Neal's waiting arms.

It was routine for them to embrace and kiss when he called, but this morning he held her longer than usual. Long enough, in fact, for Rambi to tire of waiting and come from the kitchen to sit at their feet, solemnly gazing up at them. Releasing her at last, Don took her by the hand and drew her into the living room, where he looked at his watch.

"You ready, love?"

"Yes, I'm ready."

"We've a little time, then. Let's talk." He sat, and Rambi leaped into his lap.

Cricket sat, too, frowning at him expectantly with her head tipped a little. How fortunate she was to be in love with a man so caring and considerate, she thought. A man so strong yet gentle. That with his thick dark hair and browner-than-brown eyes he was also the handsomest man she had ever known—well, now, that was just a lucky extra. She would have adored this man no matter what he looked like.

"Listen, love," he said. "Are you sure about this?"

"What do you mean?"

"That you want to do it. What about your folks? You may never see them again."

She sat there returning his steady gaze. It was nothing new, what he was saying. She quite understood that he was simply giving her a last chance to change her mind.

"We *could* try to reach Florida," he said. "If we made it, we'd at least all be together for whatever time is left."

"Don, we'd never get there." Ever since the first meeting at the professor's house she had thought about Florida as an alternative, and knew she was right. Even the main cross-country highways were unsafe now. People who used them were being killed for the food and money they carried—money wanted mainly for drugs.

Yes, drugs. That told you something, didn't it? Even with food so scarce and pollution spreading like a rampant cancer over the whole planet, forbidden drugs were still to be had, worldwide, if one had the money to pay for them.

What did the drug dealers *do* with the money, anyway? What could they buy with it, when practically everything except their own filthy merchandise was in short supply?

Anyway, the answer to the Florida suggestion had to be no. The roads were unsafe. Hardly any motels were now open. Even if you found one, the chances were your car would be stolen while you slept.

"We wouldn't get there, Don. You know we wouldn't. And if by some miracle we did, we'd only be going there to die with them. It's the same there as it is here. Perhaps even worse."

The man she loved was silent, and she knew why. He wanted her to think it through. To be absolutely certain.

To reassure him, Cricket said quietly, "You remember what my mother said in the last letter I had from her?" Rising, she went to her backpack and returned with the letter in question. "I'm taking this with me, by the way, and a photo of the two of them that I've had for years. Listen."

She did not have to search for the passage she wanted; from repeated readings she knew just where to find it. *"Darling, your father and I would join you if we could, to be part of the group you wrote about. If your friends would want us, that is. But, really, we're too old for such an adventure, and what's been happening has taken its toll on us physically. You go with your Don and don't worry about us. Just know that our prayers and love go with you both, even if we ourselves must stay here and make the best of what we have left."*

She sat there in silence with the letter in her hand, her gaze fixed on Don's face.

He took in a breath. "I suppose she's right. I just have to be sure you won't be sorry later."

She got up and returned the letter to her pack, then walked to his chair and leaned over the back of it to put her lips against his. Not the way she kissed him when they were making love. A gentler, even more meaningful way.

"Don, dear, we don't even know whether they're still alive," she said then.

"I realize that. I just thought—"

"Am I being selfish?"

"No, no, of course not."

She said quietly, "We can't be sure that what we're doing will turn out to be any better, you know. All we're sure of is that there's no hope at all if we stay here."

Don pushed himself to his feet and took her in his arms again. They held each other for such a long time, in silence, that Cricket's little dog finally barked at them. Unlike most of his breed, he was not usually a barker.

"You sure you've got everything you'll need?" Don asked.

"As sure as I can be, until I wake up some morning and discover I've forgotten something I just can't do without." She found she could still laugh, even at such a moment. "Shall we go?"

"Better take a last look around. No matter what happens, you won't be coming back, you know. Not here. A house like this—druggies will probably take it over as soon as they realize it's empty."

"Yes, I know."

"I'll wait here."

With Rambi at her heels she walked slowly through the house again, remembering. Remembering the day she had first stepped into it with Dr. Tom, wondering if some of her friends might be right in advising her not to. He might have more in mind than wanting someone close by to check on the animals, they had suggested. "Think about it, Cricket. You're young, you're pretty, and with you paying no rent for the place, he might expect you to feel you owe him." But her every instinct had told her that a man like Dr. Tom would never suggest such a thing. Not a man who sometimes spent hours trying to save the lives of stray cats and dogs that had been hurt in some of the many terrible ways such helpless creatures could be hurt. That had been hit by cars, or abused, or even shot by angry men with guns. And, of course, she'd been right.

In the bedroom she remembered, too, the first time she and Don had made love—after she had promised to marry him as soon as things got better. She recalled her expectation of feeling shame and embarrassment on undressing before a man for the first time, and her astonishment on finding she had no such feelings. And the wonder of it all, from the first gentle touch of his hands to the awesome sense of wanting to belong to him wholly, forever, when it ended.

She was still reliving that first time in bed

with him when she returned to the living room
and reached for his hand.

"All right, I'm ready."

"You're sure you want to do this now, love?"

"I'm sure. So long as we do it together."

Chapter Three

"The bastards!" Eugene Cuyler said.

It was the fourth or fifth time he had used the word in the hour and a half they had been packing, his wife realized. Each time he did, his voice became more like the angry-dog growl that usually predicted an explosion of temper.

As soothingly as she could, she replied, "Now, Cuyler, you know we couldn't have taken any of that stuff with us. So what difference does it make?"

Rowena Cuyler had long since learned not to provoke her husband with anything like a complaint. At five feet five she was seven inches shorter than he. At a hundred and sixty pounds she was fifty-five pounds lighter. True, she had grown up on a farm and was no weakling. But she had been slapped around by him enough times to have learned it was safer to be careful.

"Dammit," he said, "I was gonna give those guns and that ammo to the neighbors. That's what difference it makes. I was gonna be big-hearted and give them something to protect themselves with after we're gone and they won't have me to look after them."

Rowena looked up from filling the two back-packs they would be taking. Following his instructions, she was trying to arrange them so she would be carrying at least half of his gear along with her own, because he would have the tools and ammunition to look after. Actually, she was sure, all their fancy planning would turn out to be a waste of time once they got the canoes. The canoes would have to be big ones, and on the portages they would probably be all that the men could handle. The women would have to take care of just about everything else.

But when you were the wife of Eugene Cuyler you did what you were told to do and let him find out his mistakes later. She just wished he could have been in a gentler mood this morning, when they were about to leave their whole life behind and start out on a crazy adventure they couldn't even guess the end of.

All right, so the gunshop downstairs had been broken into while they slept last night. So what? They still had enough guns and ammo here upstairs, even if the guns weren't exactly the ones Cuyler had planned on. He still had the tools he would need—he'd long ago brought those up. And the thieves hadn't tried to steal the van in the alley. What's more, the van's tank was full of gas, with plenty more in cans in case they couldn't get any along the road even with hoarded ration tickets.

What was making him so sore, she guessed, was that the creeps had actually dared to break into the shop while he, the big hunter, was asleep upstairs. And that they'd been able to do it without making enough noise to wake him up. Maybe he was sore, too, because he hadn't rigged up a shotgun to blow apart anyone who did break in. Lots of other shop owners were doing that these days, and he could put together one that would really work, without question. Gene Cuyler could do just about anything he put his mind to.

Finished with the two backpacks, she looked up to speak again and discovered Cuyler had stepped out. Out to the van, probably, with the last of the guns he'd been cleaning and oiling for the past half hour. He had a weapon of some sort for every man in the group, he had bragged a while ago. None for the women, of course. In his world women were not supposed to do things like hunt or fish. They were to clean and cook what the men killed, and do the housework and have kids. Her own father had been pretty much the same kind of man, expecting all those things of her mother, so she should have known what to expect when she married a boy from the same farming community. Especially when she'd grown up next door to him.

He came thumping up the stairs while she was thinking about it. "You anywhere near ready?"

"I'm *all* ready, Cuyler. Just tell me this." She held up a bottle of bourbon he had put with his things, for her to pack. "Do you really have to take it?" Booze of any kind, even beer if he drank enough of it, too often put a hair trigger on his temper. You wouldn't think that would be true of a guy built like a football player, which he'd been in high school, but it was so. And if you thought Cuyler could be hard to handle when sober, just look out for him when he wasn't. There must be some kind of pent-up fury deep down inside him, like lava in a volcano, that liquor provoked to the surface.

"Go on, pack it," he said.

"I don't think I should. You know what—"

"Pack it, dammit! Somebody may get hurt."

"The professor said he'd be taking a first-aid—"

"Rowena, will you stop arguing with me, for Chrissake? It's no big deal you've got there—just a single lousy bottle—and I'm telling you to pack it."

When Cuyler "told you" in that tone of voice to do something, you did it. She obeyed him, though with her lips tight and a tightness around her deep-set hazel eyes. How would the others react when Cuyler showed them that side of himself? she wondered. They didn't know him that well yet. Actually, they'd invited him and her to join them only because he knew about guns—and owned some, of course—and could be counted on to supply the group with fresh meat. Not for a moment had she fooled herself into thinking that a quiet, gentle man like Professor Varga would have gone out of his way to include her husband if he hadn't had something the group needed. The professor hadn't even known Cuyler until Dan Frazier brought him to one of the meetings a few weeks ago.

"If you're finished there, you better take a last look around," Cuyler said.

"Cuyler." She faced him with her hands on her hips.

"Now what, for God's sake?"

"Are you sure this is what we ought to be doing?"

He gave her one of his heavy sighs that meant, plain as day, "Oh God, here we go again, but all right, what is it?"

"They're not really our kind of people, Cuyler. Not your kind, anyway." Except maybe Frazier, she thought. He's into guns a little, though not in love with them the way *you* are. But the others aren't going to understand the way you think and talk, Cuyler. Believe me.

"Whaddaya mean, they're not my kind of people? What's so different about me?"

"Nothing, nothing," she said quickly, fearing an eruption of the volcano. "It's just that—well, you know what I mean."

"No, I don't know what you mean." He was leaning against the wall now with his hands on his hips, glaring at her. "So suppose you tell me."

"Cuyler, would any of them ever invite us to their homes? As friends? To spend an evening?"

"So maybe they wouldn't. But where we're going I'll be smarter than they are. A damn sight smarter. And that'll make me the one they look up to, not just a flunky, like *you* seem to think."

"All right, all right." She never should have mentioned it. But the fact that he was so touchy on the subject proved she was right, didn't it? He knew as well as she did why he'd been invited. Being Cuyler, he just wouldn't admit it, even to himself.

"So take a last look around, will you?" he said.

"For what? I made up a list, remember? I know we've got everything."

"Look around anyhow. I don't want you telling me you forgot something when we're halfway to Varga's place."

"All right." With a shake of her head, she turned away.

"But make it quick," he threw after her. "I'll be down in the van."

Guarding your precious guns, she thought, in case some of the druggies come along. The van would be locked, of course, and nobody could see into it with the doors shut, but nothing seemed to be safe these days from people high on Halleluja. It was the most addictive drug in years, turning even teenagers into violent crazies who would do just about anything to feed their habit.

She watched him start down the stairs with the backpacks, then hurried through the house as he had ordered. There was nothing in it she would miss or even wanted to remember. Buying the gunshop and this apartment over it had been Cuyler's idea, not hers. At heart she was a country girl and always would be.

Of course, things were not the same at home now. The fish in the river out there, only forty miles from here, had something in them that would slowly kill you if you kept eating them. The crops were taking up some kind of poison from the soil. And the water—well, it might be hard to believe, but somehow the factories that had moved out from the city ten or eleven years ago had managed to ruin every well for miles around. The few folks still living out there had to have water hauled out to them. Which was really no solution, because even the city water would soon be unfit to drink, according to Professor Varga.

And it wasn't only here. All over the country the same things were happening, weren't they? So what she and Cuyler were about to do was really the only thing left *to* do, even if it seemed like the end of the world. Clinging to that thought, she quickly finished her tour of the apartment and went downstairs to the alley.

Cuyler was waiting in the van.

"There's something I forgot to ask you," she said as she opened her door and climbed in.

"Now what?"

"Did you pack some of those government kits for testing the water?"

He made a face at her. "Course I did. What am I? Stupid?"

"I just wanted to be sure."

"Well, I did."

"All right. So we can go."

She leaned back and closed her eyes, suddenly feeling tired. Somehow whenever she had to do anything with him lately, it seemed to tire her out: not the actual doing it, but expecting he would find fault with how she did it. Of course, this move they were making with Professor Varga and his crowd was enough to scare anyone. She couldn't really blame Cuyler for being uptight. She was on edge, herself.

"You going to sleep on me?" her husband said.

She opened her eyes. "I'm sorry. I didn't sleep much last night. Hardly any, in fact."

"You think I did?"

"I said I'm sorry."

He drove on in silence through a drizzle of rain. The dashboard clock said 7:30. The wiper blades squeaked because of the grit that was always on the glass lately. The streets seemed darker than they ought to be at that hour. Not so dark, though, that she couldn't see the broken store windows. Or the shadowy shapes prowling along the cluttered sidewalks. Or the other shapes, older and slower, poking through the piles of garbage in search, probably, of something to eat.

She was glad, suddenly, that she and Cuyler were about to put it all behind them. No matter what they might be blundering into, it couldn't be as bad as what was happening here.

Some of the shadowy shapes turned to stare at them as they drove through downtown. You could count on that at such an hour, when so few cars were abroad. Nothing bad occurred, though, until they were out from under the heavy gloom of tall buildings and on the freeway. Then she just happened to be looking at Cuyler when he glanced into the mirror and muttered something she didn't catch.

"What's the matter?"

"Behind us. Bunch of creeps in a car, up to something."

Even as he spoke, a big car—the kind of gas-eater you couldn't give away these days—came looming up beside them in the drizzle, and she saw the faces of its occupants turned toward them. Four people. Four boys, teenagers, young men, whatever. Their lopsided, stupid-looking grins told her all she needed to know about them: they were high on Halleluja. Only, kids their age didn't call it that anymore; they'd shortened the word to Hal.

Suddenly the car swerved into them. Deliberately.

There was a grinding noise as the two vehicles came together, and if Cuyler hadn't expected something, the van would have gone off the concrete, she was sure. If she'd been driving, it would have. But her husband's big hands had already tightened their grip on the wheel, and when he slammed his foot on the brake pedal, the van screeched to a halt.

Lurching from side to side, the car sped on by.

Cuyler moved his foot from brake to gas then, and floored the gas pedal. The van took off like a rocket. Before she could even think of protesting, the two vehicles climbed a highway overpass and were suddenly side by side again.

"Cuyler, *don't!*" she screamed. But the plea came too late. He had already wrenched the wheel over, and he was better at that kind of thing—much better—than the druggie driving the car had been.

There was a grinding thud, a second one, a third, as Cuyler did what she knew by the whiteness of his lips he was determined to do. Foolishly, the driver of the car tried to escape by speeding up. The final thud sent the car lurching at high speed into and over the guardrail.

She heard an explosion from the highway below as Cuyler drove on. In her mirror she saw a column of fire shooting up like a blowtorch flame through the drizzle, followed by a tower of swirling black smoke.

"The bastards," her husband growled, using his favorite all-purpose word. "That'll teach 'em."

For a while she only sat there in silence as he drove on down the highway. He was silent too, no doubt guessing her thoughts. At last she took in a deep breath and glanced at him.

She probably shouldn't blame him, she decided. After all, the druggies had tried to run them off the road first. And it was only luck that they'd been on the overpass when he hit back.

But, dear God, what a way to begin what she had so desperately hoped would be a new and better life. And Cuyler was actually proud of himself. His twisted look of triumph told her so.

Chapter Four

"Now then, let's go over this one last time, please, to be sure there are no questions."

The speaker was Professor Theron Varga, a tall, dark-complected man, with nearly black hair, who was sometimes thought by strangers to be Afro-American, though his ancestry was Greek. The place: his attractive, 1990s-type home a block from the university campus, on the outskirts of the city. The time: 8:27 A.M.

While speaking, the professor stood with his feet apart and his hands behind his back, as he so often did when lecturing students. As he had done, in fact, until school closed for the summer only two weeks ago, for in spite of everything, the university still struggled to hang on with a tenth of its former student body.

Those seated before Theron Varga in his living room at the moment were not students, however. All were adults, and, counting the professor's red-haired Irish wife, Sheila, there were ten of them. Even Eugene Cuyler listened in respectful silence while Varga's surprisingly soft voice droned through the crowded room.

"The plan, as finally agreed upon, is for six of us to go in Cuyler's van and five in my car, which is the largest of the cars we have available. No doubt it will be a bit crowded and uncomfortable, but a third vehicle would only add to the risk of our running out of gas."

He paused for nods of assent.

"As you know, we had hoped to maintain communication by means of CB radios in our two vehicles, but one of the sets that Cuyler finally located and installed—"

"I took them in trade for guns," Cuyler interrupted.

"So you did, Cuyler. And I'm sure you have our gratitude. However, the one in my car no longer functions, and the part needed to repair it seems to be unavailable, so we have had to devise another plan."

Again the professor's gaze wandered over the group, gauging reactions. So far, so good, he thought.

"This fallback plan, as finally agreed upon, is for Cuyler to lead the way at all times. If at any time we become separated for more than twenty miles or so, he will stop to allow me to catch up. That *is* the plan, is it not, Cuyler?"

The gunshop man nodded.

"Good. Well now, we are in agreement that it would be reckless for us to attempt to go by way of Manitoulin Island because the ferry from Tobermory may no longer be running. So after crossing into Canada we are to skirt Lake Huron's Georgian Bay on Route 69 to Sudbury, then travel west on Route 17 along the lake's north shore to our destination. Are there any questions about that?"

They shook their heads.

"Each of us has a number of the government-issued water-testing kits in his pack. Correct?"

They had some. Yes.

"And no more than his allotted twenty pounds? You've actually weighed your packs, as Cuyler suggested? You're not merely guessing?"

More nods and murmurs. They had weighed their packs. He couldn't, himself, see the point of Cuyler's being so rigid about that, but if it would make the fellow even a little less difficult, so be it.

"I trust we have all withdrawn the designated amount of money from our bank accounts?" he continued, making it a question by his inflection. Some, of course, had agreed to withdraw double—and he, in fact, triple—to compensate for the fact that others could contribute nothing because their banks had failed. But it made no difference, really. The entire banking system was in danger of imminent collapse, and in any case, once they had purchased the canoes and other necessary equipment, what good would money be to them? Their first thought had been to close their accounts entirely, but there had lingered that thin, faint hope that the government would finally pull itself together and at least some of the banks might be saved. In any case, carrying that much more cash than the group required would obviously be foolish, no? It would have to be paper money, and paper money was bound to disintegrate eventually. "*Have* we attended to that?" he asked. "All of us who could?"

The lucky ones had, they indicated.

"And have we also done our best to inform relatives and friends of our intentions? With phones out and the mail service all but nonexistent, the question makes little sense, I suppose, but have we done what we can?"

Again, they had.

"Let me remind you, then, that we have agreed on one other important matter. If at any time from now on we should find ourselves in dispute about some point of procedure, we will put the problem to a vote and abide by the decision of the majority. Right?" Because, he thought, gazing at those to whom he spoke, some differences of opinion were bound to arise in such a group.

Just look at them. Don Neal was a teacher, Lloyd Atkinson a pharmacist, Max Krist a computer expert, Dan Frazier a doctor of medicine, and Eugene Cuyler an outdoorsman experienced in the use of firearms. Well, perhaps that didn't make them so different after all, except in the case of Cuyler. But they certainly possessed different personalities.

And in that respect the women were equally unalike, were they not? Cricket Swensen, Don's girlfriend, was a gentle soul with a deeply sincere love of animals—witness the little deerlike dog she held on her lap even now, and the way it gazed up at her with such adoring eyes when she stroked it. Becky Atkinson was a briskly cheerful businesswoman who had enjoyed attending to the financial side of her husband's drugstore. Max Krist's girlfriend, Penny Bowen, had been a model. She was black, though of such a light complexion that she was often thought to be white, in the same way that he, Theron Varga, was taken for black.

And, finally, Cuyler's wife, Rowena, was—well—a farm girl, no? Or a girl of nature. Yes, a *child* of nature. Delightfully so.

There was something missing in his summation, he thought. He had included no mate for Dan Frazier. In the future, if they all survived, that could be a problem. Dan had had a wife, but the mere thought of what they proposed to do had terrified her, and soon after the group came together she had left him and fled east to join a widowed sister. Dan, himself, was a handsome and brilliant young medic who at present seemed not to mind his solo role in the mating game. But there could come a time, could there not, when he might feel himself the odd man out?

Varga suddenly realized the others were

waiting for him to finish what he had begun. He cleared his throat and again put his hands behind his back.

"Ah, yes," he said with a smile. "Well, now, if you will allow me just a few words more, we can bring this meeting to an end and begin our journey into what we all hope will be a new and better life. At forty-nine, I am the senior citizen of this group by ten years, I believe. Being that much older than the rest of you does not, of course, give me the right to claim leadership, but I should like to be thought of as—how shall I put it?—a sort of father figure. If one should ever be needed, that is. And Sheila, though a bit younger than I"—he smiled at his little joke—"wants you ladies to think of her as someone to whom you can bring your problems when they require a woman's understanding." He held out a hand, and his red-haired wife of thirty-seven, twelve years his junior, smiled happily as she rose to take her place beside him.

Again, happening to catch the eye of Dan Frazier, the professor thought of what it would be like to be a man without a woman in the days ahead. All too vividly he remembered his own three years of loneliness following the death of his first wife. Dan Frazier was Sheila's doctor. It was she who had persuaded him to accompany them on their hegira.

In fact, Dan had come to dinner last evening—the last dinner that would ever be served by Sheila in this house—and had stayed the night rather than return late to his empty home when the streets were so dangerous. After dinner she had played some of her music on the stereo and danced gaily with both of them, as though oblivious of the fact that in only a few hours her beloved recordings would no longer exist for her. He was indeed fortunate to have such a brave and lovely woman by his side.

He forced himself back to the present. "So then . . . are we ready?"

They had been waiting for him to ask it. Suddenly, as though someone had flicked a switch or turned a dial, the room filled with sounds and motion.

It had already been decided who should ride with whom, and now Varga watched them as they gathered up their gear and made for the door. Interesting, he thought, how some were so solemn, others so seemingly cheerful, as though they were embarking on a grand adventure. A question of personalities, no doubt. As he picked up his own and his wife's backpacks, Sheila took his arm and smiled at him, then matched steps with him as though they were merely out for one of their frequent morning walks. But at the door, holding him back, she turned for one last look at what they were leaving behind.

He would have put an arm around her had his hands been free. Instead he turned with her, taking in a deep breath and slowly letting it out.

"I have been so happy here, Therry," she

whispered. The pet name came as a mild surprise, though she had used it often in the first year or so of their marriage, as if to prove to herself that she was no longer one of his students. "I shall always remember this house."

"And I." He put the packs down and took her in his arms, to hold her for a moment in silence. They were the last to leave the house. Sheila shut the door behind them, then side by side they walked across the veranda, descended the steps, and crossed the narrow strip of lawn to the large black car, an Avant, awaiting them in the driveway.

Moments later, when his passengers were ready to depart, Theron Varga turned to look at the house once more before taking his place at the Avant's wheel. Tears blurred his vision.

The van had already rolled out of the driveway and was speeding down the street past the university gate. The cars that were being left behind stood silent on the Varga lawn, rather like oversized tombstones in a cemetery.

No doubt they too would soon be gone—driven away by thieves.

Chapter Five

Border crossings were not a problem these days, with so few people able to travel. Only one uniform was on duty, and he appeared to be bored.

"Where are you going?"

"Chetwood."

"For what purpose?"

"A camping trip. To get away from the horrors for a while."

"This is all the luggage you have?"

"All we expect to need. We'll be renting tents and canoes."

"You hope. But good luck. You may proceed."

The roads were in miserable condition, though, and driving at anything like the speed limit would have been foolhardy. Darkness was falling when the expedition put the Thirty Thousand Islands of Georgian Bay behind and found a motel still open near Grundy Lake.

"We've no electricity, but you're welcome to stop if you want to. You'll have to double up somehow."

"Double up? But—"

"I know. We've twenty units and you don't see any cars, but only three of the units are still usable. All the others need repairs. We've no water fit to drink, either, but I can give you bottled water."

Though seemingly only in her forties, the woman leaned against the office counter for support and gazed at them through tired, deeply pouched eyes. "The truth is, my husband and I are planning to close this place. With almost nobody traveling anymore, there isn't much point in trying to stay open. You want the three I've got?"

"Please," said Professor Varga. "And the drinking water." There was bottled water in the van, but they had better save it, just in case.

"All right." Straightening, the woman reached for keys on a board behind her and dropped them on the counter. "Here you are. Six, eight, and nine. They're fifty-eight apiece, so that'll be"—she applied pencil to paper—"a hundred seventy-four plus tax. Funny, isn't it? Our government can still collect taxes—yours, too, from what I hear—even if they can't seem to do anything else right. That'll be one-ninety-one forty altogether. What time will you be checking out?"

"At daybreak."

"I won't be up that early—my husband's sick—so I'll thank you to pay now. Cash, please. No credit cards."

"Of course." Credit cards were things of the past in the States now, too.

Varga paid her and slid the keys toward him across the countertop. With a glance at Dan Frazier, he said, "We're sorry about your husband. We have a doctor in our party if—"

"He's seen a doctor."

"And?"

"My Arthur's not the only one, he said. It's the water we've been drinking. Been bad for a long time, they're finally telling us. That's the main reason Arthur and I are closing the place and going to live with our son in Toronto. Everyone around here has to drink bottled water, and sometimes you can't get any."

Professor Varga shook his head in sadness.

"Whole world's in a mess, it seems like," the woman said. "Well, good night. Wherever you're going, good luck."

Don Neal said, "By any chance, is there a place to eat within easy driving distance?"

"No. Everything's closed."

"Could *you*, perhaps—"

"Feed all of you people? Heavens, no. I've trouble enough finding food for the two of *us*."

"I see." Don's smile was sheepish. "Well, thanks anyway." Actually, food was not that big a problem, at least not tonight. Aware that few such eating places were still open, they had bought sandwiches for an evening snack when they stopped for lunch at a highway restaurant. It wouldn't be dinner, but it would tide them over. Leaving the motel office, they talked for a time about how they would pair up, then all but the professor and Cuyler walked to their designated units. The latter two drove the car and van there and parked them. As the woman had remarked, there were no other cars.

The motel consisted of two rows of units, and the doors numbered six, eight, and nine were on the same side of the blacktop parking area, near the end of their row. While the members of the group were carrying their back-packs in, the proprietress came with plastic jugs of water. There followed murmurings of "Good night," "Sleep well," and "See you in the morning," and doors were closed. All the talking that needed to be done had been done during the hours on the road.

In unit number six, which the professor and his wife were sharing with Dan Frazier, Sheila Varga took sandwiches from brown-paper bags and unwrapped them while her husband sat on one of the two double beds and peered at a road map. A pair of oil lamps on a chest of drawers provided the only illumination. The woman had lighted them when she delivered the water. The burning oil, obviously of poor quality, was already fouling the air.

48

Dr. Frazier lowered himself onto a chair and stretched out his legs. "How far have we come, Prof? Did you look at the odometer?"

"No, but according to the map here, about three hundred miles."

"Not bad, under the circumstances."

"Not bad at all. We've about a hundred seventy to go."

"So by this time tomorrow we should have everything arranged. Thanks, Sheila." With one of his laid-back smiles, Frazier accepted a corned-beef-on-rye sandwich from Sheila and bit into it. "About the canoes, I mean. And the tents."

Sheila handed her husband a sandwich. "Did you two hear what that border fellow said when Therry mentioned canoes and tents?"

"Yes, I caught it," Varga said. " 'You hope.' It didn't sound too promising, did it?"

"Oh, come on," Frazier protested. "Hasn't Chetwood always been a jumping-off place for wilderness trips?"

"According to Cuyler."

"And he'd know. He's into that kind of thing. So there'll be outfitters there."

"If they're still in business," the professor said.

His wife sat beside him on the bed and began to eat a sandwich. When she had chewed a mouthful and swallowed it, she said, "Why do you suppose the water is bad here, so close to the lake?"

"The lake's probably polluted, Sheila," Frazier said with a shrug. "Almost all of them are."

"Or perhaps it's another case of official stupidity," she said with a frown, trying to answer her own question. "Like that city in—where was it?—that fouled its aquifer with the sludge from its own sewage plant."

"The way these lamps are fouling the air in here," the professor said, "let's hope they don't make us ill." Finishing his sandwich a moment later, he announced that he was tired and ready to turn in.

With a remark that he, too, was ready for some shut-eye, Frazier moved from his chair to pour a drink of water from the plastic jug the woman had delivered. Then he went to his bed and began to undress, but, with his shirt off, stopped and looked at the professor.

"You're sleeping in your clothes?"

"We might as well," Varga said. "It will be too cold to undress at night once we get under way."

"So it will." The doctor put his shirt back on and stretched out on his back, with his hands under his head and his gaze on the soot-stained ceiling. Varga had his eyes closed. Sheila still moved about the room.

"You know something, Sheila?" Frazier said, turning his head to look at her.

She had blown out one lamp and was leaning over the other, her red hair shining in its light as though suddenly on fire. "What, Dan?"

"I think I'd rather be back at your place, dancing to your music again."

* * *

In unit eight, Eugene Cuyler had opened the bottle of bourbon his wife, Rowena, had not wanted him to bring. Standing at the chest of drawers, he poured three inches of the liquor into a motel glass, added a more or less equal amount of water, then turned to his three companions and raised the glass high.

"Well, here's to our new life."

When all three glanced in his direction without speaking, he gazed at them in silence, dismissing them as not being worth any further effort to be sociable. What the hell—if they didn't like his drinking, let them sulk. The dismissal included his wife, who had her backpack on one of the two beds and was rearranging its contents.

Maxwell Krist had carried one of the unit's two oil lamps to a small table and was now seated there, writing in a notebook. Penelope Bowen, his girlfriend, lay on their bed, watching him.

The silence continued.

A long silence almost always made Cuyler uncomfortable. "What you writing, Max?" he finally condescended to ask.

"Nothing much. A journal, sort of."

"By hand? I thought you computer-whiz types had to use a word processor."

"I'll muddle through somehow."

"Yeah? Like for how long? I mean, where will you find more paper when that runs out?"

"That could be a problem, couldn't it? But this will last me a while, at least." Krist pushed the notebook away from him and stood up, stretching his arms above his head as if to relieve an ache in his shoulders. "Is that water fit to drink?"

"It is with booze in it." Cuyler grinned, feeling a challenge coming on. He enjoyed being challenged. Back in high school he'd got his biggest kicks in football when up against some team everyone said his team couldn't beat. "But you don't drink, do you? Or smoke, either."

"I used to. Both."

"Lucky you. You won't have to get used to going without." And that, Cuyler thought, was no joke. What the hell would he do when that time came, as it was bound to? Sure, this bottle would last a few days if he watched himself, and he had another stashed away. Maybe he could even get more in Chetwood before they took off. But he wouldn't be able to carry more than a couple. Jesus. How was he going to handle being stuck with this bunch of weirdos without something to drink now and then? Or even a cigarette when he wanted one—though he'd be better off without the coffin nails. They always did start him coughing now.

He took another sip of his drink and leaned back against the chest of drawers, watching Krist. Computer whiz, he thought. Where they were headed, what the hell good would a computer whiz be, even one who was a respectable five-eleven and weighed one-eighty? What could he contribute to an expedition like this? And why—Jesus Christ—had he brought a *black* woman along?

Maxwell Krist lowered his arms, glanced at Cuyler, and sat down again. He began writing.

Cuyler, our hunter, is watching me as I write, and I believe I can guess what he is thinking. Not only his speech but his facial expressions and body language make him an easy read. He is probably wondering what earthly use a "computer whiz," as he calls me, can possibly be on this mission of ours.

Though Cuyler was unaware of it, Krist was not only a "computer whiz." From Professor Varga's university he had emerged with a Ph.D. After earning the degree, however, he had learned to his dismay that doctors of philosophy could do little anymore but teach philosophy to others, a future that did not interest him. So, being fascinated by the seemingly endless wonders of computer science, he had sought refuge in that field and ended up owning a store whose personnel sold, serviced, and taught customers how to use computers. Yet he was still the philosopher and had never ceased trying to exress himself in that discipline also, often in forms of poetry.

At the moment, aware that Cuyler was silently sneering at him, Krist wondered how he would be able to stand the man if they were together for any length of time. Not his drinking and chainsmoking; those would come to an end when supplies ran out. But his exaggerated pride in what he considered his masculinity. And, most distressing of all, his disdain for everything gentle—or tender—or even humane.

I suppose I'll get used to him, Krist wrote in his notebook. *Obviously, we'll all have to.*

Penelope Bowen had been watching the two of them and noting the interplay of words and glances. There could be a problem shaping up, she told herself. Not right away, of course—her Max was not a man to lose his cool quickly—but eventually, when friction between them built up to create heat, as it almost certainly would.

She could understand why Cuyler had been asked to join the group, of course. Not only had no one else owned a gun; no one else even knew much about using one. But when you came right down to it, Cuyler embodied in his attitude toward life so many of the very things they were running away from. In the southeast, where she had been born, he would have been the kind of man who drove around in a battered pickup truck, brandishing a bottle of beer in one hand and having a shotgun or rifle on the seat beside him and probably a pit bull in back. The kind of man who would have called her, Penny Bowen, a nigger. Or at least thought of her as one.

Very well. She, the same Penny Bowen, had been allowed to join the group only because she was Max Krist's girlfriend. She knew that. As a woman working in a real-estate office, she had possessed no talents the group could possibly use. But she would prove to them they had not made a mistake. Always a hard worker, in the days ahead she would show them that she could be better than they were at some things. Yes. It was a promise she had made to herself, and she would keep it. What was it Max had said to her in bed that night a few weeks ago? "You know something, Penny Bowen? When you're in action, anyone might take you for a man"—probably because she was a bit on the plump side, and solid—"but relaxed you have the most sensitive, feminine face I've ever seen or hope to see. Such a truly *beautiful* face. Ah, my darling, how I love looking at it!"

That was good enough for her. Just remembering those words—and how Max had looked at her when he said them—would keep her going, no matter what happened in the days ahead.

The fourth person in unit eight, Cuyler's wife, Rowena, had also taken note of the exchange between her husband and Max Krist. Though pretending to pay no attention, she had heard every word while seemingly intent upon re-rearranging her backpack.

Why, she asked herself, did Cuyler have to treat all men as if they were—well—like threats? Or enemies. Ever since she'd known him he had carried a chip on his shoulder, even way back in grade school when most of the other boys, even bigger ones, had been afraid of him.

Couldn't he see that if he didn't make an effort to fit in, he would only end up making life miserable for everyone in the group? Including himself and her?

In unit nine Don Neal, Cricket Swensen, and the Atkinsons were eating sandwiches. Seated on the edge of the bed she would share with Don, Cricket leaned down to offer some of her corned beef to her dog.

"You know," said Lloyd Atkinson from a chair that had seen better days, "that little fellow may be a problem for you later on."

Cricket glanced at him in surprise. "Problem?"

"If Cuyler doesn't turn out to be the mighty hunter we all expect him to be, I mean. Prof has those pills he created, but will they satisfy a dog? Will a dog even eat them?"

Weighing the question, Cricket sat up and gazed at the pharmacist with a frown of respect. She liked Lloyd Atkinson. Six feet one and balding at thirty-six, he was skinny and wore glasses. He had a protruding Adam's apple, knobby knees, and bony elbows. But all his drugstore customers had liked and trusted him. Most had called him by his first name.

His remark, then, had not been meant as a put-down, as it might have been had it come from someone like Cuyler. She knew it had been offered with genuine concern.

"He's right, you know, Cricket," said Lloyd's

wife, Becky. "It *could* be a problem, don't you think?"

And she, too, was genuinely concerned, Cricket knew. Even as she spoke, Becky dropped to her knees on the threadbare carpet and with outstretched arms invited the little greyhound to come to her. Without hesitation, he did so.

Becky and she would be good friends in the days ahead, Cricket told herself. For that matter they already were, having met and talked frequently in the drugstore and at the many preparatory gatherings of the group. Perhaps it was an attraction of opposites. Becky was only five feet three and sort of dumpy, though almost always full of fun.

"But I wouldn't worry about it," Becky added brightly, with the dog's black nose and big brown eyes now only inches from her face. "The way this little guy steals your heart, I bet he'll never go hungry so long as *we* have anything to eat."

Suddenly stretching himself, Rambi placed both front feet on her left shoulder and turned his head to lick her cheek. The unexpected move caused her to lose her balance. Laughing, she fell sprawling onto the carpet.

Don Neal stepped forward to help her up. "He's a real tiger sometimes. Doesn't know his own strength."

It was meant as an apology, Becky realized. The dog wasn't Cricket's; it really belonged to and was loved by both of them.

What a nice couple Cricket and Don were, she thought. She and Lloyd were so lucky to have been paired off with them. She must speak to Lloyd about trying to maintain the arrangement when the group discussed who would be with whom in the tents they talked about.

While thinking about it, she turned down the bed she would sleep in with her husband.

Cricket was doing the same to the other bed. "Last one in blows out the lamps. Okay?"

That would be Lloyd. After extinguishing the first one, he said with a frown, "I don't suppose anyone brought a flashlight."

Don was climbing into bed beside Cricket. "Uh-uh. We couldn't see the point, when we won't be able to get new batteries."

"We could have put some in the cars, though, and left them behind at Chetwood. I was just thinking that if anyone comes prowling around in the night . . . But we're out of the city now, so we're probably safe."

Lloyd's voice trailed off as he made himself comfortable. Then Cricket's softer one came wandering through the silence. "Well, good night all. . . ."

"Good night."

"Sure. Sleep well."

"See you at daybreak."

Strange, Don thought as Cricket snuggled up to him. All the conversation had been small talk, intended mainly to relieve the tension by pushing back the silence. Why was that? Now that they were actually on the road, was it too frightening to think or talk about what they might be getting themselves into?

Chapter Six

Cuyler awoke from a dream and sat up in bed, unsure whether the sound that had aroused him was part of the dream or something else. His sudden movement awoke his wife, and Rowena turned sleepily toward him.

"What's the matter?"

"Sh-h-h . . ."

She, too, sat up, but more slowly, more quietly. Then they both heard the sound.

A scratching or scraping as of metal prying metal, it came from outside, where the van was parked.

"Don't move," Cuyler warned, and groped for the floor on his side of the bed.

Unlike the occupants of unit nine, he had seen fit to bring along a flashlight. Moreover, he had taken the precaution to carry it in from the van and place it where he could reach it if the need arose.

He had carried something else in from the van, as well: a double-barreled, twelve-gauge shotgun that now leaned against the wall only inches from the flashlight. He reached for that as he swung his feet to the floor.

On retiring, Cuyler had removed his shoes and socks, nothing else. In his bare feet now, with the flashlight in his left hand, the shotgun in his right, he glided to the door. Years of hunting had taught him stealth.

Behind him Rowena, too, scrambled from the bed—but wide-eyed with alarm, straining to see what her husband was doing.

The metallic sounds continued at the van outside.

Cuyler had not yet turned the flashlight on. At the door he transferred it from his left hand to his right armpit, and reached for the heavy bolts confronting him. The door had two of them, one above and one below the knob; by law in this country, all motel doors were now so equipped. He slid them back with only a whisper of sound, then carefully turned the knob, which required no key except from the outside.

Flinging the door wide, he snatched the flashlight from his armpit, switched it on, and jerked up the shotgun.

"All right, you sons of bitches! Get the hell away from that van or I'll blow you away!"

They must have been young people, and the one who screamed was almost certainly female. In the gritty drizzle that misted down through an eerie, spooky darkness, the flashlight beam failed to reveal them clearly. He thought there were four of them but could not be certain of that, either.

They were in a group when he splashed them with light, one apparently working on the van door with something like a tire iron and the others crowding him, pushing at him, nervously urging him to hurry.

At his yell they broke and scattered, becoming only a blur of mixed-up shapes racing for the safety of darkness.

With another yelled obscenity Cuyler squeezed off both barrels, and the twin explosions added to the confusion.

Rowena saw it all as she ran from the bed behind him. Then, as he went charging after them, she remembered the car he had run off the overpass and screamed, "No, Cuyler! Don't!"

It was true that some kids were stoned out of their minds these days. She knew that. But some were just plain hungry, too. Even the police said so. You had a right to protect yourself. You could do that. But don't go crazy. Don't shoot at every shadow.

Anyway, they'd gotten away. And behind the swerving beam of his flashlight, like some menacing figure in a nightmare, her husband was lurching back through the drizzle. He stopped at the van.

As she ran out to him, she realized the other two in their unit, Max Krist and Penny Bowen, were out of bed and hurrying along beside her, excitedly asking questions. But she had no time for them. A crisis like thieves trying to steal something of Cuyler's had to be dealt with quickly before it exploded into something dangerous.

"What happened?" she gasped, deliberately grabbing Cuyler's gun arm between wrist and elbow. "Did they break in?"

His reply was the explosion of fury she had hoped to head off. "No, goddammit, they didn't. And I'd have got them, too—a couple, at least—if I hadn't been afraid of shooting up the van."

Cuyler, she thought, they were just kids. And the one who screamed was a girl. Still tugging at his gun arm, she said, "Then they didn't damage anything?"

"They would have, for Chrissake! In another minute they'd have had this door open, damn their—"

She shut her ears to the rest of it. Actually did so, yes. It was a trick she had learned long ago in self-defense, the way you learned, back in the old days, not to hear some of the more tiresome commercials on TV. Besides, Penny and Max had reached the van now. And other members of the group, evidently aroused by the gunshots, were hurrying toward them from the other two units.

There came a barrage of questions with Cuyler snarling answers and Rowena trying to coax him into being less angry.

Don Neal said at last, "Why don't you unlock the van and give me the gun, Cuyler? I can stay out here on guard the rest of the night." He said it almost casually, as if he were saying something ordinary such as, "Why don't we have some coffee and talk about this, Cuyler?"

"No fucking way," Cuyler growled. "If those creeps come back, I want to be the one to welcome them!"

"Cuyler, you have to drive tomorrow," said Professor Varga quietly. "Come now, what Don is suggesting makes good sense. Let him have the gun."

"Cuyler, you can't stay awake the rest of the night and be alert tomorrow," Lloyd Atkinson said.

It took all of them to talk Cuyler into it, but in the end, with a face-twisting scowl, he reluctantly handed Don the weapon. Not, however, without feeling he had to say, "You sure you know how to use this?"

Don ignored the sarcasm. "I'll manage. Have you reloaded it?"

"Of course I reloaded it. Here, take this too," Cuyler added, handing over his flashlight. "By the way, Neal—why didn't that stupid mutt of yours bark when those goons were out here?"

"Rambi isn't exactly a watchdog, Cuyler."

"Then what good is he, for Chrissake?"

Before Don could reply, the door of the motel office opened and, behind a weaving flashlight beam, the proprietress came trudging toward them. The group fell silent and turned to face her as she approached.

"I heard shots," she said wearily. "What happened? Did someone try to steal the van here?"

"Some people tried to break into it," Professor Varga said.

"Who did the shooting, you or them?"

"One of us. To—ah—frighten them off."

"Anybody hurt?"

"No, no. No one is hurt."

"Well, thank the Lord for that, at least. When I heard the shooting, I was afraid it meant more trouble for me, and I've got enough troubles." She waved a hand. "All right. Long as it's only that, I'll say good night."

She turned and trudged back to the office.

With the others still standing around, Don Neal climbed into the van. Cricket, pushing her way forward, would have climbed in after him.

He held up a hand to stop her. "Uh-uh, love. You need your sleep."

"How could I sleep, knowing you're out here alone?"

"Please," he said. "I'll get some shut-eye on the road tomorrow."

Shaking her head, she stepped back and stood there looking up at him. The others, including Cuyler, were already returning to their units.

Cricket never took long to make up her mind. After only a brief hesitation, she reached a decision. "You might fall asleep," she said, and in spite of Don's protests, climbed up beside him. "Anyway, with you out here alone, I know I wouldn't."

He stopped protesting and put an arm around her.

They were sitting quietly a moment later, her head on his shoulder, when they heard a motel door clatter open and someone shouting. Snatching up the flashlight, Don switched it on and dropped from the van seat to the blacktop, turning at once to sweep the row of units with the light beam.

It was the unit-six door that had been flung open. The occupants of that one had lit a lamp again and Professor Varga stood there framed in a rectangle of murky yellow, waving his arms, while the others poured out of their units in swift response to his yells. Don took a step toward them and stopped, torn between a desire to know what had happened and his duty to guard the van.

Cricket suddenly appeared at his side, touching his arm. "You stay here," she said quickly. "I'll find out what's wrong."

She hurried away, leaving him standing there in the drizzle with the flashlight in one hand and Cuyler's shotgun in the other. The light showed him little: only a cluster of shapes moving in and out of the professor's unit, accompanied by a buzz of voices. Finally

Cricket reappeared, trudging head-down through the drizzle toward him.

"What happened?"

"Get in out of the wet," she urged, and set him an example by climbing back into the van.

He followed suit, demanding again to know what had happened.

She turned toward him, shaking her head. "While we were all out here, someone stole some of Prof's things. No one thought to lock any doors. Maybe it was the same thieves we saw. Maybe others. Who knows? They just walked in and took what they wanted."

"What did they take?"

"Among other things, Prof's wallet. So now we may be short of money."

"Oh God," Don said.

"Prof says we won't really know how serious it is until we get to Chetwood and find out what they're asking for canoes and the rest of what we need. We'll just have to wait."

Don stared at her, but in the drizzling darkness her face was only a pale blur that told him nothing of her feelings. "Cuyler should have shot them," he said bitterly.

She took hold of his hand. "No. Please. Don't say that."

He was silent.

Her grip on his hand tightened. "Don't you see?" she whispered. "If we begin to feel that way, there'll be no hope for us. Not anywhere. Not ever."

Chapter Seven

Four miles west of the town of Chutes, the temperature gauge in Professor Varga's car began to climb alarmingly. With a frown of apprehension twisting his swarthy features, Varga brought the machine to a halt at the side of the road.

Cuyler's van, on ahead, had been out of sight for the past hour.

Those with the professor this second morning were his wife, Sheila, Dr. Dan Frazier, Don Neal, Cricket Swensen, and Cricket's miniature greyhound, Rambi, who had been dividing his time between her lap and the ledge behind the rear seat. They had left the motel soon after daybreak and been on the road for four hours, averaging only thirty-odd miles an hour because the road was in such poor condition. During those four hours they had seen only three other cars and found only one gasoline station open. The station had no gas, however.

"Once in a while we get some sugarcane petrol from your country," its middle-aged proprietor had said with a shrug of resignation. "But since the latest Persian Gulf blowout there's been precious little of the old stuff. I sell some food and a few odds 'n' ends, that's all. Guess I stay open just for somethin' to do."

They had been glad for the chance to buy food. As for fuel, they still had some in the containers brought from the city, and would surely be able to reach their objective. But now this.

"For some reason the engine seems to be overheating," the professor said. "I believe we'd better find out why." Reaching down with his left hand, he fumbled for and found a knob that released the hood latch.

The hood snapped up an inch, and gouts of steam spurted out from under it.

In silence, but unhappy and grim, the three men got out and walked to the front to assess the damage. The previous night's drizzle had finally ceased. A blurred, orange-hued sun struggled to burn its way through scudding, dark-gray clouds.

Dan Frazier lifted the hood and leaned in under it.

"Watch yourself," someone warned.

"I think we probably—yes, it's not the radiator. We've lost a fan belt."

"You mean it's gone?"

"Yes. It must have snapped and fallen off."

"Oh, God. Professor, I don't suppose you—"

"Brought a spare? No. In all the years I've been driving, I've never had a fan belt break. Have you?"

"Well, no, but—"

"It isn't a thing one commonly thinks of, or prepares for, is it?"

"Wait. You suppose that gas station we stopped at—"

"No, no. It's too far. Six miles, at least."

"More than that, don't you think? Seven or eight, easily. It would take forever."

"We'll be *here* forever if—"

"Cuyler will come back when he discovers we're not behind him. Remember our agreement. He was to stop every twenty miles."

"*We* remember our agreement. Will *he*?"

"Now, now, he's not a bad fellow. Of course he will."

"If it's seven or eight miles back to the gas station, we could do it in how long?"

"Too long. And the same length of time to get back. But we're only—how far are we from Chetwood, you suppose?"

"Fifty miles, perhaps. Or a little less."

"So even if Cuyler doesn't turn back to look for us until he gets there, he'll be here about the same time one of us could get back from the gas station."

"Unless he hangs around there waiting for us."

"Which he will, at least for a while. Count on it."

"But we still have no idea whether the gas-station fellow has any fan belts. He probably doesn't, you know. All that walking for nothing. . . ."

"And only one of us could go. The others would have to stay here with the women. It wouldn't be safe to leave them alone here in the middle of nowhere."

They would stay, they decided, and got back into the car. The conversation continued, and this time the women took part.

"If Cuyler does come back and has a spare fan belt that will fit this car—?"

"He won't, of course."

"You mean he won't come back? But of course he will, eventually!"

"I mean he won't have a belt for this car. Why should he?"

"But you think he'll be able to get one in Chetwood? Is that it?"

"We hope."

"Are they hard to put on?"

Silence.

"Well, are they? Has anyone here ever *put* one on? Do any of us even know how?"

"Well . . . Cuyler will know. Count on it."

"And if he doesn't?Or if he can't get one?"

"He can probably tow us to Chetwood."

"But that could take hours!"

"Well, we've plenty of those, God knows."

"Of what?"

"Hours. Time is the one thing we have in abundance, wouldn't you say?"

The talk tapered off and finally ceased altogether. Don Neal looked at his watch and saw that midday had come and gone. Feeling a need to get out of the car, he complained of cramped legs and walked down the road toward their destination. Overhead, the sky remained heavily overcast. Even the ill-defined, burnt-orange sun had disappeared.

On reaching a point where the road curved, perhaps an eighth of a mile from the car, Don saw what appeared to be a group of figures approaching on foot, a hundred yards or so distant. There were five of them. Their gait was unsteady, apparently purposeless. One of them, leaving the others, staggered to the road's edge and almost fell there, but regained his balance and went lurching back.

Trotting back to the car, Don leaned in through an open window. "We're going to have company. Druggies, they look like. Prof, what have you got in the trunk that we can defend ourselves with if they get nasty?"

The professor tugged on a handle that released the trunk lid; then he and Max quickly got out. Pushing two spare tires aside, Don lifted out a lug wrench and a tire iron. "How many?" Varga asked anxiously. "I mean, how many of them did you see?"

"Five."

"Should we face them, do you think? Or disappear until they've gone by?"

"They might strip the car," Max said. "Take all our gear."

"Yes, yes, of course. I wasn't thinking."

In silence, backed against the car with their gazes fixed on the distant bend of the road, they waited.

The oncoming five rounded the bend, saw them, and shuffled to a stop. Stopped first to stare, then to talk among themselves. Exaggerated, limp-armed gestures accompanied the talk. One of the group kept turning his head and spitting.

"They're deciding what to do about us," Don said.

"Yes."

"Can we handle them, do you think, Max? If they get ugly?"

"We're about to find that out, I think. Here they come."

The five had stopped talking and were in motion again. As they came lurching down the center of the potholed road, two broke away and staggered to a fallen tree at the road's edge. From the looks of it, the tree had been there for some time, perhaps for years. The two gathered up a number of broken limbs while the others stood swaying in the road, watching them.

The gatherers returned to the group and made a kind of ritual of handing out limbs to the others. Each of the five, as they approached the three men at the car and the two staring women inside it, brandished a heavy chunk of wood as a club. Their gait was a slow shuffle.

Ten feet from the machine, they stopped. They lifted the clubs high. They began a kind of grotesque ballet, bending their bodies forward and back, twisting their shoulders, bending their knees. Their rags of clothing flapped about them. The stink of them filled the air.

It was a kind of dance, Don realized as he prepared to defend himself, silently vowing to keep them away from the women in the car at whatever cost. Halleluja addicts did not simply kill their victims; they felt a need to turn themselves into freaks and perform a macabre death dance first. These dregs of humanity were human hyenas feeding on their victims' terror, savoring every dragged-out moment of the feast.

Meanwhile, there was nothing the intended victims could do but wait.

Now the tree-branch clubs were being tossed aside. Each of the monstrosities had drawn from somewhere in his flapping, stinking rags a thing that glistened: a thing that suddenly spat out a tongue of shining metal as the fingers clutching it pressed some sort of button or switch. The sham was over. The collecting of the tree limbs had been only a mockery, after all. Switchblades, not clubs, were the ritual weapons of Halleluja's high priests.

The druggies began to sing, if you could call it that. To sing the obscene songs that had been their hymns of hate from the beginning. Awaiting the slashing of the knives, you felt you were drowning in slime.

To begin the attack, one of the creatures, leering from ear to ear, darted in and grabbed at the tire iron in Max's upraised hand. Wrenched it away as Max blindly swung it. Then laughed—cackled—and flung himself into the idiot dance again, waving the thing like a banner. Another darted toward Don, dodged a swipe of the lug wrench and leaped back again, stretching his mouth from ear to ear in a twisted grin.

Don tightened his grip on the lug wrench and took a step forward. Anything, no matter how hopeless, seemed better than simply standing there waiting for a mass attack.

The druggies took it as a challenge.

The war dance abruptly ceased. The chanting dribbled away to a silence even more sinister than the sung threats. In a crouch now, with knives aglint in outthrust, weaving hands, the quintet closed in.

But suddenly the terrifying silence spawned a sound. Around the bend of the road came Cuyler's van.

Cuyler, at the wheel, must have sized up the situation the moment his vehicle rounded the bend: the professor's car there at the road's edge, the three men at bay against it, the five scarecrow figures advancing on them with switchblades. The van's engine sound swelled to a roar. The big machine literally sprang forward, like a beast of prey in a death charge. The druggies took one startled look and fled.

Cuyler stopped the van with a screech of

brakes and jerked the wheel, causing the vehicle to execute a ninety-degree spin and face in the opposite direction before lurching to a standstill. When it did come to a stop, he was already framed in the driver's-side window with a shotgun.

The gun thundered.

The druggies scattered from the road into dense underbrush, one of them clutching his side with both hands as he staggered from sight.

"And don't come back, you sons of bitches!" Cuyler bellowed after them as he opened the door and jumped down.

Don Neal lowered his lug wrench and leaned back against the car with his eyes closed, waiting for a feeling of weakness to pass. Max Krist stood there breathing heavily and staring into space. The professor, scowling, folded his arms and looked at Cuyler and said, "Thank God you came. We were beginning to think you had forgotten us."

The two women got out of the car, Cricket holding her little dog in her arms. Both women were white with terror, trembling as though their world had suddenly become icy cold. Neither spoke.

"I forgot," Cuyler said. "I mean about the every-twenty-miles thing. No, what the hell, I didn't forget. I just figured you guys were right behind us and you'd catch up when we got to Chetwood." Receiving no response, he turned to frown at the car. "What happened, anyway?"

"We've lost a fan belt," Don said.

"You what?"

"Lost a fan belt. Unless you have one that will fit—which you probably don't—you'll have to go to Chetwood and try to find us one."

"But not yet, please," the professor added quickly. "Not until we are sure those—those creatures—won't return."

Cuyler was still holding the shotgun. Saying, "Let's have a look at your problem," he thrust the weapon at Max and turned to the car.

For the first time, Don realized that Cuyler had been alone in the van. "Where are the rest of your people?" he asked in sudden alarm.

"What?"

"Rowena, the Atkinsons—the ones who were riding with you."

"In Chetwood. There's a restaurant open. It didn't make sense for all of us to come back here looking for you." Cuyler leaned in under the hood and his voice changed, becoming muffled. "Yeah, you lost a belt all right. Prof, you got a spare?"

"No. It simply never occurred to me to—"

"Okay, don't sweat it." Cuyler's mop of blond hair reappeared and he straightened up. "Anybody wearing a narrow belt?"

None of the men was. With a shrug, Cuyler unbuckled his own and pulled it through the loops. Though wide, it was soft and flexible.

Taking a red-handled Swiss army knife from his pocket, Cuyler dropped to his knees then, but before going to work on the belt, looked up. "Hey, now, keep an eye out for those bas-tards," he warned. "They just might take a notion to come back. You, Max. Be ready to use that gun, you hear?"

Max nodded.

In silence Cuyler went to work, first cutting the buckle off his belt, then scoring the belt to the width he wanted. With his head under the Avant's hood again, he shortened the belt to fit. With an awl-shaped blade of the knife he bored holes in the ends of it. Finally, using strips sliced from a rawhide shoelace obtained from his own backpack in the van, he laced his improvised fan belt into place.

Less than half an hour had passed when he straightened at last and said to the professor, "All right, start her up. Let's see if I got it."

The fan turned.

Threading a length of rope through his empty belt loops as casually as though he wore a rope belt every day, Cuyler turned to the pro-fessor and said, "Okay, Prof, let's move. But take it easy, you hear? I'll set the pace. And hey, listen." He paused in the road between the two vehicles. "All of you. Don't let's talk about this when we get there, you hear? With those bas-tards stealing prof's wallet last night, we may have to *sell* these cars to buy what we need. And these days, Jesus, if a car don't have a fan belt and you can't get one for it, it don't figure to be worth much."

Chapter Eight

In better days the town of Chetwood had proudly advertised itself as a gateway to adventure. Now it was a bump on the highway, a neglected side road, a handful of stores, a shabby hotel.

Only one outfitter was still in business. Its proprietor, a large, bearlike man who leaned on his counter while talking, barely glanced at the list they showed him, then quoted a price that was out of their reach.

"Money's no good anymore, anyway," he said with an eloquent shrug, and lifted his head to look out the open door at the two vehicles standing in the road. "That car and van belong to you?"

"Yes," Professor Varga said.

"You got proof of ownership?"

"Yes, we have."

"Tell you what I'll do, then. I'll take 'em in trade for what you got on this list here. Might even throw in a few extras you're likely to need."

Varga hesitated, then turned to his companions. On reaching the town, they had picked up those waiting in the restaurant, but only he, Cuyler, and Don Neal had entered the store. The other three men and the women had elected to remain outside in the vehicles, feeling the store would be too crowded with all of them in it.

It was odd, the professor thought. At their many meetings in his home, the members of the group had often discussed what they ought to do with the car and van on reaching their destination. In the end they had decided to say nothing about their real intentions and simply leave the vehicles in some safe place, as though planning to return for them. That way, if things did not work out, they actually would be able to get back to the city. Not to stay in the city, of course—druggies would have taken over their abandoned homes by then—but to reorganize somehow and decide on some other way of surviving.

Compliance with the bearded man's suggestion, then, would mean tearing up their return ticket to civilization.

"I believe we should discuss this outside,"

Varga said. "Come, gentlemen." He walked to the door.

Cuyler and Don followed him out, leaving the outfitter leaning on his counter. At the vehicles, Cuyler said in a hoarse whisper, without a moment's hesitation, "For Chrissake, do it! Take him up on it and let's get the hell out of here before he finds out about that damn fan belt. Come on. Let me talk to him!"

They went back inside, and Cuyler did the talking. "What kind of canoes you got, mister?"

"Featherlites. In real good shape."

"What kind of tents?"

"They're in good shape, too. Zylon. Real easy to carry." He turned, took a tent pack from a shelf behind him, and dropped it on the counter. "This here's the small size. How many of you in the party?"

"Five couples, one single," Cuyler said.

"Well, I can let you have six of these small ones or two big ones. Take your pick."

"The small ones," Cuyler said.

"And four canoes. You could make do with three, maybe, but four would be safer." The man behind the counter spread his arms. "So is it a deal? For the car and the van out there?"

"And the other things on the list here."

The man took up the list again and frowned at it. "How long you folks expect to be gone?"

"We don't know," Professor Varga said.

"What do you mean, you don't know? You have to, or how will you know how much of this stuff you need?"

"Give us what we can carry," Don said.

The fellow stared at them, then shook his head and shrugged. "Whatever you say. Come to think of it, I've got some survival stuff I can throw in, too. One of those outfits in the States sent me a whole lot of samples a while back. Don't ask me what it tastes like, I never tried it, but you're welcome." He leaned on his hands again, with his bearded face between hunched-up shoulders. "By the way, you people know this country? What you're getting into? If you don't, I could maybe fix you up with a couple of guides."

"No," Cuyler said. "No guides."

"You been here before, then."

"Well . . . yeah."

"When? Since they changed the names?"

"Names of what?"

"The lakes, most of them. Happened about four years back. Like it don't matter the country's going straight to hell—we have to stay up nights changing the names of things."

Cuyler turned to frown at the professor. "Do you have your map handy, Prof?"

"It's in the car."

"Better get it, huh? And the car title Mr.— What's your name, mister?"

"Ev Watson."

"The car title Mr. Watson wants. I got mine here." Cuyler took his from his wallet and placed it on the counter.

Watson picked it up and peered at it. Nodding, he handed it back.

Varga hurried out. Returning, he showed the outfitter his title and opened a well-worn map for the man's inspection.

"Well, sure, this map's all right," Watson said. "It's got the new names on it. Not that you'll actually see any difference, of course. Lakes don't change just because some loony politician goes off half cocked and wants to rename them." He glanced at the professor's car title. "Okay. You say some of you have made this trip before?"

"My brother," Varga said.

"All the way to Hudson's Bay?"

"Not all the way. Partway."

"Did I outfit him?"

"I think not. It was someone named Bethel."

"Jeff Bethel, yeah. He died—let's see—he died six years ago. No, seven. Well, all right. Why don't you folks go across to the hotel now and make your arrangements for the night while I get started on what you need here? What time you plan on leaving in the morning, anyway?"

"We'd like to leave now," Varga said.

"This late? No way." The bearded man vigorously shook his head. "You got a good piece of walking to do before you put your canoes in the water. By the time you got there on a mean day like this, it'd be near dark and you'd have to pitch camp. Makes a whole lot more sense to stay here at the hotel and leave at daybreak."

"You'll be up at daybreak?" Cuyler asked.

"With everything ready for you. Then you

hand over those titles and the keys to the vehicles out there, and you're on your way."

The small, shabby restaurant at which some of the group had eaten earlier was part of the town hotel. The proprietor, a thin man with a pockmarked face, said he had eight rooms still fit for occupancy and no other guests, so they could have as many rooms as they liked at sixty dollars a room.

"We're Americans," Max Krist said. "How much in our money?"

"The same."

"But the exchange rate—"

"Mister, I don't fool around with any exchange rate. The way things been going, nobody knows what it is till it's already changed, anyway. First thing you know, money won't be worth squat and we'll all be back to bartering for what we need, like the Indians did."

All the usable rooms were on the second floor, he explained. The group paid for six—one for each couple and one for Dan Frazier. Then, at seven o'clock, all eleven of them met by arrangement in the restaurant for dinner.

The two waitresses who were to serve them had pushed four small tables together to make one large one. "There's such a lot of you, we thought you'd like to make it a banquet, sort of," one said with a bright smile. She was young and pretty.

Professor Varga returned the smile. "Most

appropriate, since it will be our last such meal for some time."

"You mean you're going off on a camping trip?"

"Yes, miss."

"Oh, how *wonderful* to be getting away from all the terrible things that are happening! How long will you be gone?"

It caught the professor off guard. "I beg your pardon?"

"How long do you plan to be away?"

Varga looked down the table at the others. "Well, ah, we—we really haven't decided yet."

The girl gave him a strange look as she went on filling water glasses.

It was a better meal than they had expected, considering the shortages. Or perhaps, in a place this far removed from major problems, the shortages were less paralyzing. No menu, of course. Even the restaurants still open in the city had not had menus in recent months. Everywhere, now, you took what was served to you, though in some of the better places you might be offered a choice of two or three main dishes.

The pretty girl and her fellow waitress, who was older and much less attractive, brought a soup of some wild greens that none of the group could identify, then roast chicken with mashed potatoes and carrots, and finally apple pie and the synthetic brew usually served as coffee these days. It was over the ersatz coffee that Don Neal said to Theron Varga, who sat facing him, "How old was your brother when he made this trip, Professor?"

"How old?" Varga looked thoughtful. "Well, now, let me see. Anton was four years younger than I, and did this eleven years ago . . .

And I am now forty-nine, so he would have been thirty-four if my arithmetic is correct. Yes, he was thirty-four. Were he still living, he would be forty-five."

Anton Varga, Don recalled, had been one of the first to die of leukemia in the now abandoned town of Vale, where he had been a research chemist in the very factory responsible for the fatal toxic waste that caused the death of so many. A brilliant man. In fact, according to the professor, it was Anton who had begun to develop the emergency food tablets that all members of the group now carried in their backpacks. The professor had merely finished the project from his brother's notes.

"And you say he didn't go all the way north to Hudson's Bay, Professor?"

"No, not all the way. He told me they were gone about a month. Of course, they were not looking for something as we will be. They were simply four men on a camping trip."

"But you have his diary."

"I have his diary, yes." Behind the black facial hair that Varga was allowing to grow, the professor's smile was a playful child peeking out through a bush. "Mostly, I'm afraid, it's about the quantity and kind of fish he managed to catch each day. But it may be of some help to us." Leaning forward, he looked both ways along the table. "Is everyone finished? Shall we retire to our rooms and try for a good night's sleep in preparation for tomorrow? We depart at daybreak, remember."

The farewell banquet had come to an end. Each of the men except the professor, whose wallet had been stolen, left a generous tip for the two waitresses. At the top of the old wooden staircase, as the five couples and Dan Frazier went to their separate rooms, there were murmurs of "Good night" and "Sleep well."

Chapter Nine

In the room nearest the head of the stairs, Professor Varga sank wearily onto a chair and gazed at his red-haired wife. "Well, my dear, what do you think?"

"I think you'll have to wait a minute before we can talk, Therry. I shouldn't have drunk that awful coffee." The last few words came from behind the dark-green curtain that served as a door to the bathroom.

The sounds Varga heard then told him she had diarrhea. A touch of it, at least. But the coffee could hardly be the cause of it, he thought. Not so soon. More likely it was nerves, though Sheila seldom suffered from nervousness.

After a while he heard her rattling the handle on the toilet tank, and heard her say, "Damn!"

Then the curtain swished open and she stepped back into the room.

"Wouldn't you know? The toilet doesn't flush."

With all major problems apparently safely behind them, no such minor one as a malfunctioning toilet could dull the professor's bright mood. "My dear," he said cheerfully, "we won't have toilets to contend with after tonight. Tell me now—what do you think of our little venture, so far?"

She stood before the dressing-table mirror, gazing at her reflection and running her fingers through the red hair he so admired. "Two things worry me, Therry."

"Oh? What are those?"

"Cuyler and Dan."

"M'm." Varga continued to gaze at her but stopped smiling. "Are you saying we shouldn't have brought them along?"

"Maybe it's too early to say, but Cuyler . . . well, isn't he . . . that is, wouldn't you say he represents too much of what we're trying to get away from? The way he talks, I mean. His attitude."

"He was able to repair the car today, Sheila. If we hadn't brought him along, we might not be here tonight."

She walked to the bed and sat on it, looking into space. Then, still silent, she rose and began to undress.

"And what about Dan?" the professor said. "What problem do you have with him?"

"It's a problem I think *he* has, Therry. Or soon will have."

"Being the odd man, you mean?"

Forgetting she had brought no nightwear, Sheila took off the last of her clothes and now stood there naked—not the Irish beauty she must have been when young, but at thirty-seven still a handsome woman, softly curved in all the right places. With her hands on her hips, she faced him. "Therry, think about it a minute. We're going to have six of those small tents you talked about at dinner, no? And in all but his there'll be two people to keep each other company and help each other stay warm at night when the weather turns cold. Dan is going to be all alone."

The professor frowned at her, seeing not a naked woman but a man alone in a tent at night in a wilderness.

Sheila stepped into her panties and reached for her bra. "Now, that was real smart of me, wasn't it? I forgot we're not undressing for bed anymore. Hey. Are you coming to bed, or do you just plan on sitting there?"

"It *is* something to think about, isn't it?" her husband said.

"What is?"

"I have a feeling you're right. Dan should have brought someone. But it's too late now."

In room two, Max Krist broke a slice of home-baked bread he had brought up from the restaurant and handed the larger slice to Penny

Bowen. The room they occupied was a twin of the one the Vargas were in, with the same dark-green curtain for a bathroom door, the same double bed, the same two shabby chairs and small dresser. With her shoes off, Penny lay back on the bed and nibbled at her half slice of bread while talking.

"You know, I'm glad about the tents, Max," she said.

Max had placed one of the two chairs at the dresser and was writing in his notebook. He looked across at her and smiled. "That we'll have some privacy, you mean?"

"Uh-huh. I was scared half to death we'd all be using one big tent, or maybe two."

Max went to the bed, sat on the edge of it, and leaned forward to kiss her. He had to wait for her to stop chewing, but then made such a thorough production of it that she tossed away what was left of the bread and threw her arms around his neck. By the time he finished, she was holding him close and making small moaning sounds. Their lovemaking had always been a happy mixture of tumble and tenderness.

"If we weren't going to have any privacy on the trip, do you know what you and I would be doing tonight?" she whispered against his beard when she could speak.

"We can do it anyway."

"But not all night, like I planned. That's what I would have done—made love to you the whole night long, and never mind how tired we'd be in the morning. Now we can just do it like always, and get some sleep." Her mouth sought his again, and when that kiss ended she said, "What were you writing in your notebook?"

"What happened today."

"To them, you mean? The car breaking down? The druggies?"

"That, and the rest of it. Mostly thoughts."

In spite of his being a doctor of philosophy, Max had always treated her as though she were every bit as smart as he was. She wasn't, of course, but it was certainly nice of him to pretend she was. "Anything I should be thinking about with you?" she asked.

"I'm concerned about Cuyler, Penny."

She frowned. Why was it that whenever Cuyler's name was mentioned, she always remembered she was not white? Since meeting and falling in love with Max she had almost never given it a thought until Cuyler came into their lives. Was it because she could read the man's mind when he looked at her? Because she could see his word for black people in those cold hazel eyes of his?

"What about him?" she said.

"I'm not sure. Perhaps I don't feel entirely safe with him," Max replied, in the hesitant, extra-quiet way he always spoke when probing his own thoughts. "It bothers me, for instance, the way he has already pushed Prof and the rest of us aside and taken charge. I'm not sure I want him in command."

"He can't be in *command*, Max, can he? Didn't we agree to put things to a vote?"

"We did, of course. But I'm afraid we may be in for some surprises."

Penny put her arms around him again and pulled him down on her. It wasn't time for the anticipated lovemaking yet; they were both still fully dressed, and she knew he would finish writing in his notebook before coming to bed. But when alone with this man, this computer expert who wrote philosophical poetry, she always felt full of love and eager for him to know it. She might not always understand the things he said and wrote about, but she knew she would be lost without him.

Max, leaning over to kiss her again, looked into her face and knew well enough what it was that troubled him most about Cuyler. Knew, too, that he would not be telling her. It was not Cuyler's taking charge of things, but the way the man's voice changed when he spoke to Penny, as though with a woman of her coloring he didn't even have to pretend to be civilized. It was the lengthening of the man's usual scowl and the extra glint in those cold eyes when he looked at her.

Most of all, it was the feeling that one day Cuyler would say what he was thinking, and would have to be challenged for saying it.

The Atkinsons had room three.

While walking down the hall from the top of the stairs, five-foot-three Becky had been her usual self, clinging to the arm of her Ichabod Crane husband and gaily laughing at one of her own jokes. But on reentering their room she had suddenly become solemn, turning to him and saying with an anxious frown, "Lloyd, I just thought of something. Did you bring an extra pair of glasses?"

Lloyd's stringbean body seemed to freeze in midstride. "Uh-oh, did I? I don't remember."

"Oh God," she said. "*I* didn't pack an extra pair for you. I'm sure I didn't."

Hurrying to the two backpacks on the floor beyond the bed, she had picked his up, placed it on the bed, and opened it. Now she had its entire contents spread neatly on the bed for inspection. It was the way she had been in their drugstore—swift and efficient, with no wasted motions, though in the drugstore she had seldom been so tense as she was at this moment.

Without his glasses Lloyd would have a terrible time, she knew—and he was always losing or breaking them. He could see things close up, to be sure—could even see to read without them—but anything even ten feet away was little more than a blur to him. "They're not here," she moaned, turning to face him. "Lloyd, what are we going to do? There won't be a place here to have a pair made; I'm sure there won't."

Her stringbean husband took in a deep breath and simply stood there by the end of the bed, staring back at her.

"What are we going to *do*?" she repeated.

Suddenly his pent-up breath exploded and his whole body sagged with relief. "They're in my jacket," he said. He had worn a long-sleeved, rain-resistant jacket all day because of the intermittent drizzle. Damp weather made his chest ache.

Striding to the closet where the jacket was hanging, he found the glasses in the garment's left breast pocket. "Whew!" he said. "Don't ever scare me like that again, lady!"

With the glasses clutched in a shaking hand, he sat on the bed and looked at her.

She stood by the dresser, returning his stare.

Suddenly she went to him and held out her hands, and he clasped them.

Later, when they had put the light out and were in bed together, both in their underclothing, Becky said, "It looks as though we won't be sharing a tent with Don and Cricket, after all."

"Right. We won't."

"But we'll have a tent of our own. That will be even better."

"M'm."

"Is something the matter, darling?" She knew there was. She could always tell.

He did not answer.

"Lloyd? What is it?"

"I keep wondering if we should go through with it," he said in a low voice. "After what happened today—the way Cuyler forgot about the car and had to go back for it . . ."

"You don't like him much, do you?"

"Does anyone?"

"I suppose not. But he'll change, I think,

once we're under way. When being macho isn't so all-important."

"I hope to God you're right."

"Once we find the kind of place we're looking for, he'll be more like the rest of us," Becky said. "I feel sure of it."

Turning, Lloyd moved closer and pressed his face to her breast. "You know those bumper stickers that used to be so popular when we were younger? The ones that said 'I'd rather be fishing' or 'I'd rather be sailing'—that kind of thing?"

"Uh-huh. What about them?"

"I think I'd rather be running a drugstore."

Room four was like the others except for the pictures on its walls. There were two. One was an old photo of a wilderness waterfall with the caption "Mississagi River" written in faded ink on its bottom. The other was a print of a plaid-shirted fisherman in a canoe, on his knees to net a large red trout.

Rowena Cuyler, Professor Varga's "child of nature," sat with her shoes off on the edge of the bed, methodically massaging her feet. Her husband came from the bathroom with a glass half full of water and went to the dresser, where he completed filling the glass with bourbon from his bottle.

"Should you be drinking that water?" Rowena asked.

"You drank it at dinner," he said with his back to her.

"Yes, but I asked that little waitress—the pretty one—and she said they boiled it."

"What the hell." Cuyler lifted the glass to his mouth and drank a third of the bourbon and water down, then tipped the bottle over the glass again.

"She said the whole town boiled its water."

"Why? What's wrong with it?"

"What's *wrong* with it? Good grief. Where have you been living for the past five or ten years? On the moon, maybe?"

"Hell, we'll be drinking lake water from tomorrow on," Cuyler said, holding the bottle up to see how much bourbon remained in it. He might as well finish this one off tonight, he told himself; then he wouldn't have to backpack a near-empty bottle.

Rowena finished massaging her feet and lay back on the bed with her hands clasped beneath her head. There was no point in talking about the water any more, she decided. Cuyler might pretend not to care—he was good at not caring—but he had heard enough warnings on TV and seen enough of them in the newspapers to know there was a real problem. Why else, for heaven's sake, would both their own government and Canada's be handing out free testing kits for people to use? There was no point, either, in asking him to cut down on the bourbon. That problem would be solved only when he ran out of it.

What would he be like when that happened? she wondered. More even tempered? A little easier to live with, please God? Or would it make him even worse?

She remembered a newspaper clipping he'd shown her once, when he was playing football in high school. Eugene Cuyler, it said, was the kind of boy who always played as if he had a grudge against every member of the opposing team.

Cuyler had shown it to her with pride.

Her husband emptied the bourbon bottle into his glass, walked to a chair, and sat. "Well, what do you think?" he said.

"What do I think about what?"

"How we're doing so far."

"All right," she said. "We're doing all right, I guess. They're nice people."

"They're a bunch of weirdos, you mean. We get on the trail tomorrow, and I'll bet you not one of those guys even knows how to pick a canoe up and carry it."

"They can learn, Cuyler."

"Sure, sure, they can learn. But who'll have to teach them? Me, that's who. I'll have to teach every one of them every goddamn thing, like how to carry a canoe, pitch a tent, make a fire . . ." He turned on his chair to look at the fisherman in the canoe, netting the red trout. "Even how to do that, most likely."

"So, then, they'll be glad to have us along," Rowena said. "What's wrong with that?"

"I'll be doing all the damn work. That's what's wrong with it."

The liquor was talking, Rowena thought, and she had better change the subject. "Anyway," she said, "I was real proud of you today, the way you fixed that car. We all were."

"What do you mean, *we*?"

"*They* were, then. But, Cuyler, we're all together in this now, can't you see? We have to be, if it's going to work."

Cuyler finished his drink and glanced at the empty bottle on the dresser. Frowning, he shifted his gaze to his backpack, which lay within reach beside his chair. There was another bottle, a full one, in the pack. Did he want to open it here or save it?

Save it, he reluctantly decided. There'd be times in the days ahead when a drink would be more important than it was right now.

He began to undress. "You taking your clothes off tonight?"

"Why?"

"Come on, do it. It'll be our last night in a bed."

She looked at him. He hadn't made love to her in more than a week, but evidently he wanted to now. It must be the liquor. Not that liquor always turned him on. Sometimes when he got drunk he only became the football player with the grudge and slapped her around.

She took her clothes off, but slowly, waiting for some hint of which Eugene Cuyler she would have to deal with. But Cuyler was busy taking his own clothes off. She still did not know what to expect when he stepped naked to the bed and looked down at her.

"You know something?" he said. "Prof thinks you're pretty special."

"Does he? You mean he's said something to you?"

"He don't have to. Are you blind, you haven't noticed how he looks at you—like you're a pitcher of cream fresh from the cow and he's real deep-down thirsty?"

"Cuyler, stop it," she said. "Don't say crazy things like that."

He got into position the way he always did, without any love talk or touching or kissing to make her feel good about it. Then, with his eyes only inches from hers, he worked his mouth into a scowl and said something that spoiled it for her even before he started.

"Let me give you some advice," he said. "If that old bastard ever makes a pass at you, you tell him real quick to back off, you hear? Or he won't be alive to enjoy this 'haven' we're looking for, even if we find it."

In room five at that moment, Don Neal and Cricket Swensen were also in bed together, and had been for some time. Cricket's little greyhound, Rambi, lay on a chair with his head on his front paws and his eyes wide open, watching them.

Like the Cuylers, Don and Cricket had taken off their clothes and were about to make love.

But with them, making love was much more than a mere physical act. Always, from the beginning of their relationship, it had been a profound statement of their love for each other.

They lay face-to-face with their arms around each other, their bodies one body. "You know something?" Don said with his lips close to hers. "This may be our last time in a real bed."

"For a while, maybe. Not forever."

"What do you mean?"

"Do you know what I see when I close my eyes?"

She knew how he would answer that, Cricket told herself with an inner smile. He would say something like, "What do you see when you close your eyes, darling?" This man who had been such a wonderful teacher of kids with special needs would never let her down at such a moment. And when he said it, his voice would be gentled by the understanding that was so much a part of him. Especially in moments such as this.

"What do you see when you close your eyes?" he said.

"I see a log cabin by a lake somewhere. A lake of clean, sweet water. And in the cabin I see a homemade bed much nicer than this one because we built it together. Maybe a smaller bed, too, for a child. The way it must have been years ago before all the overcrowding, the pollution, the drugs, the greed." She pressed her body hard against his. "Isn't that what you see, darling?"

101

"Yes," Don said. "That's what I see, too."

And they lived happily ever after, he thought, as in a fairy tale. But fairy tales were only fantasies, weren't they? The only reality Cricket and he could cling to was that they had each other and would be facing the future together, whatever it held for them.

Chapter Ten

In room six, Dr. Dan Frazier lay on his bed, gazing at the ceiling, and thought about the wife who had left him. Where was she now? he asked himself. Was she better off, safer, than she would be if here by his side, or had her flight to Miami, to join her widowed sister, been a frying-pan-into-the-fire thing? Miami was said to be right up there with New York, Los Angeles, and Chicago on the list of the worst nightmare cities.

What, he wondered, were the couples in the other rooms doing? What were they talking about? Why did he feel so alone?

In the beginning he had been stunned when Ellen elected to flee to Miami rather than become a member of the professor's group.

Theirs had not been a bad marriage, only an unexciting one, and the thought of taking part in the hegira without her had frightened him. Then, strangely, he had been almost relieved to know he would not have to think for two—glad he would be free, without the obligation to look after a wife or girlfriend as the other men in the group would have to do. Face it. With Ellen having deserted him, all the problems of marriage had fallen from his shoulders and left him feeling years younger.

Why, then, did he feel so alone now?

Still fully dressed, he got off the bed and went to the dressing table to peer into the mirror there. Thirty-nine, he thought. Two evenings ago he had danced with the professor's wife, Sheila, in her living room, and felt like a teenager.

Striding to the door, he stepped into the hall and closed the door behind him.

As he went down the hall to the head of the stairs, assorted sounds reached him from behind the closed doors of the other rooms. People were talking; some were moving about. His was the only silent room, he realized with a frown. At the foot of the stairs he slowed his pace—must not seem to be too eager, too much in a hurry—before entering the restaurant where the group had been served dinner. Striving to appear only mildly interested in what he was doing, he leisurely made his way to a table and drew back a chair.

The place was empty and silent.

"Hullo!" he called out. "Is anyone here?"

In the empty restaurant, his voice and the footsteps he heard seemed a bit spooky, as if he were an actor in some sort of horror movie. The door to the kitchen swung open and one of the two women who had served them appeared.

But not the one he had hoped for. Not the young, pretty one. Did he want this one?

She saw him and came to the table where he sat. "You're back? Is there something you want?"

He looked up at her. "I—ah—was wondering if you have any of that coffee left?"

"You want coffee?"

"Please, if you have some."

"I'll see." She went away. God, she was homely. Even the way she walked was homely, as if only her legs were capable of movement. What rotten luck. The other had been young and fresh, with such a pretty smile.

She came with a cup of coffee, an envelope of what passed for sugar now, and a tiny paper cup of imitation cream. "You want anything else?"

He frowned up at her. "Where's the other young lady?"

"Alison? Gone home. I'd be on my way home, too, if you hadn't walked in." Obviously she was not happy about having to wait on him.

"I'm sorry. I didn't realize it was so late. Are you the last one here?"

"Except for the night clerk I am, yes. And it's

a half-mile walk to my house." She had her hands on her hips now and was glaring at him. "And I don't like walking home in the dark these nights, I can tell you. So if you could take that coffee up to your room . . ."

"I'm sorry." He stood up. "But wait. Why don't I walk you home? I could use the exercise. I've been riding in a car all day."

The frown faded. "You mean it? You really want to walk home with me?"

"I'd like to."

"What will your wife say? No, I remember now—you're the one who didn't have anyone. At supper, I mean. All the others did, but you didn't."

"That's right. I'm alone."

"Just give me a minute to get my bag, then," she said, and hurried back to the kitchen.

It was strange, he thought as he walked along the broken sidewalk with his hand on her arm. Except as a doctor, he hadn't touched a woman since Ellen, and it was pleasant to be walking up through the town with this one, even though he had no idea where she was taking him or what would happen when he got there. At this hour the town seemed all but deserted. They passed a row of stores, all of them closed and some boarded up. The sidewalk ended when the stores did, and he found himself walking through weeds and grass at the edge of a road that appeared to have been blacktopped once but was now mostly dirt.

"What's your name?" she asked.

"Dan Frazier."

"I heard some of them calling you Doc at dinner. Are you a doctor?"

"Yes, I am."

She turned her head to look at him with some interest. "When you get back from your trip, why don't you think about staying here in Chetwood. We sure could use a doctor here."

"You don't have one, you mean?"

"We did—old Doc McGovern—but someone broke into his house one night about three months ago and shot him. Someone after drugs, most likely. He had his office there in his home."

"You mean you have a drug problem here, too?"

"Lord, yes. Name me a place that doesn't."

Night was coming down. The trees beside the road had lost their individual shapes and become a single wall of shadows. "What's your name?" Ian asked her.

"Martha."

"Well, Martha, I don't know what I'll be doing when I come back. I'm not even sure I'll be coming back."

Without breaking her stride, she turned her head again to frown at him. "Just you, you mean, or all of you?"

"All of us."

"Where are you going, for heaven's sake?"

No one had ever before put the question to him in such a way, as if injecting it with a hypodermic needle. He had to let it take effect for a

107

moment. Then he said soberly, "I don't think any of us know. At least, we won't until we get there."

"You mean . . ."

"We're a little like those ancient mariners who set out to explore an ocean, not knowing whether they'd find a new land or drop off the world's edge."

With her head turned in a way that had to be causing her neck to hurt, she continued to gaze at him as they walked along in the deepening dark. "Well, anyway," she said at last, "if you do come back here, just remember we need a doctor." And then: "Here's where I live."

The house was a small one, standing alone in darkness just off the road. At the door Martha took a key from her handbag.

"You live here by yourself?" Dan asked.

"I do now. My husband took some fellows on a fishing trip last year and they came back without him." She turned the key in the lock, straightened, and looked at him. "You never did drink your coffee back there at the hotel, Doc. Would you like some here?"

"I would."

"Come on in, then. I'll make some."

She had electricity, he was surprised to learn. Back in the States, at least in his state, that would be highly unlikely in a country home half a mile from the nearest small town. As she went through the house to the kitchen at the rear, she turned on light after light and through an open door he caught a glimpse of a neatly made double bed.

"Have a seat," she invited, waving him toward a kitchen chair.

He sat. While she put water and coffee in the coffeemaker, he said, "You say your husband *took* some men fishing. He was a guide of some sort, you mean?"

"He worked for the power company. But he did guiding, too, when Ev Watson needed someone. I went along sometimes, to help out."

"Watson is outfitting us," Dan said. "Unless there's more than one man of that name in the business here. Where did this happen? Where did your husband disappear, I mean."

"Lake Fletcher, they call it now."

Dan thought he had seen that name on the professor's map. "I believe that's one of the lakes on the route we plan to take. What actually happened—if you don't mind talking about it?"

"Nobody knows what actually happened. They got there all right, the other three said. They'd been there several days. Then one morning when the others woke up, Dan was gone."

Frazier, who had been talking more or less shotgun style while looking around the kitchen, swung quickly on his chair to focus his gaze on her back as she stood at the stove. "Your husband's name was *Dan*? Like mine?"

She must have caught the disbelief in his

voice. She turned to face him. "That's right. His
name was Dan. Dan McNae, spelled N-a-e. I'm
Martha McNae." A smile brushed her homely
face, vanishing almost at once. "It's something
to think about, isn't it?"

It certainly was, Dan thought.

She set the table with two small plates, two
cups and saucers, some silverware. Then she
brought a plate of what he guessed were oatmeal cookies and, finally, the coffeemaker. In
silence she poured the coffee. Then: "Like I
said, they just woke up one morning and found
him gone," she said. "Ev Watkins and another
man went up there and looked for him, but
they never found anything. He just disappeared
off the face of the earth, seems like."

"Drowned, perhaps?" Frazier suggested.

"If he fell in off the shore, maybe—which is
sort of cliffy in places, Ev said. There wasn't a
canoe missing." As she leaned over the table to
pour his coffee, he noticed for the first time
what she was wearing. Strange. Ellen had
always accused him of being blind when it
came to what women looked like—meaning
what they had on, or sometimes how they did
their hair.

She, Martha McNae, was wearing a sort of
silvery shirt—or blouse, he guessed it was—
with long sleeves that fastened at the wrist, and
a black wool or flannel skirt, and when she
leaned over to pour his coffee he found himself
looking at her breasts. She wore a bra, but her
breasts were full and the bra too old and loose

to confine them. She might be homely in the face, he thought—though now that he had spent some time with her even that was questionable—but there was certainly nothing wrong with her body.

"Sugar?" she asked.

"No, thanks."

"Milk? I've a can of evaporated. We don't get it fresh anymore."

He shook his head. "Please sit down."

She sat, and his gaze met hers across the small table. No, he decided, she was not homely at all. She had a fine, strong face and good brown eyes. Her mouth might be a little large, but her lips were attractively full and soft-looking. All in all, she was a handsome woman.

But now, for some reason, they seemed to have run out of things to talk about.

Trying to think of some way to break the silence, he ate an oatmeal cookie and sipped his coffee. They had stopped looking at each other. At last, almost in desperation, he said, "Don't you find it lonely, living here by yourself?"

"Sometimes."

"Is it safe? For a woman to be alone out here, I mean."

"Well, folks do tell me I should have a dog. But I had a big black Lab I was really fond of, and when he passed away last year I just didn't feel up to getting another."

They talked about her dog, each of them groping for words to keep the conversation alive. They finished their coffee. Martha McNae stood up and took in a breath.

"Well, Doc? Are you ready?"

"For what?"

"Why, to go to bed with me, if that's what you came here for." She seemed genuinely surprised. "That *is* what you came for, isn't it?"

Staring at her, he put both hands on the table and slowly pushed himself to his feet. "Oh Lord," he said. "Was I that obvious?"

"Well . . ."

"I'm sorry," he blurted. "It's just that I'm new at this kind of thing. I never looked at another woman while I was married, or even thought about it after my wife left me—until tonight. Then, when I realized I was the only loner in the group . . ."

"You thought of Alison."

"No, no, wait. I just wondered what would happen if I went downstairs and—"

"It wouldn't have worked out," Martha McNae said. "Alison has a boyfriend she's crazy about." Her attempt at laughter told him that while she was trying very hard to seem worldly, she was in fact nervous, perhaps even a little frightened. But then she stepped forward and placed a hand on his left shoulder. "Doc," she said, "I haven't been with a man since I lost my husband, and I've been pretty lonely, too. I guess what I thought . . . well, I said to myself, he's nice looking and he's a doctor, so it will be all right."

112

Frazier stood up and took her into his arms.

When he kissed her there in the kitchen it was a wholly new experience. Never before had the touch of a woman's lips on his given him such a sensation of being reborn, of having stepped from one world into another. He was still in a kind of dreamworld when they walked together into the bedroom and undressed and got into bed together. Then the sensation of being reborn was repeated.

With Ellen, making love had always been a cut-and-dried thing, a mere going through the motions. This woman used her lips and hands to bring out feelings he had never even heard of before except in certain books he had glanced at out of mere curiosity and dismissed as unreal.

But when she awakened what had so long been asleep in him—what, in truth, he had never dreamed was there at all—they spent the best part of an hour making love to each other and then fell asleep like children tired after a session of play. It was four in the morning by his watch when Frazier opened his eyes. The light was still on in the bedroom.

He was on his back. Martha, still asleep, lay on her side with her head on his shoulder and one leg over both of his. Reluctantly he nudged her awake.

"Hey. We have to talk."

She pressed herself against him, voicing little sounds of pleasure. "Talk about what?"

"I have to go. My crowd leaves at daybreak. Martha, listen." He made it urgent. *"Why don't you come with us?"*

She opened her eyes at that. Opened them wide and looked at him. "Why don't I do *what?*"

"Come with us! They'd approve, I know they would. They think it's wrong for me to be alone when all the others are paired off." He waited for an answer, but none was forthcoming. "Martha? Will you?"

"Oh my God," she said in barely audible voice. "I'd love to, but you don't even know where you're going."

"What does it matter?" He began touching her again, but not the way he had before. Not caressing her. Just wanting desperately to hold on to her. "Wherever we end up, whatever happens, we'd be together. We'd have each other."

She pulled away, and he knew he had tried too hard, had frightened her. "Wait," he begged, but she was out of bed, reaching for her clothes. Was dressing in such frantic haste that she already had her skirt and bra back on before he could extricate himself from the bedsheets and reach for her.

"No!" She turned away to escape his hands. "No, no, Doc. You're crazy!"

Naked, he stood beside the bed with his arms limp at his sides, wanting to cry. "But didn't you feel just now . . . ?" Dear God, how could she not have felt it?

She was putting her blouse on, and answered

114

him with her arms in the air. "Doc, I don't know what's got into you, but—" The garment settled into place, and she shook her head at him. "Me go off into the bush with you and those others? Not even knowing where you're headed, or if you'll ever come back? No, no, Doc. I may be lonely here, but at least I have a place to live and something to eat." She backed away. "Be sensible, Doc. Get dressed now and go. Please. Don't make me sorry I let you walk me home."

It was no use, he realized. She must like him or she could never have made love to him that way, but she hadn't any understanding at all of what he and the others hoped to do. If he could spend a few days with her he might be able to make her understand, but he hadn't a chance in the short time left before daybreak.

Martha had left the bedroom. In silence, defeated, Frazier began to put his clothes back on.

She was waiting by the front door when he finished. When he stepped forward to kiss her good-bye, she put out a hand to stop him. "Uh-uh," she said, shaking her head as she retreated from his reaching hands. "I like you, Doc, but just go. Please."

When he stepped out the door to begin the half-mile walk back to town, he felt as though he were leaving something of himself behind. All the way to the hotel he cried tears of helplessness at being unable to change the way things were.

Chapter Eleven

Daylight was still a gray haze when they assembled in the hotel restaurant the following morning. They would have to carry their own food from the kitchen to the tables, the cook informed them. "Both of our girls live a good way out of town, and we couldn't ask them to walk here in the dark. It'd be too dangerous."

So, Frazier thought sadly, I'm not to see Martha McNae again.

After a simple breakfast of eggs, toast, and coffee, they went across the road to the outfitter's store and found Ev Watson waiting for them with piles of food and other supplies lined up on his grimy counter. The size of the piles brought gasps of consternation. It had been one thing to see these items listed on a sheet of paper. This was something else.

The big man leaned on his counter, looking more like a bear than ever. "I been thinking," he said. "Seems to me you folks ought to fix those packs of yours a little different. If you go dividing this stuff up amongst the lot of you, you'll be forever trying to figure out who's got what. Right?"

No one answered him.

"So"—he shrugged—"if I was you, I'd put all this food, for instance, in one pack. Or two, if it'd make the one too heavy." Turning to a mound of plastic bags, he took them up one by one and checked them off against his list. "You got flour here. Rice. Coffee. Tea. Dehydrated vegetables and fruits. Macaroni. The usual small stuff like salt and pepper. And there's some other stuff here, too, that I figured you'd be glad to have. What I'm saying—if you divide all this up between you, you won't know where anything is when you come to fix a meal. You agree?"

They did.

"Same with this other stuff." Walking along behind his counter, he waved his hand over a much larger assortment of items that included blankets, axes, and a cooking outfit. The latter consisted of nested lightweight pots and pans, a folding reflector oven, sturdy plastic plates and mugs, the expected silverware, and a solid-looking coffeepot that would also serve for making tea.

"You see what I mean?"

They spent the next twenty minutes rearranging their packs. In the end, those to be carried by the women held not only each bearer's personal belongings but those of her man as well. The men's packs contained food, supplies, and the five small tents. Dan Frazier, having no woman to carry his personals, would take care of them himself, along with the cooking outfit.

The bear nodded his approval. "Better. Lots better. None of 'em's too heavy, either, seems to me. If they do seem a mite heavy at first, you can leave the canoes behind at the early portages and four of you walk back for them. We done that often with the old wooden canoes, I can tell you. Step up here now and watch me."

On a sheet of brown paper from under the counter, he drew a rough map showing the road they must follow to reach the lake. "You have about a mile to go before you come to the trail that leads in to the lake itself. You'll see a sign: Dunsmore. No way you can miss it." He waited for their nods. "Anything else I can do for you here? No? Then suppose we go out back and see about the canoes."

Until last year, he explained, he had kept his canoes in a boathouse at the lake. "As a convenience to my clients, you understand. What I done in those days was load people and their packs into my truck here and drive them to the lake to save them the walk. But I quit after thieves broke into the boathouse and made off with two of my best canoes. A man has to be more careful these days. Anyway"—he shrugged—"my truck's out of commission now. Transmission's busted and I can't find no one to fix it. So I keep all my canoes in the back room of the store, and this morning, before you come over, I moved yours out into the yard."

It was daylight now as they stepped out into his yard. The sun had not yet risen, but the sky was clear, and apparently they were to be spared the drizzle of the previous day. "You know how to carry these?" Watson said, stopping beside an overturned canoe.

"I've carried wooden ones," Cuyler said. "These don't look so different."

"They're different. Don't be fooled because they're green. This Featherlite stuff is tough as steel, but lighter'n anything we ever had before. Here, I'll show you."

Stepping forward, Watson reached under a canoe for a pair of paddles. As if he had done it a thousand times and could do it in his sleep, he flipped the craft right side up and lashed the paddles side by side to the two middle thwarts with strips of nylon rope already in place for that purpose. That done, he grasped the gunwales and smoothly swung the craft upside down over his head. When he lowered it into place, the paddles acted as a yoke to distribute the canoe's weight evenly to his shoulders, and his head disappeared into the space between them.

His voice came out muffled. "It's real easy, see? You got any questions, any of you?"

"We'll be okay," Cuyler said.

Watson returned the canoe to the ground, stepped back, and turned to peer at Cuyler. "You being the one with the know-how, I'd sort of help the others out at first if I was you. Be easier for them. But they'll get the hang of it quick enough."

"I'm sure we will," Professor Varga said. "So, has the moment of truth arrived?" He turned to look at the others. "Are we ready to go, gentlemen? Ladies?"

There were murmurs of assent.

Varga took the keys to his car from his pocket and extended them to the outfitter. Cuyler, with a scowl, did the same with his van keys.

"Good luck to you," Ev Watson said. "But remember, a deal's a deal. If you decide to call it quits up the line somewhere and turn back, the vehicles belong to me." He dropped both sets of keys into a shirt pocket. "Tell you what. Why'n't you let me put those backpacks in the van and drive them up to the lake for you? I could take the ladies along, too, if they like. Four of you fellers'll have to tote the canoes up there, though. No way can I carry those."

"I prefer to walk," said Cricket Swensen

without hesitation. "You can take my pack, and thanks, but I'm walking with my boyfriend."

The other women echoed her decision. Watson shrugged. "Well, then, all of you just bring your packs to the van, if you will." He turned to direct a scowl at the lineup of packs. "You got your names on them? Yeah, I see you have. Good idea, they being new and so many of them looking alike. Just hope you used waterproof ink that won't wash off in the rain. Well, then . . ." He walked to a gate in his backyard fence and swung it open.

They carried the packs to Cuyler's van. The men, all except the professor, returned for the canoes. Then, in single file, with the canoe bearers leading the procession, the eleven began their journey. Cricket's little dog, who had thoroughly investigated Watson's store and yard, trotted happily along beside the column. The road they followed was the one Dan Frazier had walked the night before with Martha McNae.

As they neared her house, Frazier felt his heart pounding. Last night was still the strangest, most unforgettable night of his life, its events so vivid in his mind that all else seemed scarcely worth thinking about.

Would he see her again? Would she come to the door when they passed? She must, she must! After all, an expedition of this size could not be an everyday thing, even here.

But what if she were in town? What if she

had already been at work in the hotel when they left Watson's place?

To see better, he raised the bow of the canoe he carried. And just ahead, on his left, was the house.

What a disappointment! In his mind it had been an enchanted cottage, a dream house. In reality it was only a drab gray box that looked forlorn and abandoned. Or was it disappointing only because she was not there in the doorway, as he had so desperately hoped? And because *he* felt forlorn and abandoned?

Ah, Martha, if only you had said yes . . .

The door opened as he stared at it. And there she was.

Frazier stumbled out of line, so excited he lost his voice and was unable to call out to her. With the canoe still balanced on his shoulders, he stumbled, almost fell, but regained his balance and went staggering toward her.

She took a step forward as if to greet him, but stopped and stood motionless on the porch, in front of her open door.

Frazier managed at last to swing the canoe to the ground.

"Martha—"

The others had halted in the road and were watching him in amazement, but he was not aware of it.

"Martha—thank God!" He stumbled again, on the single step up to where she stood. He had his arms out. "Martha, come with us! Please!"

When she took a step back, her eyes wide and staring, he knew he had gone about it wrong. Knew he should have kept himself under control and remained calm.

"Martha, I'm sorry. . . ."

She stopped retreating and simply stood there in the doorway, a picture in a frame, not quite clear because of the shadows. Afraid to go closer lest she disappear altogether, Frazier resisted an almost overpowering impulse to reach for her.

Be calm, you idiot. You've frightened her!

"Martha—darling—think about it. You can't stay here much longer in any case. What's happening everywhere will happen here too, and then it will be too late. Please, please come with us. They *want* you to. Ask them!"

She continued to stare at him from the doorway, her hands now gripping the sides of it so fiercely he could see the whiteness of her knuckles. She shook her head. "No, no . . ."

"Why?" he begged. "We can have a life together, like these other couples! A *good* life, Martha. Last night you felt the way I did. I know you did. Oh God, Martha, please . . ."

He could not help it. He stumbled forward, reaching for her.

Had he been wrong about why she opened the door? Had she done so to leave for work, not just to watch him and the others trudge past? It had to be that. Because now, instead of running back into the house and slamming the door shut in his face, she unexpectedly ran *at* him, pushing him so hard he staggered backward off the porch and fell to his knees in the yard. By the time he had recovered from the shock of it and struggled to his feet, she had fled past him and was far out of reach, racing down the road with her hair flying.

Not even once did she turn her head for a backward glance at him.

She didn't feel any of what you felt last night, Frazier. The truth is, she didn't feel anything at all. Stop being an idiot.

The others were still motionless in the road, waiting to see what he would do. Biting his lip, he walked over to his canoe and swung it up into position. No one spoke when he rejoined the group. It simply came to life again, as though what had taken place at Martha's cottage were merely part of a videotape that had been frozen for a few minutes and then allowed to run again.

No, there was a flaw in that analogy. One member of the group did acknowledge that something unusual had happened. As Frazier put himself in motion along with the others, Cricket Swensen's little dog suddenly appeared at his feet to trot along beside him, curiously looking up at him.

Why hadn't Martha listened? Dear God, why hadn't he been able to say something to make her understand that her only hope for survival was to do what he and these others were doing? So what if it was crazy? So what if it failed to work and only hastened the end for them? For those who didn't try to do *something*, the end was inevitable anyway.

In spite of the canoe, he turned to look back. The house—that house in which for a few glorious moments he had felt reborn and wholly alive again—had mockingly disappeared, and so had she. A little while later they came to the sign Ev Watson had told them about. Bearing the words LAKE DUNSMORE, it was a weathered wooden thing in the shape of an arrow, directing them down a pair of sandy ruts that curved mysteriously from sunlight into woodland shadows.

They turned down it.

Ten minutes later they had to step off the road to let Cuyler's van pass, with Ev Watson at the wheel.

Soon after that, they arrived at the lake and found the van awaiting them at what had to be the boathouse Watson had talked about. The backpacks were already unloaded.

With his big hands on his hips, the outfitter watched them ready the canoes. "You figured out how you'll split up in those?" he asked. "Be best if you do it by weight, I should think. Not that any of you weigh a whole lot."

It was one of the many things they had discussed back in the city, at some of their meetings. They told him so.

He shrugged. "In any case, you can make changes later if you have to. Got another suggestion for you, based on my experience with sports who never did this before. I'd suggest you don't try to go straight across this lake but stay close to shore. Be safer till you get the hang of those canoes. And I'd make camp over there if I was you, 'stead of trying to go on farther today. With most of you being new at this, and no guides to do the bulk of the work, it could take you quite a while to get those tents up and fix yourselves something to eat."

"That would seem to be very good advice, Mr. Watson," Professor Varga said. "We thank you."

"Well, then, I'll be getting back." Watson climbed into the van and waved good-bye. "So long. Best o' luck! Hope you find whatever it is you're looking for."

Chapter Twelve

In the last canoe to leave shore and glide out onto the lake were Cricket Swensen, Penny Bowen, Don Neal, and Cricket's dog. Cricket had the bow paddle, Don the stern. Max Krist's girlfriend sat amidships with a hand on each gunwale.

Before they were a hundred yards from shore, Rambi had finished investigating the backpacks and settled down at Penny's side to gaze wide-eyed at the unfamiliar world opening up before him.

In the canoe just ahead were Lloyd Atkinson, Sheila Varga, and the professor. In the one ahead of that were Max Krist, Becky Atkinson, and a very quiet Dan Frazier, who appeared to be paddling as though in a trance, merely going through the motions.

In the lead canoe was Eugene Cuyler, with his wife plying the bow paddle. "Better let me go first," the gunshop man had suggested. "Just me and Rowena. We have the guns to look after, and we can carry some extra gear in place of a third person." Not once had he let his precious collection of guns out of his sight. Now, tied in plastic to make them waterproof in case of rain or accident, they lay within reach, close to his feet.

It was understood, however, that the arrangement was subject to change. In the days ahead, most of their waking hours would be spent in the close confines of these four canoes, and it was important for those traveling together to be compatible.

At the moment, though obviously feeling he was in charge, Cuyler was actually taking someone else's advice. Instead of heading straight across the lake to the portage on the far side—as he had talked about doing—he was staying close to the heavily wooded shore as Ev Watson had suggested.

Don Neal looked past Penny Bowen and Rambi and said to the woman in the bow of his canoe, "No problems, Cricket? Everything all right?"

"No problems!" she called back cheerily, without turning her head.

"You, Penny?"

"None here, either. I'm loving it." The black

girl did turn her head. "I can't get over that out-fitter, though, demanding the car and van for four canoes."

"And tents, Penny. Don't forget the tents, and the rest of what he gave us."

"He took us, though. You know he did."

"Well, at least we're on our way."

On their way, yes. Don's gaze traveled ahead to the other canoes, each of them creating a spearhead of wake in the almost dead-calm water. At last, he thought. After all the weeks of planning and preparation, they had finally put the past behind them. If the future turned out to be anything like this moment of fulfill-ment—this "moment of truth," as Prof had called it—he would be content. A quiet lake, a moosebird shrilling in the top of a pine, the whispery wing-throb of wild ducks high in a cloudless blue sky . . . it was a magic world so different from the sordid, dangerous one they had left. On shore, darkly mysterious woods were relieved occasionally by multicolored walls of rock rising from patches of sandy beach.

They were doing this in the footsteps of the early explorers, Don mused. Of Indians and fur traders and Jesuit fathers. He was beginning to feel like an explorer himself. And he was with the woman he loved.

His gaze traveled ahead to Dan Frazier, in the canoe behind Cuyler's. What had happened back there on the road from town to the lake, when the doctor had startled them all by breaking ranks and running to the gray cottage? Dan had offered no explanation, then or since. The woman in the doorway had been their waitress the evening before. The homely one. Why had Dan wanted to talk to her? What had they been talking so excitedly *about*?

A sudden sound from shore interrupted Don's musings. Pausing in the midst of a paddle stroke, he turned his head. Cricket followed suit, and Penny Bowen also turned her head. Like statues, the three gazed at the point on shore from which the sound seemed to come.

Something was crashing through the underbrush there. Something big.

Suddenly a large brown shape leaped from an explosion of growth at the lake's edge. Hurtling out over the water, it landed with a huge splash and seemed to head straight for the canoe on an attack course.

"Cricket, go!" Don yelled.

Both of them dug deep and sent the craft lunging ahead, out of the thing's path. Both looked back when aware that the danger of a collison was over. There was no pursuit. The creature had not been attacking them, after all. A bull moose, it stopped at that moment, turned, and swam slowly back to shore. All in the four canoes watched it as it scrambled awkwardly out of the water and disappeared into the forest.

Cuyler waited for the other canoes to catch

up to him. When they had done so, there was a discussion.

"He may have been trying to outrun deerflies that were annoying him," Professor Varga offered. "That is, if deerflies attack moose. I don't know. My brother wrote in his diary that he saw them drive a running deer nearly crazy once, until it reached a lake and plunged in."

"Anyway," said Cuyler, "if there's a few of those suckers around, we won't be short of meat."

In single file they went on again. On to the end of the lake. And yes, Ev Watson had been right, they agreed. They were tired. At least the paddlers were. Muscles ached that had never ached before.

A small wooden sign in the shape of an arrow, nailed to a tree, bore the stenciled words POR. TO J.L. 72 CH. That translated, they decided, into "Portage to Jones Lake, 72 Chains." Almost a mile. All agreed they would be a weary lot when they got there, as Ev Watson had predicted. Too weary, at any rate, to make a proper camp and prepare a decent meal. They should make camp here and continue the journey in the morning.

Cuyler said, "Prof, you want to test the water? See if it's okay to drink?"

"And if it isn't?" Lloyd Atkinson said.

"We can use the tablets," said Sheila Varga. Her husband, not trusting the purification tablets issued by the government along with its testing kits, had made up some of his own.

Professor Varga tested the water and shook his head. He filled a water bag and dropped in two of his tablets. "In an hour or so," he said.

Cuyler cut some tent poles and suggested they watch him put up his tent. With Rowena helping him, the task took but a few minutes, after which, armed with a machete, he disappeared into the forest to cut pine branches for bedding while the others struggled with their shelters. By the time all the tents were in place he had made half a dozen trips, returning each time with his arms full. "Got some balsam here, too," he announced triumphantly. "Makes an even better bed. Now let me show you how to use this stuff."

The tents supplied by Watson were larger than pup tents but not tall enough for a man to stand erect in. For this task, however, Cuyler would have been on hands and knees anyway. Working from the head of the bed area to the foot, he layered the pine and balsam boughs in a compact spread, tucking the butts of the topmost layer deep into the greenery beneath. Over this soft cushion went the blankets, and the bed was finished. Cricket's dog promptly pronounced it satisfactory by bouncing up and down in the middle of it with yelps of delight.

"You got it?" Cuyler asked, pushing himself to his feet.

They had it, they assured him.

"Okay, then. While you guys fix up your beds I'll find us some firewood and try for some fish. I dunno about the rest of you, but I'm hungry."

He disappeared from the lakeside clearing again, this time with an ax, and soon they heard him at work not far away. This time he returned with an armload of dry wood.

"Poplar, most of this is. Good firewood."

The tents had been set up more or less in a circle. Cuyler dropped his firewood near the center of it and turned to his wife. "Show them how to make a fire, hey? I got more important things to do." Without waiting for a reply he strode to his tent, swapped his ax for a fly rod, and made for the small, sheltered cove where they had drawn up the canoes.

A moment later they saw a canoe glide out from behind a screen of trees, with Cuyler in its stern and the fly rod lying across the thwarts in front of him. The band of his felt hat now bristled with fishing flies. For a while they watched him, admiring the way he handled the craft. Then they went about their chores.

When Cuyler returned two hours later, the men had long since finished and the women were impatiently waiting to prepare a meal. He had three small trout on a string and wore a scowl that discouraged comments or questions.

"It's the wrong time of day," he said angrily. "That is, if there's any fish in this bastard lake at all. I had to troll for these and look at them—too small. Watson should've told us, damn him. If he had, we wouldn't have made camp here."

He had cleaned the trout at the lake's edge. Now he thrust them at Rowena. "Won't be enough, God knows, but you got rice and other stuff to go with them." His face still a thunder-cloud, he strode to their tent and disappeared into it, to emerge with a bottle of bourbon. Defiantly he stood there glaring at them, with the bottle tipped to his mouth.

His wife, her lips tight-pressed, glanced at the others and quickly turned away to begin the meal.

In preparing that first meal, Rowena unob-trusively took charge but welcomed the other women's help. They cooked rice and steamed the three trout in some of the professor's puri-fied water. Discarding the bones, they added the fish to the rice and served the mixture with ban-nock cooked in a fry pan. The group sat around the fire and ate without much talk, Cricket and Don sharing theirs with a hungry Rambi.

Over the coffee that followed, Becky Atkin-son, the pharmacist's wife, said vaguely, "You know, I'm not sure that fish tasted quite right. Am I the only one?"

"No, you're not," said Sheila Varga. "I noticed it too."

"One of them was a funny color," Max Krist added.

They looked at the fisherman.

Cuyler shrugged. "Tell the truth, when I caught that third one, I wasn't sure what it was. I mean, I knew it was a squaretail like the oth-ers—you could tell that by its shape—but I never saw a squaretail milky gray before." Scowling, he turned to the professor. "Maybe it was a new breed? Or a cross?"

"Or a mutant," Varga replied quietly.

"Or what?"

"This past year or so we've heard a lot from Europe and Asia about mutants. Not fish—animals. In one case, even humans."

Cuyler stared at him. "You mean like the bigfoots?"

"Like the sasquatch, yes. And the yeti. If, indeed, those are mutants. At any rate, the reports have been from highly respected sources, so it would not surprise me greatly to find mutant fish in these waters. Especially at this stage of our journey, so close to our pretty civilization."

"You mean it'll be okay when we get farther along?"

"I most devoutly hope so," Varga said.

There was a silence. Then Cuyler, his meal finished, tossed his empty plate aside and rose to his feet. "Jesus," he said. "If the fish here are weirdos, I'm going after some meat before dark. Sure as hell I'm not gonna be a vegetarian." Muttering, he strode to his tent.

When he reappeared a moment later, he had a small automatic rifle in his hands, one he had proudly described earlier as "the latest from the Middle East and the best little killer on the market today." With it he vanished into the woods again.

Just before dark he returned. Professor Varga and others, brewing a pot of tea at the fire, looked up and asked the expected question.

Cuyler strode past without a reply and they

heard him in his tent, raging at his wife. They saw Rowena come from the tent a moment later and walk to the lake's edge. She was still sitting there with her arms about her knees when darkness wiped the last faint reflection of sky glow from the lake's surface. Then she rose and trudged slowly back to her tent, passing those at the fire without a word.

"So sad," murmured Professor Varga to his companions. "So very sad."

"And not a thing any of us can do about it," observed Max Krist, the philosopher, who had been recording the day's events in his notebook.

Chapter Thirteen

Three days later, alone in his tent, Max Krist again wrote in his notebook.

"Cuyler went fishing with Lloyd Atkinson today, and this time it was Lloyd who hooked a strange-looking fish. They brought it back to show to us, but we have not eaten any of the suspicious-looking ones since Sheila Varga became slightly ill at the first lake. Actually, Sheila blamed the hotel coffee rather than the fish—said she had diarrhea before that, at the hotel—and did in fact recover quickly, but I suspect her husband is right in thinking that the odd fish we have encountered are mutants. Before embarking on this journey I read everything I could find about this region, and believe

I know what the fish in these lakes are supposed to look like.

"Today, while Dr. Frazier and I were out searching for dead wood for the fire, he explained his odd behavior on our walk from the town to the first lake. I was mildly surprised, because I had put it out of my mind. All of us had, I'm sure. He seemed to want to talk about it, though. It would seem that he and the woman who lives there—one of our two waitresses at the hotel—had spent the previous night there at her home, and he is convinced that he fell in love with her and she with him. The first part of that I tend to believe—he was so obviously desperate to talk to someone about it. But I hardly expect to look up one day and see her paddling a canoe across some deep-woods lake in a mad attempt to overtake us!

"We are camped on our fourth lake now, and the water is better, Prof says. He tests it, of course, at every new lake we come to. Soon, perhaps, we shall be able to stop using the tablets. Food has not been a problem. Among us we have quite an assortment of fishing equipment—at Cuyler's insistence, even the non-anglers among us brought some sort of gear—and fishing has become a recreational thing for nearly everyone. Not all of us actually *catch* fish, but those who do are able to keep us well supplied. Too, Cuyler goes hunting at every opportunity and has brought back both game birds and small animals. As might be expected, soups and stews have become staples of our diet.

"We owe much to Cuyler, I must admit. But in a less laudible way—unfortunately—so does his wife. Yesterday morning she appeared with a red welt on her cheek which she claimed was caused by the zipper on a sweater she had used for a pillow. This morning she explained away a larger, uglier bruise by saying that she had fallen during the night when leaving their tent to go to the bathroom.

"But I must give this up now and turn in. We plan to rise at daybreak to begin the portage to something called Fergus Lake. Fergus? I wonder which patron of our lake-renaming politician answered to that name. And was he Angus Fergus, say, or Fergus McAngus?"

On Fergus Lake the following afternoon, Cuyler paddled his Featherlite along a heavily wooded shore a mile from camp and cursed the lake for being uncooperative. "A whole hour we been out here, and not a single fucking strike," he complained. "What're you using now?"

His canoe-mate this afternoon was Don Neal. "The red-and-gold streamer you handed me a while back," Don said.

"That, huh?" Cuyler took off his hat and studied the array of flies on its band. "You know what I think? If there *are* any fish in this lousy lake, they're not trout. Didn't Prof say his brother caught pike in some of these lakes? And bass?"

"I really don't know, Cuyler. I haven't read his brother's diary."

"What we need is some live bait, I say. Come on, reel in and let's find some."

Fergus was a long, narrow lake walled in by forest, and they were more than a mile from the clearing where the group had made camp. But they were close to shore, and before long found a grassy opening where they could safely beach the canoe. Together they drew the craft out of the water.

"What kind of live bait are we looking for?" schoolteacher Don Neal asked.

Having fished for more than an hour without even a strike, Cuyler was in one of his dour moods—as much a result of injured pride, perhaps, as their failure to find food. "What the hell do you mean?"

"Cuyler, be a little patient with me. I'm new at this. Are we after worms?"

"Christ, no. You can't dig in this stuff, even if we had a tool to dig with."

"What about a knife?"

"You can't dig with a *knife!*"

With an effort, Don kept his voice level. "So . . . back to square one. What are we looking for?"

"Something small that jumps or crawls or wiggles, for God's sake. Anything that even moves, grab it."

There was no path for them to follow. At

some of the earlier lakes there had been, but after the first two days the only trails they had found were the marked portages linking bodies of water. Still, after struggling through thick woods for some fifteen minutes, the two came to what Cuyler said was probably a deer or moose run. For two hundred yards it snaked around large gray boulders close to the water's edge.

Suddenly Cuyler, in the lead, lurched onto his knees and thrust out his hands. His yell— "Got you!"—exploded like a gunshot in the forest quiet. Scrambling to his feet again, he turned triumphantly to Don and held out his prize.

It was a frog, but a strange-looking one, more yellow than green, with three eyes in a head much too large for its legs and body. For some reason—perhaps because of the extra eye—Don felt sorry for it.

Cuyler must have felt something too, if only a touch of uncertainty. "What do you think, huh?"

"It's too big, Cuyler. Don't you think it's too big?"

"Well . . . oh, shit, I suppose so." Cuyler spat in the face of the squirming creature and hurled it full-force against a nearby boulder, where it hit with a sodden thud. Fragments of flesh flew back with such force that some of them splattered against Don's pants, and one stuck to his neck.

He winced as he tugged a rag of handkerchief from his pocket and wiped his neck clean. "Did you have to do that, Cuyler?"

"Did I have to do what? What the hell are you bitching about now?"

"Did you have to kill it? It was only a frog, Cuyler. It wasn't doing us any harm."

"It had three eyes, for Chrissake! *Three* of them. What the hell's got into you, anyway? Here we are in a world gone stark raving mad, all poisoned and sick, and you bitch about what I do with a dumb frog that's got too many fucking eyes!" Cuyler spat again, this time on his hands before wiping them on a clump of grass. "You nature boys make me sick," he added under his breath—but loud enough, perhaps intentionally so, for Don to hear.

Don glanced at him—a movement of eyes only—and, in silence, continued the search for bait.

Soon afterward, Cuyler captured some crickets and a smaller frog with only the usual number of eyes, and the two men returned to the canoe. But it was late. A setting sun had splashed the calm waters of Fergus Lake with what looked like red enamel and set the tops of the taller trees on fire.

"We better start back," Cuyler said. "But I'll troll on the way. Maybe our luck'll change."

Using combinations of lures and live bait, he caught three large lake trout before they reached the campsite on the opposite shore. With the canoe pulled up and turned over, he handed the string of fish to Don. "Here, you clean them. I'll have to go find some firewood."

He was wrong about the firewood, at least. Some of the others had rounded up a supply and were in the process of getting a fire started. Little by little, Don thought, the group was learning how to do what had to be done. Before long, perhaps, Cuyler and his know-how would not be so necessary.

Dan Frazier, for instance, had fashioned a crude bow and some arrows, and had been practicing with them in anticipation of the time when Cuyler would run out of ammunition and not be able to bring in the occasional small animal or wild duck he now managed to add to their food supply. A rare grin appeared on the doctor's face as Cuyler and Don approached the fire.

"I don't think we'll be needing those tonight," he said, dismissing Cuyler's fish with a languid wave of the hand. "Take a look in the pot."

Don did so. "Smells good, at least. What is it?"

"A rabbit stew," said Frazier, still grinning, "And *that*"—pointing to the homemade bow leaning against his tent—"is what got us the rabbit."

"Three eyes, you say?" said Professor Varga with a frown that all but squeezed his own eyes shut.

The meal was finished. Cuyler's trout had

been used, after all, to supplement the rabbit stew. As daylight turned to dark the pilgrims, as Max Krist now referred to them, sat talking about the fire. Cricket Swensen's Italian greyhound lay at her feet, as attentive as though he understood every word.

"That's right, three eyes," Cuyler replied with a snort. "And a head way too big for the rest of it. Damndest-looking frog you ever saw."

The professor shook his head. "It is so sad, don't you think?"

"Sad?"

"But of course, Cuyler, of course! For years now, man has either poisoned the creatures who share this planet with him or wantonly killed them off. We keep catching mutant fish. Today you encountered a three-eyed frog. Because of man's greed, assorted seals, turtles, whales, dolphins—I could go on and on—are nearly as extinct as the dinosaur." Varga sighed, shaking his head. "Do any of you realize how many creatures were on our endangered-species list before it was given up as an exercise in futility?"

"And no one cares," said Max Krist.

"Oh, some of us care, Max. Some have cared for a long time. But we are so pitifully few, and so helpless to do anything about it."

Cricket Swensen reached for a stick and began to poke at the fire. "In a sense, that's why we're here, isn't it? When you can't do much about an impending catastrophe, you try to save yourself by running away from it."

"Getting back to that weirdo frog," said Cuyler, "whaddaya suppose caused it to grow an extra eye, Prof?"

Varga let silence take over while he considered his reply. The others waited, Cricket thinking that with the firelight flickering on his untrimmed beard, the professor looked a little like a portrait in an old illustrated Bible she had once owned. In fact, all the men did now. Cuyler had advised against shaving, warning them that the ever-present blackflies and midges would find them easy prey if they did, even with frequent applications of what he called fly dope. In any case, they had been too busy for such nonessentials.

The professor finally spoke. "Why a three-eyed frog? Who can say with any certainty? By definition, a mutant is the result of a rapid change in hereditary characteristics. But who knows for sure what is causing so many such changes in our world today? For years we have ignored warnings about the dangers of toxic waste, landfill seepage, acid rain, et cetera. For years we have known the probable consequences of cutting down our trees to make room for more and more houses. . . ."

"Meaning the price we're paying for the population explosion," Lloyd Atkinson said.

"The population bomb, yes." Apparently forgetting where he was, Varga rose to his feet and began pacing back and forth with his hands clasped behind his back, as though he were in a classroom. "Back in ninety-one there were something like five point three billion persons on this planet, I believe. And what is the count now? Nine billion? Ten? We can't double our number again without paying a fearful price, you know. Already South America and Africa are disaster areas.

"And our *climate* is changing," he continued. "*We* have caused it to change. With factories still belching contaminants into the air, and every year fewer and fewer trees to absorb them, we in our stupidity have been doing our utmost to make our only world uninhabitable."

Seeming suddenly to realize where he was, the professor stopped pacing and sat down. "I'm sorry." He shook his head. "This doesn't help us much, does it?"

"I wonder if nature may be getting even," Cricket said.

Varga turned his head to peer at her. "Striking back, you mean? That thought has occurred to me, too. Or if not *nature* getting even, as you put it, this tormented planet on which we live. What if, after all, our earth is a living organism and we humans are actually no more significant than fleas on a dog? Is it so difficult to imagine the earth's losing patience at last and turning on its tormentors?"

"Well, excuse *me!*" Cuyler snorted.

"What did you say, Cuyler?"

"I said count me out. If I'm just a flea on a mutt, or whatever you just said, I'm heading for the sack. Come on, Rowena." He grabbed at his wife's hand.

Rowena tugged the hand free. "I'll be along in a minute, Cuyler. This is interesting, what Prof is saying."

"Dammit, come *on!*" Again he grabbed her hand, this time jerking her to her feet.

Night had fallen. Without further protest Rowena allowed herself to be led from fireglow into darkness, leaving behind a silence unbroken except for the small sounds of the fire.

After a while Professor Varga said with a sigh, "Well, should we put out the fire and turn in? We do have to be up at first light to break camp."

When the others responded by getting to their feet, he stood up with them, shaking his head. "I wasn't too bright, was I? Perhaps I should have anticipated that such a man would not appreciate being told he might be only a microscopic irritant on the epidermis of a living earth."

Not sure he was finished, the others respectfully waited before going to their tents.

"But," he said, concluding his lecture, "we can't deny that it may be a possibility confronting all of us, can we? At least it is something we might begin to think about."

Chapter Fourteen

This time the sign at the start of the trail had read POR. TO F.L. 160 CH, and according to the map they carried, the F.L. meant Fletcher Lake.

Fletcher, Dan Frazier recalled as he lowered his canoe at the end of the two-mile carry, was the lake where the husband of Martha McNae had disappeared.

Usually Cuyler, not he, was the first over a portage, but this morning the gunshop man had been more than happy to relinquish the lead. Half a mile back, convinced he had seen a deer, he had snatched up his automatic rifle and gone into the woods after it.

Needing a rest, some of the others had stopped to await the outcome while three, including Frazier, continued on. Without meaning to, Frazier had forged ahead. Now he stood alone at the lake's edge, stretching the ache out of his arms and pondering what Martha McNae had told him.

So this pretty body of water, all aglitter in bright morning sunlight, was where it had happened. This was where the other Dan in Martha's life had vanished while guiding some sports on a fishing trip.

What, actually, had happened here? The man had been a guide, hardly likely to make some careless mistake. Had an argument of some sort precipitated an act of violence?

It could well have been something like that, Frazier decided. An unforeseen act of violence followed by panic . . . the body disposed of so no one would find it. Otherwise, why hadn't it been discovered by the Chetwood men who came here in search of an answer? Unless, of course, McNae had drowned and was somewhere on the bottom of the lake here. This Fletcher Lake appeared to be as large a body of water as any they had yet encountered, and was undoubtedly deep.

How large was it, anyway? An estimate was difficult from where he stood, because a heavily wooded point of land, jutting out on his left, partially blocked what lay beyond. The lake *felt* big, though. It felt very big indeed.

As he stood there gazing at it, a family of merganser ducks swam into view around the point and caught his attention. He counted nine of them. Suddenly they saw him, or something else frightened them, and all nine quickened their pace to race madly along near the shore, quacking up a storm.

The two adults led the parade, with the little ones strung out behind. And, yes, it was his presence that had caused the sudden rush in search of safety, for the one bringing up the rear kept turning to look at him, its curiosity apparently overruling its fear. Each time it did so, the inspection ended with a squawk and a cocky flirt of its head as it worked its feet like pistons to overtake the others.

The little guy had a sense of humor, Frazier thought with a grin.

Windfalls along the shore there were like giant pickets in a blown-down fence, some of their tops far out in the water. Each time the merganser family found its escape route blocked by one, all in line except Tail-End Charley swung out around it. Charley refused to be detoured. Those fallen trees that were not too high he leaped over like a hurdler. Those too high to hurdle he plunged underneath, popping into view on the other side at the same headlong pace.

Frazier laughed aloud.

Suddenly an unlikely burst of gunfire shattered Frazier's euphoria, and he swung about to look back up the portage. Into view came an inverted canoe wearing the arms and legs of a man.

With a practiced stoop, Max Krist slipped out of tumpline and yoke, then squirmed out of his pack and looked back up the trail. "Sounds as though Cuyler may have got something," he said.

Frazier nodded.

Max faced the lake again. "What a pretty place! Seems hard to believe anyone was ever here before us."

"I've been watching that family of ducks." Frazier turned to point, but had to lower his half-raised arm and shake his head; the mergansers had disappeared. "You got here just a minute too late, Max. There were nine of them. Beautiful things. The gunfire must have scared them."

"Maybe it's a good thing."

"What is?"

"That they took off before Cuyler got here."

Frazier looked again at where he had last seen the ducks. Not once, he realized, had he thought of them as being something to eat. Perhaps he might have if there had been only one or two of them instead of a family, and no precocious little guy at the tail of the procession making him laugh.

At the lake's edge Max had scooped up a handful of water and was tasting it. "I wonder how this will test," he said. "Be nice if we could stay here, don't you think?" He lowered himself onto a patch of leaf mold sprinkled with clumps of fern and the wild orchids called lady's slippers. "Aren't you getting a yen to settle down somewhere, Doc? At least for a while?"

"I guess we all are."

Lloyd and Becky Atkinson arrived then, followed soon by all the others except Cuyler and Rowena. Rid of their packs and the canoes, they sat to rest and discussed the sound of gunfire, which all of them had heard.

"If he did get a deer, they may need help with it," Lloyd said, tilting his glasses to the sun while wiping some kind of yellow pollen off the lenses with a handkerchief. "Should some of us go back, do you suppose?"

"I suggest we wait to find out," said Professor Varga. "He'll call if he needs assistance, I should think."

"Would we hear him?"

Varga smiled. "He would let us know somehow. Be sure of it."

But when the missing couple appeared some fifteen minutes later, Rowena had only her pack to carry and Cuyler only his canoe and pack—unless the scowl on his face could be considered an added burden. When the pair had shed their loads and were resting with the others, Don Neal said carefully, "We heard you shooting, Cuyler. What happened?"

Cuyler glared at him. "I missed the son of a bitch, that's what happened."

"The deer, you mean?"

Cuyler was examining a thumb that appeared to require his full attention.

"*Was* it a deer you shot at?" Don persisted.

Cuyler looked up. "I thought it was, for

Chrissake. All I got was a quick look at it. Anyhow, I missed." He pushed himself to his feet and strode to the lake's edge. There, turning his head, he said defiantly, "There's no law against missing once in a while, is there?"

"I think," said Professor Varga, quickly rising, "we had better see what the rest of this lake looks like and decide on a place to make camp."

As Frazier had suspected, the lake was a large one. Larger, in fact, than it appeared to be on the map they carried. The campsite agreed upon was a strip of flat land on the far shore, atop a low face of rock.

Professor Varga tested the water and found it cleaner than any they had yet encountered. Not safe enough to use without his tablets, but so nearly as to encourage him to say, "Maybe the next lake will be the one we're looking for. Or the one after that."

Making a camp was routine work now. The men put up the tents and sought bed boughs. The women gathered firewood and built a fire. Here on the Fletcher cliff top the tents were laid out in a row and the fire was built against a handy flat stone that would serve nicely as a dining table.

But no one had caught any fish this morning, and Cuyler had failed in his attempt to bag the deer. The meal consisted of Professor Varga's survival tablets and a soup made from some of

Ev Watson's dried vegetables. Afterward, no one was surprised when Cuyler, his meal finished, went in silence to his tent, reappeared in silence with his automatic rifle, and disappeared silently into the forest.

"Poor fellow," the professor remarked. "He is most unhappy about losing that deer."

"He's a lot more than unhappy," said Rowena. "None of you know my husband yet. He's mad clean through."

"Were you with him when he shot at the deer and missed?"

"No, I wasn't."

"Well, anyway," Lloyd Atkinson said, getting up, "I think I'll try for some fish in case he's unlucky again. Anyone want to come?"

"I will," said Don Neal.

"*I'm* going to have a bath," Penny Bowen announced. "Even a swim, if the water isn't too cold."

"Back in the city it was cold every time we had a power outage," Cricket reminded her. "Which was about every other day toward the end, I seem to remember."

"But this water is *cold*, Cricket!"

Yes, Cricket thought, the lake would be cold. They would step into it with trepidation, shivering even before their bare feet touched it. The men still joked about a time, two lakes back, when Max had dived in off a ledge some six feet above the water and, on making contact with the water, had shot back up again like a missile fired from a submarine. Or so they claimed. But it was encouraging how quickly everyone had become adjusted to what they had thought would be hardships. To sleeping in tents, for instance, and cooking over open fires, and keeping their clothes and themselves clean without benefit of washing machines or bathtubs. Much of the time it was even fun.

She and Penny walked along the ledge together, descended to the little beach where the canoes were drawn up, and took off their clothes. They walked into the water holding hands and laughing, and it was cold—yes, it was cold!—but after the first shock they made a game of it. They got wet all over. They soaped themselves, being careful to use no more soap than was necessary and to carry the bars to the beach, not throw them, when finished. Then they dived in and splashed around for a few minutes before running out, laughing and shouting, to snatch up towels and rub themselves warm.

Don Neal and Lloyd Atkinson came down to the beach while this was going on. Each carried a fishing rod. On their way to the canoes, they waved without stopping. "Warm it up for us, will you?" Don shouted. "It'll be our turn when we get back." By the time the men had launched a canoe and disappeared around a turn of the shore, the women were finished.

Gone most of the afternoon, the fishermen returned with enough lake trout for the evening meal. They cleaned the fish at the water's edge and handed them to Rowena Cuyler at the campfire.

"Cuyler isn't back yet," she said. "Do you suppose something's happened?"

Lloyd shrugged. "Not to him. Anyway, he's got his gun."

"We haven't heard any shots," Don said. "He's probably still looking for something to shoot at."

"He was in a mean mood. I'm worried."

"Do you want us to look for him?" Don asked. "We can if you—"

"No, no. Not yet, anyway." Rowena pretended to be busy with preparations for the meal. "Take it easy awhile, why don't you? You've been out on the lake a long time, and it's been a hard day."

Thinking back over the day's demands— breaking camp at dawn, lugging canoes and gear over a long, hard portage, setting up a new camp, searching for bedding and firewood— Don forgave himself for feeling a bit done in. But it was a relief to know he could stand up to such a routine. They were all more fit than they had been, he realized.

In his tent, finding Cricket resting in her underwear after her bath in the lake, he removed his boots and lay down beside her.

"You smell good," he said.

"I'm afraid you don't, love. Among other things, you smell of fish-cleaning and canoe-carrying."

156

"I should take a bath, hey?"

"Not now. I can see you're tired. But before tonight—yes—it would be nice if you did."

Don was alone in the tent when he awoke an hour later. Reaching out to lift a flap, he saw the others at the fire, which had been lit for the evening meal. Cuyler, he noticed, was not one of the group. When he pulled his boots on and went to join them, he found them wondering what to do about the gunshop man.

Less than a moment later there was a crackling of underbrush at the edge of the campsite, and Cuyler himself suddenly appeared there.

When he saw them all staring, Cuyler stopped and glared back. It was a challenge, Don thought. Then the hunter came striding across the camp and thrust his weapon at Rowena.

"Put this away, will you? And bring me a drink."

"Your liquor's finished," his wife said. "You finished it last night."

"Jesus."

"Sit down," she said. "You're tired."

Sinking onto one of two dead logs the men had placed near the fire to serve as benches, Cuyler leaned forward and held his hands to the flames. "I'm cold." He looked up. "Aren't the rest of you cold, for Chrissake?"

No one had noticed any special chill in the air. It always turned cool after sundown.

"Must be where I was," Cuyler grumbled. "There's a small lake—pond, I guess you'd call it—a couple of miles back in there. Anyone got the map handy?"

"It's in my tent," Professor Varga said. "Shall I get it for you?"

"Yeah, yeah. I don't remember this lake being on it—maybe it's too small—but let's have a look. Damndest place you ever saw—dark, spooky—but Jeeze, I saw a squaretail jump that must've gone six pounds, and I'm going back there in the morning and get that sucker. You just watch me." With the same challenging stare they had seen when he emerged from the woods, Cuyler leaned back from the fire. "Anybody want to come with me?"

"Why, yes," said Dan Frazier quietly. "I think I'd like to."

"You sure? It's no picnic getting through that bush."

"I'm sure."

"Okay. But we'll have to leave early. And hey"—this time Cuyler directed his scowl at the others—"I saw some berries back in there. High-bush blueberries, huckleberries, I dunno what they are, but there's a whole lot of them and some are ripe and a bunch of little birds was eating them, so they must be safe. Why'n't a couple of you come along with me and Doc and pick some? We could have some blueberry pancakes before we run out of flour."

Lloyd Atkinson leaned toward his wife and reached for her hand. With their heads together they exchanged a few words, then looked at Cuyler.

"Becky and I would like to go along, Cuyler. To pick some berries, that is. Not to fish. If it's all right with you."

"Sure it's all right," Cuyler said. "We'll leave after breakfast."

Chapter Fifteen

Frazier emerged from his bachelor tent at day-break, shivering in a clammy mist as the flaps rustled back into place behind him. It was a different world from that of the day before. Everything in it was drenched with dew. The lake was a sheet of quicksilver with not a whisper of breeze to ripple it. From somewhere close to camp came the harsh cry of a whiskey jack.

At the fireplace, Cuyler finished whittling a fuzzstick and with some birch bark that had been stored under cover, managed to get a fire going. He turned his head as Frazier approached. "Morning. You got your tackle ready? Fly rod? Some flies and stuff?"

"I laid everything out last night, before I turned in."

Cuyler aimed a scowl at the tent occupied by the Atkinsons. "No sign of the other two yet. You suppose they still want to come?"

"It isn't the driest morning we've had."

"Yeah." Cuyler looked up as though reading the sky. "It might actually rain, too. I figure coffee and some bannock for breakfast." He had already mixed flour, water, and baking powder, his version of the pan bread. "That okay with you?"

That would be fine, Frazier told him.

"Why'n't you go over and see if they still want to come?"

Frazier nodded and walked away, wondering why it was so necessary for them to leave at such an early hour. After the evening meal yesterday, the group had discussed future plans and decided to stay here at Fletcher Lake to rest for a few days. Was there some reason they had to get to Cuyler's little lake so early? Something to do with the fishing, perhaps? Or was Cuyler a man who had to keep proving himself?

But he did not have to wake the Atkinsons. When he was halfway there, the flaps of their tent opened and Lloyd and Becky appeared, fully dressed and apparently eager to get started. Happy to know they had not changed their minds, Frazier waited for them, then walked back to the fire with them.

Cuyler finished cooking his bannock and

served it from the frying pan, to be eaten out of hand. "Coffee's ready, help yourselves," he said. They ate standing up, walking about in the morning mist to keep warm, because Cuyler had built a fire only large enough to cook on.

The mist was still present when they finished and were ready to leave the still-silent camp. "Are we taking a canoe, Cuyler?" Frazier asked.

"Hell, no. We'd never get a canoe in there."

The two men carried fly rods in lightweight plastic cases, each of the Atkinsons a folding water bucket in which to collect berries. Cuyler led the way. No one had ever cut a path to the little lake or pond that was their destination, Frazier soon realized. Perhaps the guides who brought fishing parties here to Fletcher did not know about it. Or perhaps they considered it not worth visiting. Probably the latter, because no sooner was Fletcher Lake out of sight than the going became fiercely difficult.

This was not a wilderness of tall trees with a floor of moss or pine needles. It was a jungle of giant spruce, twisted jack pines, slender white birches, and half a dozen other species Frazier could not even identify, rising out of tangled undergrowth almost all of which seemed to be specially equipped with thorns to discourage intruders.

"I can't imagine blueberries growing in a place like this, Cuyler," Becky Atkinson said.

"They don't. They're in a patch of meadow, kind of, about a half mile this side of the pond. You'll see."

162

On reaching the spot, they found Cuyler's description to be on the mark. He had been right about the berries, too. Whether they were blueberries or huckleberries—or, in fact, some other kind—no one in the group was botanist enough to know. But birds were feeding on them, as he had said. Startled by the intrusion, a cloud of chickadees rose to fill the sky.

Becky picked a berry from a bush as high as her waist and popped it into her mouth without hesitation. She chewed it and swallowed it. "Tastes fine to me," she said with a grin. "Come on, Lloyd, let's get to work!"

"See you in camp, then," Cuyler said. "Unless we get some fish in a hurry and you're still here when we come back."

Half an hour later the fishermen reached the lake or pond that was their destination, and pushed through a wall of brush on its perimeter to stand at the water's edge. Frazier froze in his tracks, gazing at it with a feeling of awe and wonder.

There was something primeval about the place, he decided. Something hushed and secret, as though this dark little body of water had been hidden here since the beginning of time. It belonged not to man but to the wild things of the forest. To the family of mallards cruising leisurely in the dense gloom of the far shore. To the doe and her spotted fawn that stood in knee-deep water nearby with their heads uplifted, staring at him. To the heron that walked on stiltlike legs in the shallows.

There was not enough wind to touch this secret place. Deep water undercut the bank on which he stood, yet every stone, every blade of grass on the bottom was magically clear until the bottom fell away and disappeared in darkness.

"God damn!" Cuyler glared at the two deer. "Why didn't I think to bring a gun, for Chrissake?"

At the sound of his voice the doe leaped from the lake with her fawn in dainty pursuit, and both disappeared. The mallards took flight with a noise like machine-gun fire. The heron lifted a pair of wings that seemed broad as tent flaps, and with its long legs dangling beneath its slate-blue body, soared majestically away.

Then—suddenly—came the black flies.

Hundreds of the little two-winged insects swarmed to the attack, darting in to inflict their painful bites. Cuyler, cursing them, snatched a bottle of repellent from his pocket and smeared some of the smelly liquid on his face, neck, wrists, and hands, then passed the bottle to Frazier. "But go easy with it," he warned. "This is all we got."

In spite of the repellent, the flies continued to attack for a time, making a sound like the hum of vibrating power lines in a high wind. Then they went away.

Frazier turned, frowning, to his companion. "How can we fish this place? If we try to cast, we'll hang up."

"You know what a roll cast is?"

"Sorry, no."

"I'll show you. Watch me."

Cuyler put his rod together, attached the reel, ran the line through the guides, and bent on a leader. From his hatband he selected a dry fly that bristled with dark hackle, and affixed that to the tapered end of the leader. Holding the rod horizontally in front of him, he gave its tip a quick flip. The line looped gracefully and rolled out over the water, the fly pausing for a second in midair, then fluttering down like a thing alive.

"You got it? Just don't try to backcast."

"I'll see what I can do," Frazier said.

Cuyler made no move to reel his line in. Evidently he felt the spot belonged to him. Backing out, Frazier made his way slowly along shore in search of another such opening. Not for some time was he able with any comfort to get through the brush to the water's edge again.

Then, when he stood there, readying his rod for a try at imitating Cuyler's roll cast, he looked down and forgot about fishing. As before, the bank here was undercut, the water several feet deep but so clear he could see every smallest object on the bottom. What he saw was a turtle the size of a dinner plate tugging at something dark that looked like the torn, shredded remains of a man's clothing, through which something even more unexpected, more startling, became partially visible as the turtle continued its efforts.

It was—it had to be—the skeleton of a man.

Frazier jerked his head up and yelled across

the water at his companion. "Cuyler! Come here!"

"What?"

"Come here! There's a body in the water here!"

Cuyler reeled in his line and disappeared from view. But Frazier, his thoughts already racing, did not wait. Sitting down, he removed shoes and socks, rolled up his pants legs, and slid off into the water. By the time Cuyler reached him, all that had been on the bottom except the skeleton itself lay on the bank.

Cuyler crashed in through the brush, saw what lay there, and stopped short. Looking down, seeing what was in the water at Frazier's feet, he said hoarsely, "Jesus Christ!"

"I know who it is, I think," Frazier said. He held up part of a belt, with a buckle attached. A single initial—the letter *M*—was incised in the brass of the buckle. "Martha McNae's husband disappeared from a camp on Fletcher Lake, Cuyler."

"Whose husband?"

He hadn't told Cuyler about Martha, Frazier realized. Only Max Krist. "You remember when we were walking from Ev Watson's to our first lake? The house I stopped at? The woman I talked to? I believe this is her husband, Cuyler."

"Looks like he was fishing here and something happened."

"Or just exploring. I don't see any rod."

"Or he tangled with a bear, maybe," Cuyler said. "It attacked him here and slapped him unconscious. He fell in and drowned. I heard of that happening once. Or he could have been just standing here and had a heart attack. Anything can happen when a guy's alone. Here." Extending a hand, he helped Frazier back onto the bank. "What do we do about him?"

Yes, Frazier thought, what do we do? Was there any way he could get word to Martha? Going back there was out of the question, of course. Yet she ought to be told.

Standing there on the bank, he looked down at the white bones on the lake bottom and shook his head. It was impossible to get word to her. Quite impossible. Unless, of course—a chance in a million—they met someone who happened to be going that way.

"Lend me your knife, will you, Cuyler?"

Cuyler did so, and Frazier cut the buckle from the fragment of belt, wondering what kind of creature had eaten part of the belt away. And, for that matter, what inhabitants of the lake had stripped the flesh from Dan McNae's bones. Freshwater crabs or crayfish, perhaps? Assorted creepy-crawlies? The body had been here a year or more.

He put the buckle into his pocket. "Cuyler, I'll let you do the fishing, I think."

"Whaddaya mean?"

"I'll go back to where we left Lloyd and Becky. Help them pick berries."

Cuyler shrugged. "Whatever you say. But this guy's been here a long time, Doc. I can't see what the hell difference—"

"Good luck, Cuyler. Good fishing." But if you catch anything, I won't be eating it, Frazier thought.

"You think you can find your way back there?" Cuyler said.

"I'm sure I can."

Not far from the lake, Frazier saw the doe and fawn again, though only as flickers of color moving through a clump of trees off to his right. They were gone almost before he could be sure he had seen them.

Ten minutes later he had another surprise, not so pleasant.

Off guard because the going was not quite so difficult here, he was thinking of the belt buckle in his pocket when a sudden growl brought him up short. It had come from behind him. He twisted himself about, nearly losing his balance. Framed between two pines not twenty feet away was a huge black shape.

His mouth went dry. For a few seconds, no part of his body seemed to work, though his right hand still clutched the fly-rod case he carried. Never before had he seen a black bear, or any other kind of bear, in the wild.

His mind mechanically tried to estimate the creature's weight—four hundred, perhaps four hundred fifty pounds? Numbed by the sight of such a massive beast standing there on its hind legs, apparently ready to charge, he shrank back and heard himself struggling for breath.

Did the bear intend to charge? Its rounded ears were laid flat, the way an angry cat's might be, if that meant anything. But the common black bear of the forest was not usually ferocious, was it? He seemed to remember reading that it was not. That the sight of a human being usually sent it lumbering in swift retreat.

He raised his fly-rod case as a club, just in case—though what good a blow from a plastic tube might do, he had no idea. Still facing the bear, but with his left hand groping behind him to be sure he would not back into a tree, he very slowly retreated.

Dropping back on all fours, the bear turned and disappeared. Not in swift retreat as the book had suggested, but leisurely, as though bored.

Frazier let his breath out, not aware until then that he had been holding it.

What was it their woodsman, Cuyler, had said back there at the pond while looking at the skeleton? That Dan McNae might have been slapped into the water by a bear? It made more sense now—didn't it?—than his earlier thought that the man might have been killed in an argument with someone he was guiding, and the body deliberately hidden. Violence, after all, was more to be expected in a big city than here in the big woods.

Suddenly the stillness of those same woods was shattered by a sound of screaming.

Chapter Sixteen

At first, Frazier thought it was an animal. Or perhaps a bird. But when it continued, and he realized he was close to the clearing where the Atkinsons were supposed to be picking berries, he knew the source of the sound was Becky Atkinson.

He broke into a run.

A man's voice reached him then, close enough for him to make out shouted words. "Becky, what is it? Becky, where are you?" The voice was followed by a thud, as of someone falling, and a hoarse cry of "Oh God! Oh, good God . . . Becky, I can't see! I've lost my glasses! Becky, where are you?" All this while the woman's screams continued.

Then the screaming ended, and Frazier

heard a sound like the flapping of a bird's wings—a very large bird's wings—and saw a huge, dark, birdlike shape disappear among tall trees to his left. The noise of its going went with it, leaving only the sounds made by the man as he thrashed about in search of his wife. A man, Frazier recalled, who could scarcely read a billboard without his glasses.

Frazier had been running toward the sounds. Now he burst into the clearing where the berry bushes grew, and there, not twenty feet away, was Lloyd Atkinson. With both arms outstretched, Lloyd stumbled blindly about, still calling his wife's name but sobbing it now in desperation. Tripping over something on the ground, he would have pitched forward on his face had not Frazier reached him in time to catch him.

"It's all right. It's all right, Lloyd. I've got you."

"Doc? Oh, thank God. Thank God you're here. She was screaming, Doc. She's hurt, she must be hurt. But I can't—"

"Stay here," Frazier ordered, suddenly no longer a misfit in a wilderness but a medic facing an emergency. "Sit down and let me find her." When Lloyd protested, the request became a command. "Do as I say! Wait here and don't move!"

The other sank to his knees and raised a trembling hand to point. "She was—she was over there somewhere when she screamed. . . ."

Frazier hurried in that direction, weaving his

way through thickets of berry bushes toward the clump of tall pines into which the bird shape had disappeared. He did not have to go the whole way. First his right foot thudded against a plastic bucket half full of berries. Then he tripped over the woman he was looking for and would have fallen had not a sapling stopped him.

Recovering, he sank to one knee beside her. "Oh, my God . . ."

It came out as a whisper that seemed to repeat itself over and over—or was that only his mind at work? Becky Atkinson lay on her back, and at sight of her he thought of an old movie that had been made years and years ago and still appeared occasionally on television—or had, until most of the TV stations folded. A Daphne du Maurier story, done as a movie by Alfred Hitchcock. *The Birds*.

Because the eyes staring up at him were only empty holes full of blood, and the mouth he had heard screaming was only a ghastly red gash now. And the rest of Becky Atkinson's face and throat . . . only something with a beak and claws could be responsible for what had been done to her. Something savage and monstrous.

The blood covering her neck made it impossible to seek a pulse there. He reached for her wrist, but knew even before he touched it that life had already fled. The pulseless wrist proved him right. For a moment he could only kneel there, staring at her and wondering how to tell the half-blind man he had just left. Then he saw something on the ground a few feet beyond her. Still in a daze, he got to his feet and stumbled forward to look down at it.

A feather? It had to be, of course, though he had never seen one so large and could not even imagine the size of the bird it must have come from. More than two feet long, the feather was banded or barred in varying shades of brown. Mechanically he picked it up and turned it over and over in his fingers, telling himself he had to examine it but knowing he was only waiting for the courage to do what had to be done next. Then Lloyd Atkinson began calling to him— "Have you found her, Doc? Is she all right? Is she?"—and he knew he could no longer postpone the inevitable.

Still clutching the feather, he walked back to where he had left the man. Helped him to his feet. Told him in stumbling, broken speech what he had found. Showed him the feather and was glad Lloyd could not see it well enough to comprehend. And finally, with a supporting arm around the sobbing man's waist, he led Lloyd to the scene and was glad again that Becky Atkinson's husband could not see very well.

What should he do now? Leave the stricken man here and go for Cuyler, or take him back to camp and return with Don and Max for the body? Going back to camp would be easier; for some reason, he did not want Cuyler's companionship at a time like this. But first, returning to where he had found Lloyd, he retrieved the fly-rod case he had left there and put the feather into it for safekeeping.

The walk to camp seemed endless. Every step of the way, a stunned Lloyd Atkinson sobbed out a continuing condemnation of himself for what had happened. For what he obviously felt he had criminally *allowed* to happen.

He had lost his glasses when he first tried to respond to Becky's screams, he said. Then he had been unable to find her. "If I'd got to her in time I would have been able to prevent it, Doc. I know I would. Whatever it was that attacked her didn't kill her right away. She kept on screaming."

A branch, he said, had knocked the glasses from his face as he was running toward the screaming. Frantic, he had not known whether to hunt for them or keep trying to reach her. "And I did the wrong thing. I tried to find them and stepped on them instead. Oh, my God, if I hadn't been so stupid and clumsy I could have saved her. I know I could. . . ."

At the camp, Frazier administered a sedative from the first-aid kit, and Sheila Varga suggested putting the distraught man in Frazier's tent, where he would not be reminded so acutely of his loss when he awoke. Then Frazier showed the others the feather he had found and told them what had happened, being careful to add that he had not seen it happen and could only assume, from the presence of the outsized feather, that Becky Atkinson had been attacked by some monstrous bird. Leaving Professor Varga and the women to watch over the patient, he returned to the clearing with Don Neal and Max Krist. On the way back, each took a turn at carrying the body.

Cuyler was the only one absent when the group assembled at the fire site then. The weeping had ended. Though the shock of Becky Atkinson's death still held them in its grip, they were able to discuss what had to be done.

Becky ought to be buried before nightfall, Rowena pointed out. "Otherwise, even if we put her in her tent and tie the flaps, some wild animal might get to her."

"We could make a grave somewhere over there, don't you think?" said Sheila Varga, pointing to a clump of white birch trees at the edge of the campsite. "And put up a simple cross with her name carved on it somehow? You could do that, Max. You're artistic."

The men took turns digging the grave, using the only two camp spades the group owned. Don Neal and Dan Frazier made the cross out of green poplar limbs, with Max Krist carefully carving the dead woman's name on it. As the body was laid to rest, Penny Bowen recited words remembered from a prayer book.

Ten minutes later, Cuyler walked into camp with a string of large trout.

They told him what had happened, and Frazier handed him the feather.

He reached for it, drew his hand back as

though the feather might burn his fingers, then took in a breath, reached again, and took hold of it.

"It looks like—it looks like a hawk feather. But Jesus, I never heard of a hawk so big." Fiercely scowling, he looked at Frazier. "You say you *saw* it, Doc?"

"I said I saw something that *looked* like a bird. It flew away when it heard me coming."

"Jesus," Cuyler said again.

Frazier said, "I suggest we take turns standing guard with that machine gun of yours, Cuyler. Starting right now."

Cuyler had recovered. "It's an automatic rifle, for Chrissake."

"Whatever. That bird, or whatever it was, may be aware of our presence here. If everyone agrees, I'll take first watch."

Professor Varga wagged a hand in protest. "No, no, please. Let me take what's left of daylight."

"I'll volunteer for second, then. Who wants to follow me?"

It was agreed that Cuyler, Don Neal, and Max Krist would follow Frazier, and each man's stint would be two and a half hours long. By that time night would have ended and they could break camp.

"Okay," Cuyler said. "If that's settled, how about some supper?"

They looked at one another in silence.

"Is anyone hungry?" Sheila Varga said. "I know I'm not."

Cuyler stood wide-legged, his fists on his hips. "Now, just wait a fucking minute, will you? I spent the whole lousy day catching those trout, and I'm starved." When no one answered him, he turned angrily to his wife. "Dammit, Rowena, get a fire going! I want some supper!"

Rowena made a fire. She cooked him a trout supper. While he ate it, she sat with him in silence, staring into space. When he finished, she went to the lake and washed what needed washing while he went to their tent, brought out the automatic rifle, and made sure Professor Varga knew how to use it.

It was nearly dark when Rowena returned from the lake. All the others except her husband and Varga had retired to their tents. Still seated, Cuyler looked up at her, waiting for her to say something.

She only stood there gazing at him.

Suddenly he exploded. "Dammit, don't look at me like that! It wasn't *my* fault, what happened! I was half a mile away, for Chrissake, trying to make sure we wouldn't starve tonight!"

Still silent, Rowena turned from him and walked across the campsite to their tent.

After a while he followed her, leaving the professor alone at the fire.

Sheila Varga could not sleep. Why, she wondered, had Cuyler been so uncharacteristically hesitant when shown the feather? From the

day they had traded their vehicles for canoes—
even before that, in fact—he had been the one
who took everything in stride and was always
so sure of himself. Had the feather held some
special meaning for him?

She tossed and turned, vainly trying for a
comfortable position on the bough bed she
usually shared with her husband. It was important to get some sleep, she felt, because she was
not the strongest member of the group and
they faced a hard day tomorrow. When, oh
when, would they reach a nice lake where they
would be safe and could stop running? A place
where they could build the cabins and begin
the new life they had so long talked about?

What, she asked herself, must poor Lloyd be
thinking, faced with the prospect of living that
new life alone? But he wouldn't be entirely
alone, would he? He and Dan would surely
decide to build a cabin together now. It would
be foolish for them to build two when one
would do. . . .

For an hour Sheila tried to turn off her
thoughts so that sleep might take over. But they
would not be turned off. As quickly as she
drove one subject from her mind, another
moved in. At last, surrendering, she got up,
pulled her boots on, and went out to sit with
her husband at the fire.

"I might as well be here with you, Therry. I
can't sleep without you." Gazing at the lake,
she saw a pair of loons swimming through a
lane of moonlight. Turning to look behind her,

she saw white birch trees framing the cross at Becky's grave. The so-called civilization from which they struggled to escape seemed a world away, all but forgotten. "It—was so pretty here, Therry. Are you all right?"

Leaning from their bench log, the professor added a piece of wood to the fire, then put an arm around her. "Yes, yes, I'm all right," he assured her. "But I'm glad you're here with me."

Cricket Swensen lay in Don Neal's arms, with her head on Don's shoulder. Rambi was in his customary place at their feet.

Though they had been motionless and silent for some time, all three were still wide awake.

Cricket said suddenly, without preamble, "First Dan finds a skeleton in a pond, then poor Becky is killed by some strange kind of bird. . . . Oh God, Don, I wish I knew what's happening."

"So do I, love. But I don't think the two are connected."

"You don't?"

"You heard what Dan said about the skeleton—how the woman in Chetwood told him her husband disappeared here at Fletcher a year ago. You saw the belt buckle with the man's initial on it."

"Well, yes—I suppose. But the bird, Don. Were you watching Cuyler when Dan handed him the feather?"

"If you mean did I notice he was astonished—"

179

"No, no, we were all *astonished*. With him it was more than that. It was something almost—almost *furtive*, as if he'd been keeping a secret from us and was suddenly afraid we knew about it."

"Wait a minute," Don said.

"What?"

"I've just thought of something. Prof is out there alone. Why don't I take Rambi out to keep him company?"

"You weren't listening, were you?"

"Of course I was listening. You think Cuyler has been hiding something from us, and when he saw the feather . . . And I did notice something, yes. He reached for the feather, then pulled his hand back as if he didn't want to touch it. I had a feeling we'd have seen him turn pale if he didn't have his beard." While talking, Don had reached for his boots and begun to put them on. "What about it, hon? Rambi, I mean. Don't you think I should take him out there?"

"What if he runs away?"

"He's not that brave. It's dark out there beyond the fire."

"There's moonlight," Cricket said, peering at the tent flaps. "But yes, I think you should." Sitting up, she watched him reach for the dog's leash and put it on. "Don?"

"Yes?"

"If the hawk does come, will it make a noise? I mean, will Rambi *hear* it coming, do you think?"

"Doc said it made a noise when it flew away from Becky."

"Yes . . . he did, didn't he?"

"I'll be right back," Don said. And to the dog: "Come on, little guy. You have to earn your keep tonight."

When he rose to his feet outside the tent and strode toward the fire with Rambi at his heels, he was somehow not surprised to see two figures, not one, seated on the bench log in the glow of the flames.

In Dan Frazier's tent, Lloyd Atkinson lay alone in bed, still deep in a drug-induced sleep. The tent flaps were open. Frazier sat on the ground just inside them, where the moonlight could reach a pad of paper he held against one knee.

He wrote on the paper with a ballpoint pen, the only one he had brought with him, and hoped the ink would not fade with the passage of time. It might be a very long time, he guessed, before anyone read what he was writing.

27 June

To finder of this message, greetings. My name is Dan Frazier, and I am a friend of Martha McNae of Chetwood. Please, if you can, see that the accompanying letter and belt buckle are delivered to Martha by whatever means possible. I enclose a hundred-dollar bill to pay you for your trouble.

I urge you to read the accompanying let-

ter—I have no envelope in which to seal it, anyway—so that you will understand its importance. God bless you for your help.

After reading over what he had written, Frazier carefully tore the page from the pad, laid it aside, and began his letter to Martha.

My dearest Martha, I pray this will reach you somehow, so that you will know at last what happened to your husband. Yesterday one of our party discovered a small pond, about two or three miles from here, that is not on our map. This morning he and I went there to fish, and I discovered on the bottom, close to shore, the skeleton of a man who apparently fell in or was pushed in by some animal—perhaps a bear, for I encountered a large black bear on my way back. Scraps of the man's clothing still clung to his remains, and I examined them carefully in hope of finding something that would identify him. I found this belt buckle with the initial M on it. If it belonged to your husband, perhaps you will recognize it.

Martha, I am so sorry about this. Still, I am certain you would rather know the truth than go on for the rest of your life wondering what happened. Why do I feel so strongly that had you known about this when I asked you to come with me, your answer might have been different?

The Dawning

My dear, I still believe with all my heart that we were meant for each other. As the days pass and the miles between us increase, that conviction grows stronger and stronger. So does my heartbreak at knowing I will never see you again.

Take care of yourself, dear lady. Know that I will always cherish those few glorious hours we spent together.

Dan Frazier.

In the tent shared by Max Krist and Penny Bowen, Max brought his journal up to date.

We are standing watch tonight against the possible return of a thing that killed Becky Atkinson today while she and Lloyd were picking berries some distance from camp. Dan Frazier, who caught a glimpse of it as it flew away, describes it as a huge bird, and Cuyler, when shown a feather found by Dan, said it was a large hawk. I must note that on being shown the feather, Cuyler behaved strangely, as though it had some special significance for him. He actually seemed unwilling even to touch it. Until today I would have said that our Mr. Cuyler was a man incapable of fear, but perhaps I have overrated him.

I know without question that I am capable of fear, for in a few minutes it will be my turn to stand watch, and while the strange bird has thus far not put in an appearance, I am certainly apprehensive.

In her sleep my Penny is restless and keeps murmuring the name of the woman we buried this afternoon. As for me, I keep thinking of Becky's husband—how he will feel when the sedative Dr. Frazier gave him wears off and he fully appreciates how different his life will be from now on.

The thing that had killed Becky Atkinson did not return.

In the morning, while the women prepared breakfast, Dan Frazier placed his letters and the belt buckle in a tube of birch bark and sealed its ends with spruce gum heated at the fire. Then with Don Neal's help he gathered stones for a marker.

After breakfast the two men added their stones to those at the fireplace, forming a cairn some four feet high. High enough, Frazier hoped, to attract the attention of anyone passing by in a canoe on the lake, even if that person were not seeking a place to make camp.

The marker finished, he topped it with a six-foot-high birch pole to make it even more conspicuous. Then he carefully placed the roll of bark containing his letters where it would be protected as much as possible from rain while still being visible enough to attract attention.

It was the best he could do. *Please, God*, he silently prayed, *let someone come along and find it.*

An hour later, after breaking camp and loading the canoes, all members of the group gathered at Becky Atkinson's grave to say their farewells. Then in silence they resumed their journey into the unknown.

Chapter Seventeen

On the map it was called Hutchins Lake. After an exhaustingly long portage they reached it—cold, weary, but hopeful—at three o'clock on a rainy afternoon.

The water in the two lakes after Fletcher had tested clean. If this one did, and if it seemed to suit their purpose in other ways, they would stay at least long enough to revive their spirits and renew their energy. Perhaps it would even prove to be the final refuge they had so long been seeking.

More than a mile long, half a mile wide, Hutchins was dark and gloomy this afternoon because of the rain. No one felt like trolling for fish during the search for a campsite. But soon after the search ended and the canoes were unloaded, the rain stopped.

By now the men were expert at pitching the tents. In less than an hour Don Neal and Professor Varga were back on the lake in one canoe, Cuyler and Max Krist in another, hoping to catch fish for the evening meal. The others would build a fireplace and search for bed boughs and firewood.

The two canoes separated, Cuyler and Max heading for a likely-looking cove not far from the camp, Don and the professor for the opposite shore. As Don paddled, Professor Varga sat in the bow, facing him, and rigged both rods.

"Tell me something, Prof." Don was thinking of the grave they had left behind at Fletcher. "Do you suppose that big hawk could have been a mutant? I didn't know hawks attacked people."

"It could have been. Like some of the fish we've caught, and the three-eyed frog you and Cuyler found."

Remembering how Cuyler had spat on the frog and hurled it against the boulder, Don winced. "But what's causing these mutations, Prof?"

"I suspect it's the same sort of thing that caused so many among the dog and cat population in the city. You saw some of the really scary changes that took place there. Or if not exactly the *same* pollutants, others that have been carried here by wind and rain. The rain we had all day today, for instance. Didn't you wonder what new poisons it might be bringing with it?"

"You're saying that even if we find a clean lake that suits our purpose, we've no guarantee—"

"That it will stay clean?" Varga shook his head. "Who knows? But with the cities dying, at least the *industrial* pollution is likely to stop being a problem, and that, of course, has been—" Suddenly the professor's head jerked up. "Hey! Did you see that?"

Don had seen it. Just ahead of the canoe, within casting distance, a good-sized trout had exploded from the lake in a welter of quicksilver, then plunged out of sight again.

"Aha!" Varga thrust a rod at Don, all but losing it over the side in his eagerness. "Let's cut the idle talk and do something productive! We can discuss the woes of the world later!"

Don took the rod and laid down his paddle. As the canoe lost momentum, a second trout broke the surface less than twenty feet away, at the edge of a patch of limp weed-tops that floated like lace on the water. With the craft drifting gently toward the weeds, both men began casting.

Watching his companion in action, Don had to smile. At the start of the trip, Professor Varga had been far from "the compleat angler." Insisting he had fished only twice in his life, he had been reluctant even to try. But now, having learned to handle rod and reel with increasing skill, he was quite the enthusiast.

At the moment he could have been posing for a sportsman's-calendar photograph. Rod nicely balanced in right hand, gaze glued to a dry fly sitting cockily on the water, he was the perfect picture of an ardent angler praying for a giant strike!

Any cameraman taking such a picture would have a dramatic background for it, too, Don thought. While Prof and he had been discussing mutants and pollution, an ominous band of clouds had formed above the nearby forest. Behind it loomed a solid, oncoming mass of premature night.

Suddenly, like a collapsing tent, darkness descended upon the canoe and its occupants. A streak of lightning slashed down through it. Thunder rolled. Heavy drops of rain mottled the lake's metallic sheen.

At precisely the same instant, the lake exploded under Varga's dry fly and the sky opened up to discharge a deluge.

"I've got one!" Varga yelled.

The downpour and a howling wind drowned his outcry as in the excitement of the strike he forgot the cardinal rule of canoe fishing and leaped to his feet. Before Don could even grasp the gunwales and try to steady it, the craft flipped over and pitched them both into the water.

Don had been a swimmer in college. Instinctively he dived straight down to escape being trapped under the canoe, then turned and searched the water above for his companion. The professor was not hard to find. Just under the surface, he appeared as a dark shape with all four limbs in frantic motion.

Don swam up to him, grasped him by an arm, and got him to the surface. In a lake suddenly gone dark and wild under that howling wind, the canoe was nowhere in sight. But shore was not far off. Swimming on his back, holding the other's head above water, Don struggled through a sea of wave-tossed weeds and lily pads until his feet at last found bottom. There he rested, holding the professor erect, until both had recovered enough to struggle through massed driki to solid ground, where they collapsed exhausted.

Then in a few moments the rain stopped, the wind died, and the lake grew calm. The storm had been but a squall, after all. But the canoe was gone, carried away by that howling wind, and might be anywhere. The only way for them to return to camp was on foot through a trailless, now dripping forest. Unless, Don pointed out, Cuyler and Max in the other canoe had seen what happened and came for them.

Still seated on wet ground, soaked through and shivering, Professor Varga wagged his head. "They couldn't have seen us in that blinding rain, Don. I'm sorry I was so stupid. I really am."

"Forget it, Prof. Such things happen."

"What about the canoe? Shall we be able to find it later, do you think?"

"I believe so. It won't sink, at any rate."

"Will the rods? With the weight of the reels to pull them down?"

"I don't know. We can look for them tomorrow. I do know we ought to start walking, if you're up to it." Don struggled to his feet. "We've a long way to go, and darkness will come early in weather like this."

Fearful of becoming lost, they followed the shore. But it was difficult, and progress was slow. At times the brush was actually impenetrable, forcing them to wade in the water where driki and windfalls made every step an achievement.

In a tiny clearing within sound of the waves slapping the shore, Don finally called a halt. "This doesn't make much sense, does it? Pushing ourselves like this, we're likely to have an accident."

"I agree. And I'm exhausted."

"It will soon be too dark, anyway." Don looked around. "This is as good a place as any to spend the night, seems to me. Do you have matches for a fire? Afraid I don't."

Varga shook his head. "Another lesson learned. Never go anywhere in this country without matches."

"It's going to be a long, cold night, Prof."

They sat side by side, arms about upthrust knees, and for a while only gazed in silence at the lake, which was just visible through a screen of trees and brush. Both were wet, cold, tired. Presently the professor lifted a hand to scratch at his beard and said tentatively, "Don, were you ever a scout?"

"Boy Scout, you mean? No."

"I was. And I seem to remember a project we worked on at one time. Let me think."

The beard-scratching continued. Varga's eyes all but closed. "Yes, I *do* remember! We were supposed to be learning how to make a fire in the woods in just such an emergency as this. What we need—" He pushed himself erect. "See if you can find some dry birch bark, will you? With all this debris around, there should be some somewhere. Or dry moss, perhaps. Or both. I'll get the rest of what we need." Even while speaking, he groped in a pants pocket for his knife, then in a shirt pocket for a square plastic envelope that held a leader. "By heaven, I think we can do it! Yes I do!"

"Dry birch bark?" Don repeated, rising. "Or dry moss?"

"Or anything else that will burn easily!"

They plunged into the woods on their separate errands.

Varga was the first to return. In ten minutes he had collected a green alder branch and some chunks of wood kicked from the dry heart of an old windfall. On his knees, knife in hand, he went to work. By the time Don reappeared, the professor was nearly finished.

"Thought I'd have to walk all the way to Hudson's Bay," Don said with a groan. "But I finally found a pile of brush with a dead birch on the bottom." He held out a roll of white bark.

"Don't drop it!" Prof cried in alarm. "The ground's wet! Just hold it, please, till I'm ready."

The preparations required a good half hour, but in the end he had two flat slabs of dry wood, a miniature bow made from the alder branch and a length of the leader, and a round, dry stick some eight inches in length. In each of the flat slabs he had gouged out a depression to accommodate an end of the stick.

"Now then, I form a loop in the leader . . . like this . . . and feed the stick through it. And with the lower end of the stick in the bottom slab, and the top end in the top one, I hold the contraption in place so . . . and spin the stick by pushing the bow back and forth . . . like this. And—Don, I think it will work! I really do!"

Don, too, was excited. "What do *I* do? Shred some bark and—"

"Yes, yes! Shred some bark and pack it around the stick while I spin it. By heaven, if this works we ought to get merit badges! Are you ready? Set? Let's go!"

For long, tense moments, dry stick spun unproductively in dry slab. Varga rested and tried again. Still nothing happened. They swapped tasks for a third attempt, and just when both were about to admit failure, a tiny wisp of smoke curled up through the heap of birch bark shreds, and a flicker of flame followed.

"It works, it works!" Varga shouted.

Half an hour later they proudly sat around a warming fire and talked.

"Everything's good that happens," Professor Varga said with a grin. "Now we'll know how to make a fire when our matches run out. So what if it's time-consuming? Time is one thing we'll have in abundance, isn't it?"

An old windfall of yellow pine, easily kicked apart, had provided more than enough dry firewood. The flames lit up the clearing.

"What was it you were saying about Cuyler, Prof?"

"That he seems to be growing more—angry, is it?—every day now. As though he wishes he had not come with us. You know"— again the characteristic half-closing of the eyes as the professor searched his mind—"for all the fact that he's by far the best outdoorsman among us, he isn't really a *lover* of nature, is he?"

Don remembered the three-eyed frog and shook his head. "No, I don't believe he is. He likes to hunt and fish, especially to hunt, but—"

"But not for the hunt itself. More for the killing. When he goes off with one of his beloved weapons and *doesn't* find something to kill, he is unhappy. By the way, he is also unhappy, it seems to me, that some of us are occasionally finding food with our homemade bows and arrows. Have you noticed?"

"I've noticed."

"He didn't anticipate that, I'm sure. And did you see the look on his face when Max and Penny were working on a snare? As though he felt—well—betrayed?" Varga lay back on the ground, using his linked hands for a headrest. "And speaking of guns and snares, are you as hungry as I am right now?"

"I'm certainly hungry."

"Still, have you noticed something? That we eat less here in the wilderness than we did before? I do, at least."

"All of us, I'm sure."

"Yet in spite of all we are called upon to do—in the physical sense, I mean—we seem to be getting stronger every day. Which makes an interesting point, wouldn't you say?"

Don's laugh blended nicely with the crackling of the flames. "That we should have changed our eating habits long ago, you mean? I'm sure we should have. Though toward the end we hadn't much choice in the city, had we? We ate what we could get."

"And there's something else I've noticed," the professor said quietly. "How you and Cricket always share what you have with your little dog, even when we're tightening our belts. It's a thing I've admired about you."

Don gazed at the ground to hide his embarrassment. "Well, Prof, you know what Cricket said from the beginning. If Rambi couldn't come with us, she wouldn't, either. She loves the little guy. I mean really loves him."

"She loves all animals," Varga said, nodding. "It troubles her, I'm sure, that we have to kill some for food. Another thing that troubles her—that to some extent troubles all of us, I believe—is Cuyler's offensive language. It's getting worse, you may have noticed."

"I've noticed. What makes a man act like that, Prof?"

"Yes, what does? I'm not a psychologist, but my guess is that in his case he is trying to conceal a feeling of inferiority— a feeling he may not even be aware of, mind you, but that is there nevertheless. He knows we don't like it. And as he sees us becoming less and less dependent on him, his fear increases. What we can hope for, I suppose, is that in time he—"

A yell from the lake cut the professor short. He and Don were on their feet in an instant, peering out at the dark water.

Into the outer fringe of the firelight glided a canoe, propelled by the man they had been talking about. Alone in it, Cuyler expertly maneuvered the craft as close to shore as was possible, then called to them again. "You guys okay?"

"Yes," Don shouted back. "We're all right."

"Saw your fire. Can you wade out here? I can't get in any closer."

"Wait. We have to put the fire out."

"You won't be able to see me if you do. It's black as a nigger's balls out here tonight."

"We can't leave the fire burning," Don argued. "If a wind should come up again . . ."

"All right, all right. But hurry it up, will you?"

Having nothing in which to carry water from the lake, Don and Professor Varga had to stamp out the fire they were so proud of. It took time, and again Cuyler yelled a complaint. "What the *hell* are you guys doing? Come on, will you? Let's get out of here!"

They finished extinguishing the fire. In total darkness they struggled out through the driki and climbed, wet to the waist again, into the canoe while Cuyler clung to an overhanging tree limb to steady it. They thanked Cuyler for coming for them. They apologized for having kept him waiting.

"Okay, okay," he said grudgingly. "I guess you're right. We don't want to burn the fucking woods down. What happened to you guys, anyway?"

"You and Max didn't see what happened?" Don asked.

"No, we didn't. We saw that hellacious squall coming and made for camp in one big hurry. Then, when we got there and looked for you guys, you'd vanished." Cuyler plied his paddle with powerful strokes, the water gurgling about its blade and forming tiny whirlpools of silver that slipped out behind like a string of beads. "Hey, we figured you'd gone ashore somewhere to wait it out, that's all. But when you didn't turn up at camp, we began worrying. And then we saw your fire." He stopped paddling and scowled at them. "I guess the squall tipped you over, huh?"

Professor Varga said, "Well, yes. But if I hadn't—"

"You're right, it tipped us over," Don said quickly. "And we lost both rods, unless they're still floating and we can find them tomorrow. But we made it to shore and tried to walk to camp until we saw we wouldn't be able to get there before dark. So we built a fire and—"

"You were damn lucky you had matches," Cuyler said in a voice that was part sneer.

The canoe had rounded a point of land. Just ahead, a small fire glowed in the darkness. By its light Don recognized the campsite.

"Yes," he said quietly. "Weren't we?"

Chapter Eighteen

In the Vargas' tent, Sheila slept little that night. Time and again she awoke and propped herself on one elbow to study the face of her husband. He was in a different position each time, but his breathing was always loud and raspy, as though his nose and throat were full of phlegm.

He had caught a bad cold, she knew. Dan Frazier said it was nothing to fret about, but she knew her Therry better than any doctor could—even Dan—and she was worried. No matter how proud Therry might be of having made a fire without matches, the accident had taken its toll. A man of his age, who had never really been strong, could not be wet and cold for such a long time without paying a price.

This time when she awoke and looked at him, the tent was pale with daylight and he was having even more trouble breathing. Poor Therry, she thought. Somehow she must persuade him to stay in bed today and rest, no matter how big an argument he gave her. What if—dear God, what if something happened to him? How could she go on without him? Lloyd Atkinson might manage without his Becky, but she could never keep going without Therry. She relied on him for just about everything.

Gazing at him now, with the dawnlight on his bearded face and the tent full of the harsh sound of his breathing, she pictured herself back in their apartment, dancing with him to their favorite music. What a wonderful dancer he was! And what fun they always had dancing together! That was probably why he had asked her to marry him, and why she had said yes even though he was twelve years older. When she was in his arms, and the Greek in him was directing his feet, the difference in age just didn't matter. Nor did the fact that he was Professor Theron Varga and she a nobody born in Dublin of a barely literate mother and a father who had bragged horribly about how many of the "other side" he had slain in his violent lifetime. Bragged so hard that mother had finally fled with her two children to the States, thank God. Brother Danny was a priest in Boston now, perhaps trying to make up for the fact that Father, for all his killing and boasting about it, had never been much of a Catholic.

Had, in fact, only killed because he thought it made him important in the eyes of his cronies. Like Cuyler, she thought.

As if in response to the thought, she heard Cuyler's voice at the tent next door, calling Don Neal to get up because they had to go look for the missing canoe. It was like him, wasn't it, to wake the whole camp when he didn't have to?

The voice aroused her husband and he struggled to clear his nose and throat, then realized she was leaning over him and said, "Hullo, there. It's daylight, isn't it?"

"It is, but you're not to get up."

"Why not?"

"Because Dan says you've caught a bad cold and you need to rest today." She smiled at him and ran her fingers through his beard. Actually, she liked him with a lot of hair on his face; he was a crazy kind of lover—all Greeks were supposed to be, weren't they?—and the beard made it even more exciting. "So you stay right here," she ordered, "while I go see about some breakfast for you."

"All right."

She was surprised. "You mean you're not going to give me an argument?"

"Not just now, at any rate. Dan's right, I think. But"—a frown half closed his eyes—"Don will expect me to help him find the canoe we lost."

"No he won't, Therry. He and Cuyler are going after it."

"Then I'll rest for a while, at least."

"And I'll soon be back with your breakfast."

She went outside, closing the tent flaps behind her, and walked over to the fireplace to make a fire. A morning mist lay like a shroud over lake and forest, hiding the far shore and blotting out the tops of tall pines at the edge of the camp clearing. It was a strange, gray world in which the tents—only five of them now, with Lloyd having moved in with Dan—seemed not to belong, somehow. From the far end of the lake came the crazy, laughlike cry of a loon, in her opinion the weirdest of all the weird sounds in the wilderness.

She heard a sound at the lake's edge then, and saw Don Neal and Cuyler launching a canoe. The camp here was on a knoll above a weedy inlet. As the canoe glided out to the lake proper, with both men paddling, it left a wake on which the weeds and lily pads of the inlet rhythmically rose and fell, as though the dark water there were breathing. While she watched it, Rowena emerged from the Cuylers' tent, stretching her arms above her head and yawning.

"Hi, Sheila. You up already?"

"I need to get Therry something hot."

"First we need a decent fireplace." With the accident disturbing their routine, no one had gotten around to building one yesterday. "Give me a hand, will you?"

There were green logs already cut and barked. Working together, the two women laid a pair of them in a V with the open end toward the lake to catch the slight breeze coming off the water. Pinecones and slivers of bark gathered the previous day were soon blazing inside the V, and on top of those Rowena laid split sticks of ash and cedar. About the time the sky turned red in the east, forecasting sunrise, a bed of red coals was ready.

The others were up and around by then, but breakfast was skimpy because no one had replenished the food supply with fish, small game, or birds the day before. Sheila carried hot tea and a bowl of oatmeal to her husband in his tent. The others settled for coffee and some of the professor's food tablets. Then Max and Lloyd Atkinson went fishing.

Lloyd's glasses, Sheila noticed, were held securely in place this morning by a thin strip of cloth apparently torn from a handkerchief. Having lost one pair, he was taking no chances.

An hour later the morning mist had disappeared and the sun was pleasantly hot. Rowena, coming from her tent with an armful of soiled clothes, said, "I'm for doing my laundry and taking a bath. Anyone want to join me?"

They all would, they decided. With Prof and Dan the only men left in camp, the time was appropriate for bathing. In a few minutes all four—Sheila, Rowena, Cricket, Penny—had carried their laundry to the shore of the inlet.

From the beginning, that weedy inlet had seemed to be a haven for wildlife. As the women reached the narrow strip of sand at the water's edge, a roaming beaver protested their intrusion with a resounding slap of its tail on the quiet water before sounding; an osprey circled in search of fish; a red-crested woodpecker hammered a gaunt pine, making the bark fly; a swift brown streak in the brush might have been mink, fox, or otter. Then silence took over and they had the place to themselves.

"I'm not sure I like this," Penny Bowen said, peering into the water. "I feel safer when I can see bottom."

Sheila dropped her burden of clothes to be washed—her own and her husband's—and sat on the sand to take off her boots. "It's only leaves that have fallen in, Penny. There'll be sand under it."

"Do any of these lakes have leeches?" Rowena asked.

"Leeches?"

"You know. Bloodsuckers. Like in that old movie, *The African Queen*, where Humphrey Bogart tows the ship through a swamp and gets covered with them?"

No one knew if there were leeches in Hutchins. "We haven't seen any yet on this trip," Cricket protested. "Aren't they warm-water things?"

"Maybe. *I* don't know. But this place *looks* like it would have leeches in it." Rowena's shudder appeared to be extravagant, but Sheila guessed there was something real under the exaggeration. "Anyway, if we stay at this lake, I hope we find a better campsite."

Naked except for a long-sleeved shirt, which

she had left on in case midges or blackflies put in an appearance, Sheila knelt in shallow water and began work on her laundry. Those winged pests had not been a problem here so far, thank heaven. In fact, the whole scene was about as peaceful as it could be. Close by on her left, Cricket hummed a song while rubbing soap on a pair of Don Neal's pants. On her right, Penny and Rowena worked close together, quietly chatting.

Yes, it was a peaceful place. It made all the big problems seem small for the moment. Becky should be here.

"There it is!" Don Neal cried. "Over there in those weeds, Cuyler!"

Cuyler, in the stern, held his paddle motion-less in the air and leaned forward, squinting. They were in a small cove on the far side of the lake.

"Yeah. That's it, all right."

Only the bottom of the missing canoe was visible. Close to the brushy shore, half hidden by weeds that grew a foot or more above the surface, it looked like a large dead fish or animal that had been floating there belly up for a long time.

Cuyler dipped his paddle again.

Don, in the bow, caught hold of the other canoe with both hands as the two craft came together. With a grip on it, he turned his head. "Got it. But we can't turn it over here. Water's too deep. Can we take it farther in?"

Cuyler did not like being told what to do. He had not liked having to search for a canoe lost by someone else in the first place. The narrowing of his eyes, the set of his head and shoulders, made these things clear. But with clever use of his paddle he maneuvered both canoes through the weeds to a point where Don could step out into water that was only waist deep.

There, after a struggle, Don was able to turn the lost canoe over. Under it was a single paddle.

"Lucky," Cuyler grunted. "A chance in a million, you ask me."

Don tossed the paddle on shore, then pulled the craft through the weeds to a leaf-layered bank just wide enough to accommodate it. He turned it over again and emptied it, with Cuyler sitting motionless in the other canoe and offering no comment. A distance of some thirty feet separated them.

"You don't think we might find the second paddle?" Don called.

"You can look for it if you feel shit-lucky this morning. Me, I want some fish to eat tonight."

"What about the rods? Is there a chance they might be floating somewhere?"

"You could look. Like I say, I'm goin' fishin'." Cuyler lifted his paddle. "Is that canoe okay? You can get back to camp in it?"

"I'll be all right, Cuyler."

"See you later, then." With a perfunctory flap of the hand, Cuyler departed.

* * *

206

Sheila finished her laundry. With a bar of soap clutched in one hand, she stood up to stretch the kinks out of her arms and back. Having taken her shirt off to wash it, she was now wholly ready for her bath. The others were still on their knees, doing their laundry.

"Watch out for those leeches, Sheila," Penny called with a laugh.

Sheila turned her head. "I wasn't the one who asked about leeches. It was Rowena."

"Anyway, watch out."

Sheila took a step forward and stopped. She took another. A third one carried her beyond the small area where she had swept the sandy bottom clean while washing her clothes. Now her bare feet were ankle deep in a paste of soft, slimy leaf mold that felt as though it had been there since the beginning of time. A shudder seized her. She stopped.

The others were watching her. Even without looking back, she knew it. "What's the matter?" Rowena called.

"It's cold! Can't you see I'm shivering?"

"Rub yourself," Cricket advised. "Sometimes that helps."

Obediently Sheila massaged her thighs and hips, shifting the bar of soap from one hand to the other to do so. But what she had called shivering only became more violent. She crossed her arms over her bare breasts and hugged herself. That didn't help, either. She must really be something to look at, she thought—a naked redhead standing not quite waist-deep in a wilderness lake, shaking like a leaf, afraid to go in any farther.

Afraid of what? This was crazy.

She forced herself to advance two more steps and almost lost her balance. When she had steadied herself again, the dark water was above her waist, hiding the most private parts of her body from view. So why did she feel that everyone left alive in the whole wide world was staring at her? Not just the three women she had come here with, but everyone.

And why did she feel she was standing ankle-deep in something that was—was *alive?* Something that might suck her down and devour her?

Oh, dear God . . .

She couldn't walk in any farther. And she was too afraid to dive, though what she was afraid of she had no idea. But she had to get wet all over. She couldn't soap herself without getting wet, for heaven's sake. So the only way to handle this was to close her eyes, fall forward, and let the water flow over her. But never again would she do this here. Never, never, never. If the group decided to stay at this lake, they would absolutely have to find a better campsite.

The others were really laughing at her now.

"Go on, Sheila! What are you waiting for?"

"If you stand there like that any longer, the fish'll think you're bait!"

"What's the matter, Sheila? It isn't *that* cold!"

She twisted herself about to look at them. All three had stopped work and were waiting to

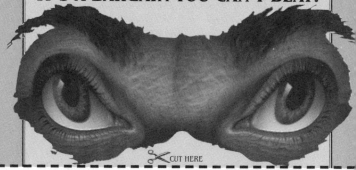

see what she would do. Never in her life had she felt so foolish, so naked.

Therry would be ashamed of her. Really. And with reason.

Well, then, no more of this! Absolutely. Sucking in a big breath, she managed to take two more forward steps—long ones—without losing her balance.

Then from her throat burst a scream of terror so shrill it flushed birds from some of the tallest trees bordering the inlet. And they—the birds—further shattered the stillness with shrill cries of their own.

In the dark water directly in front of her, apparently waiting for her, loomed something huge and green. Something like a frog that was far too large to be a frog. Something with three eyes.

As the shadowy creature sprang at her, its cavernous mouth suddenly yawned open, all white and lustrous inside. A long, curving tongue flicked out.

Still screaming, Sheila flung up her arms and tried to retreat. But the three-eyed thing was at home in the water, and she was only a hapless intruder whose feet could find no purchase on the inlet's slimy floor. With her arms wildly flailing at nothing, she lost her balance and fell over backward.

Of the others, Cricket Swensen was the nearest. While not close enough to observe every smallest detail, she saw most of what happened. Rigid at the water's edge, eyes frozen open and hands clenched in midair, she saw the three-eyed creature leap. Saw the huge white mouth gape open and the tongue flick out to snare Sheila's struggling body. Saw the huge mouth snap shut as though routinely swallowing a captured insect. Saw the creature languidly turn about and disappear.

Suddenly, just above where it had vanished, a single huge bubble shot up from the depths and exploded, sending a crimson froth in all directions. Some of the froth splashed on the sand at Cricket's feet, some on the washed clothes she had spread out to dry.

Not until then did she cry out, while Penny Bowen ran screaming toward camp and Rowena Cuyler continued to kneel there, swaying from side to side and crying over and over in a kind of moan, "Oh holy Jesus! Oh my God!"

Chapter Nineteen

Dan Frazier heard the screaming when he emerged from the Vargas tent, where he had been looking after the professor. Knowing where the women had gone, he broke into a run for the inlet.

He was nearly there when he saw Penny Bowen stumbling toward him, still gasping out what would have been screams had she not been fighting for breath. Penny saw him at the same instant and ran to him. In his arms, uncontrollably shaking, she sobbed out her account of what had happened.

"Go sit with Prof," he told her crisply. "Don't wake him—he's asleep now—just stay with him." That was not for Prof's sake, but for hers.

Because until she regained her self-control she should not be alone.

He ran on. At the cove he found Cricket and Rowena clinging to each other at the water's edge, gazing as if hypnotized at a patch of pink froth floating on the water a few yards out. As he approached, they turned toward him.

"Is this where it happened?"

Yes. This was where it had happened. But they were in shock, barely able to tell him about it.

Frazier looked for a weapon and saw a piece of ash the size of a walking stick. He snatched it up. Ready to strike out at anything that might confront him, he strode into the water. "Here?" he called back on reaching the patch of froth.

Yes, they indicated.

He poked around in the waist-deep water, fearful of losing his footing on the slimy bottom. Finding nothing, he strode back to the waiting women.

"Let me get this straight." God, it was hard to stay calm. But he must. He had to. "Penny said she was swallowed up by a huge frog-thing with three eyes. Is that what you saw?"

Yes. A frog-thing, a monstrous frog-thing, with three great bulging eyes.

"It dragged her down?"

It had dragged her down.

"Then disappeared?"

Yes. It had disappeared.

"In which direction? Did you see?"

Cricket Swensen said between sobs, "It went straight out, at first. Then it seemed to veer off that way." She pointed toward the end of the inlet.

"Stay here," Frazier said. "Get back from the water, but stay here unless you see it again. If you see it, yell and get out of here fast." Leaving them, he walked slowly along the water's edge in the direction Cricket had pointed. When a normal-sized frog suddenly leaped into the water from a lily pad just in front of him, he froze in his tracks.

For half an hour he searched both sides of the cove. Whenever he looked back at Cricket and Rowena, they were staring either at him or at the patch of pink froth on the water. He poked with the stick he carried, disturbing a second small frog, a six-inch newt, a dragon fly clinging to a weed stalk. He saw a school of minnows swimming. He watched a bronze-colored crayfish scurry under a rock. But he saw nothing that looked like a giant three-eyed frog.

Sick at heart, frightened, he returned to the women. "I'd better walk you to camp," he told them. "Then I'll come back here and go on looking. Wait. Take these clothes you've washed. Don't leave them here."

They gathered up the clothes, including those the missing woman had spread out to dry. Rowena, he noticed, shrank from touching a shirt of Sheila's that had a half-dry gob of the pink froth on it, but picked it up in spite of her revulsion. With everything collected, he led the way back to camp.

"When you've put those things away, why don't you sit here," he said, pausing by the bench log at the fireplace. "I'll get Penny and check on Prof."

Rowena said, "What should we do with Sheila's laundry?"

"Well—"

"Most of it will have to be washed over."

"Yes," he said vaguely, finding it difficult to shift mental gears. Yes, of course, even if Sheila would not be wearing her things again, they could not be discarded, could they? Nothing of Becky Atkinson's had been discarded. Because here in the wilderness all clothing was precious and that of both lost women must be kept in reserve for the inevitable time of need. If, of course, *any* of the group survived long enough to need it. Troubled by that thought and by his inability to slam a door on it, he went to the professor's tent and found Penny Bowen seated inside.

She looked up at him as he entered. She had been crying, he saw, but the tears that streaked her face were dry now. "He's asleep," she whispered.

Nodding, Frazier went to his patient and bent over him, to listen to the sound of his breathing. The rasping was muted now, the struggle for breath less pronounced. "Come," he whispered to Penny.

She followed him out.

As they walked to the fireplace, he saw a canoe on the lake. Don Neal was alone in it. The plan, he recalled, was that if Don and Cuyler found the lost craft, Don would return with it while Cuyler stayed to fish.

Cricket and Rowena were at the fireplace. He led Penny to them and said, "Prof is still asleep. And Don's coming, so I'll ask him to help me. If Prof wakes up, please be careful how you tell him. Perhaps it would be better not to say anything until we're all together."

Their faces told him they would be only too glad to let him do the telling. Leaving them there at the fireplace, he walked down to the lakeshore, where Don was beaching the canoe.

They talked. "What do you know about frogs?" Don said when the first shock had passed. "Do they stay in one place pretty much, or do they move around?"

"I have no idea. But this couldn't have been a frog, no matter what they say. Huge. Three eyes—"

"It was a three-eyed frog Cuyler killed. And it had an oversized head, at least. I was with him, Doc. I saw it."

"But big enough to swallow a human being?" Frazier fiercely shook his head. "I just don't believe it."

"We've come across some strange creatures. Those mutant fish we caught. The big hawk that attacked Becky." Don looked toward camp. "Should I ask Rowena for a couple of Cuyler's guns, do you think?"

Frazier shook his head. "If you're feeling as shaky as I am, we might end up shooting each other." He eased himself into the canoe and stepped forward to kneel in the bow. "Let's make sure she's not somewhere in the inlet first. You paddle, unless you're tired."

"I'm all right."

They searched every inch of the inlet, Frazier peering down into the water with his face just above the surface. Finding nothing there, they exchanged roles and with Don in the bow extended the search along half a mile of shore in either direction.

Max Krist and Lloyd Atkinson, returning with fish from the far end of the lake, paddled over to see what they were doing and took part in the search. Then Cuyler, on *his* way back to camp, saw them and changed course. When told what had happened, he too joined in.

The search continued until darkness put an end to it.

At camp, the women had a fire blazing but were simply waiting there, not yet trying to put a meal together. The men beached the canoes and joined them, no one stopping to clean the fish that had been caught. A few moments later, while Frazier was still searching for words to report failure, a sound from the direction of the Vargas' tent made all in the group turn to look in that direction. They saw the professor crawl out through the flaps, unsteadily rise to his feet, and come shambling toward them.

"Uh-oh," Cuyler said under his breath. "I better get some of those fish cleaned." He hurried away into the darkness.

Frazier went to meet the professor and, with an arm around him, gently led him to the fire. "Sit here, Prof," he said, easing the sick man onto a bench log.

Seating himself, Varga peered suspiciously, through half-shut eyes, at the row of staring faces. He looked down at Cricket's little Rambi, who sat there with head cocked and ears alert, studying him. He peered at the row of faces again. "Is something wrong?" he said at last. "Where—where is Sheila?"

"Prof, we have some bad news." As a doctor, Frazier had had to do this before, and knew what to expect. Or, rather, knew he could *not* know what to expect. "We think something has happened to Sheila."

Varga only looked at him and waited.

"She—you need to be strong for this, Prof. We think she's—gone."

"Gone back, you mean? No. She would never do that."

"I mean *gone*, Prof."

Varga reached up to rub his eyes, then let the hand fall. "I don't understand. What are you trying to tell me?"

"We think—we don't know for sure, Prof, but we think there's been an accident."

"Are you saying she is dead?"

Frazier could not bring himself to repeat the word. He could only nod.

The professor continued to stare at him for a

moment, then looked at the others. "Tell me," he said at last.

Frazier turned to Cricket Swensen. "You were closest to her when it happened, Cricket. Can you?"

In a faltering voice, Cricket told what she had seen. Then Frazier took over again and told the professor how he and the other men had spent most of the day searching. He spoke slowly, stopping repeatedly to answer Varga's barely audible questions. By the time he had finished, the professor was simply sitting there, gazing into space again.

"Shall I give you something to make you sleep?" Frazier asked.

Varga shook his head.

"Are you hungry? You haven't eaten anything all day."

"I'm not hungry. But go ahead with your dinner. Please. I'll just sit here where it's warm."

Cuyler, back with some fish, had been standing at the rear of the group. He stepped forward now and handed the fish to Rowena, saying, "I left some in the lake." He meant he had put some in a plastic bag and submerged the bag in the lake's cold water to keep the fish fresh. It was a routine procedure now when supply exceeded immediate need.

Glad to have something to do, the women focused their energy on preparing the meal while the men moved about, trying to help but mainly getting in the way. Professor Varga sat with his head bowed, apparently lost in his own private world.

They ate in silence. When all were finished, Frazier again urged the professor to take something and finally persuaded him to consume some tea and a few mouthfuls of the trout. Then with a hand on Varga's shoulder Frazier said gently, "We'll look for her again in the morning, Prof. As soon as it's light enough."

"We'll never find her," Cuyler said. "And we ought to get out of here. What if that damned thing comes after more of us?"

Frazier sent him an angry look. "Not until we're certain." Of course, Cuyler was probably right about Sheila. They would not find her. But in any case, Prof still had a bad cold and was in no shape to travel. Another day of rest was a necessity.

Cuyler shrugged and stood up. "In the morning, then. We look for her till noon and break camp after lunch. Even that'll be rough. If the map's right, the next lake is a good four miles from here."

There was a long silence. The professor put an end to it by saying in a monotone, "I am not leaving here until I know for sure what happened to her."

Max Krist said quietly, "That may not be possible, Prof."

"Then I stay here, no matter what the rest of you do."

The silence returned as they looked at one

another. Then Frazier stood up, walked over to Varga, and reached for the older man's hands. "I'm sleeping in your tent tonight, Prof," he said. "Let's turn in now, shall we?"

"Let's all turn in," said Rowena Cuyler. "We need to be up real early."

Midnight came and went. A porcupine ventured from the bush and waddled across camp to investigate a scrap of trout near the now-dead fire. From a jack pine at the edge of the clearing came the mournful cry of a screech owl.

In the tent occupied by Cricket Swensen and Don Neal, Cricket awoke and rose on one elbow to look at her companion, who lay on his back. "You're awake, aren't you?" she said.

Don reached up and put his arms around her. At their feet the Italian greyhound opened one eye, then closed it.

"No, wait," Cricket said. "Something's been bothering me. We need to talk."

Don gazed up at her, expecting her to continue. When she did not, he frowned and said, "Talk about what?"

"There's something I don't understand. Ever since we got here to—what's the name of this lake?"

"Hutchins."

"Ever since we got here to Hutchins, Rambi has been playing around that inlet where the frog—where Sheila was seized today. I mean really playing around, running up and down in shallow water after minnows and turtles and things. So if that big frog was hanging around there, why didn't it take *him*? Haven't you wondered?"

"I can't say that I have."

"But isn't it something to think about?"

"I guess so. Unless, of course, the frog wasn't there all that time. We don't know that it was."

"Tell me something. Do you sometimes get a feeling we may never find a safe place to settle down in? A feeling we may go on like this until there are none of us left?"

"Don't talk like that," Don said. "Don't even think like that." He drew her gently down into his arms and held her close, with her head on his shoulder. "No more talking now, huh? Turn your mind off and go to sleep."

But, he thought, it was something to think about, wasn't it? If frogs were territorial, staying pretty much in one place, why *hadn't* Rambi been taken?

Chapter Twenty

All next day the search for Sheila Varga continued.

The professor would accept the assumption that Becky Atkinson had been killed by a hawk. Even ordinary hawks were large birds. He could not, he insisted, wholly believe the women's story of a frog large enough to swallow a human being.

Something had attacked Sheila, of course. Because of the blood on the water, he must concede that. But it had been an otter, perhaps, or a beaver. Certainly not a frog. And whatever it had been, it might only have drawn blood in biting her, then later let her go. She might still be alive somewhere, wandering about in shock.

The others, sympathetic, agreed to search

with him despite their conviction that nothing would be found—and despite their fear that Sheila's killer might strike again. But though Rowena Cuyler, in particular, stayed close to him, striving by word and action to help him in his grief, the professor did not last long. His fever had weakened him. He was further robbed of strength by the shock of knowing his beloved Sheila might be lost to him forever. At midmorning, Rowena and Penny Bowen took him back to camp and put him to bed.

The others, keeping their promise to him, went on with the search until dark. But though every chain of the lakeshore was eventually explored either on foot or by canoe, the quest turned up nothing.

At the evening meal, when Cricket Swensen prepared a plate of food for the professor, Lloyd Atkinson took it from her and carried it to Varga's tent along with his own. The two men ate together, mostly in silence. When they had finished, Lloyd said, "Would you like me to move in with you for a while, Prof? So you won't be alone? I've been through this, remember."

"Thank you, but no. I'm still not convinced."

"Convinced?"

"That she is gone. I'll be in much better shape by tomorrow, and we'll find her, I'm sure."

Lloyd touched him on the hand. "Of course, Prof. Try to get some sleep now, okay?"

Later, when Lloyd himself was dropping off

to sleep in the tent he shared with Dan Frazier, he heard voices from an adjoining tent. It was the one occupied by the Cuylers. The voices woke Frazier, and both men listened.

"You had a great time with old Varga today, didn't you?"

"What do you mean?"

"I mean you practically held his hand the whole goddamn day, that's what I mean! You think I wasn't watching you?"

"Cuyler, stop it. The poor man needs all the help we can give him."

"And he has an idea you're pretty special. He's had his eye on you from the start. You think I'm blind?"

"Cuyler, for heaven's sake, *everybody* tried to be nice to Prof today; it wasn't just me. Everybody felt sorry for him." A pause. "Except you, maybe. I'm not sure you're capable of feeling sorry for anyone."

"So now the fucking frog is *my* fault, is it?"

"Don't twist my words around!"

"I suppose I invented the damned thing. Jesus."

"Cuyler, I didn't say—"

"I heard what you said!" The sudden loud slap that followed could have been Cuyler's hand striking his wife's face. "So shut up, will you, for Chrissake. And stay away from him tomorrow, you hear? I don't care if he did lose his wife. I'm not sharing mine with him."

The voices ceased. Lloyd Atkinson sadly

shook his head and looked at his companion. "Poor Rowena. Doc, what makes a woman put up with that kind of abuse?"

"What makes *us* put up with it?" Frazier replied. "And how long do you suppose we'll go on doing so before we finally come to our senses?"

After breakfast in the morning, the group discussed how and where to continue the search, Prof vowing he was well enough to stay the distance this time. But Cuyler declined to participate.

"I'm going after a deer," he said sullenly. "And someone better go with me, because I'm gonna get me one this time and I'll need help hauling it back here."

Chin in hand, Max Krist studied him. "Why do you want to kill a deer *today*, Cuyler, when you know we'll be moving on tomorrow and will have to carry it with us?"

"Because I'm sick and tired of eating fish and pills every damn meal, that's why. And who said anything about taking it with us? We'll eat what we want and leave the rest." Cuyler looked around in anger. "So who's coming with me? You, Don?"

"If you like," Don Neal said with a shrug. They wouldn't get a deer anyway—Cuyler hadn't killed one yet—but even something small would be a welcome change.

In a few minutes the camp was deserted, Cuyler and Don departing in search of a deer, the others in search of Sheila Varga. The morning was pleasantly warm, the sky a brilliant blue.

For the first half hour or so, Cuyler seemed to enjoy the hunt for its own sake. He joked a lot. He took time to blaze an occasional tree with the sheath knife he always carried, so they would have no difficulty finding their way back. But as time passed and nothing presented itself to be killed, the joking ceased and he became morose. Tense, excessively alert, he twisted constantly from side to side, searching the forest shadows for something to shoot at. For Don, unhappily trailing him, it was less like a hunt for food than watching a jungle war film in which a soldier stalked a dangerous enemy.

Twice something brought Cuyler to a halt by moving into his line of vision. Once a fat porcupine waddled out of some underbrush, unaware that intruders had entered its domain. Cuyler froze, took aim, followed it for a moment with his gun muzzle, then let it go. Next time it was a bird of some kind—one that appeared to be all legs and scrawny neck. Again Cuyler stopped short and seemed about to squeeze the trigger. In both instances, not until the creatures disappeared unharmed was Don sure that his companion would not blast them into oblivion.

He wants to kill something, Don thought. He won't quit until he's done it.

They no longer exchanged pleasantries. No

longer spoke at all. Furious because a deer would not offer itself for the sacrifice, Cuyler was now wholly the soldier in the jungle war film. His every movement suggested that his desire to kill had become an obsession.

Suddenly he froze again, this time not even flapping a hand behind him as a warning. Don stopped too, peering past him into a clump of brush from which had come a sound of dead twigs crackling.

A deer? At last?

Don almost laughed. Perhaps would have laughed, had he not been so tense. This time the creature that appeared was neither porcupine nor bird, but a skunk. At least, it had the black and white markings of a skunk. These days, one could not be certain. In any case, it was a small one, perhaps a baby.

Cuyler had taken aim the moment he saw it. Now, with his legs spread wide again and a finger on the trigger, he actually began to tremble. Don could see his head shake.

And this time the hunger to kill was too acute. Cuyler's finger tightened. A series of thunderclaps shattered the forest stillness. The tiny black and white animal flew through the air in a bloody rain of bits and pieces.

Remembering the three-eyed frog that Cuyler had hurled against a stone, Don remained silent.

An hour later Cuyler angrily admitted defeat, and they returned to camp empty-handed. Those searching for Sheila returned empty-handed, too. And after a long discussion at the evening supper fire, Professor Varga grudgingly agreed to leave Hutchins Lake in the morning.

They broke camp at daybreak. The long portage brought them that afternoon to the most promising lake they had yet encountered. Lake Collier, it was called on the map. Professor Varga tested the water and pronounced it safe. "And I mean really safe. Not a trace of any pollutant."

The lake offered half a dozen good campsites. Before dark they had decided which was the best and set up camp. Cuyler in half an hour caught enough fish for the evening meal. Afterward, Varga alone went to bed, reluctantly admitting fatigue. The others sat about the fire, talking.

"It's certainly the prettiest lake we've seen yet."

"And large enough."

"With plenty of fish. What's in here, do you think, Cuyler?"

"Hard to say. Those were lakers I caught. There could be other kinds of trout and the usual small stuff. We'll know soon enough. Anyway, we can fish other lakes too if we stay here. Take a day off now and then just to go fishing, I mean, like you'd do if you lived in a city."

Filled with hope and excitement, they talked for more than an hour. Was this Collier really

the lake they had been looking for? The end of
their tiresome and tragic journey? The beginning of the future they had planned on? The
talk ended only when Max Krist said with a
yawn, "Let's pack it in for tonight and get some
sleep, shall we? Prof has to be here before we
can vote on it, anyway."

But even after they had retired, the talk went
on.

It was a warmer-than-usual night. In tent
number one, Cricket and Don had taken advan-
tage of that fact and gone to bed naked. They
had made love. Now they lay in each other's
arms, tired, content, but still too excited to
sleep. Their little dog, disturbed by the lovemaking, had settled down at the tent entrance,
his head pushed halfway out between the flaps.

"Don?"

"M'm?"

"Do you think we should stay here?"

"Well, it's just the kind of place I've been pic-
turing—far enough in to be clean and safe, not
so far north that we'd need to become Eskimos
and live in igloos."

"And it's beautiful. Everything about it is so
beautiful. If we stay, how long will it take us to
build a cabin, do you suppose?"

"With that homemade bed you were talking
about?"

"Uh-huh. And other furniture. But the bed
first, of course."

"Depends,"

"Depends on what?"

229

"For one thing, how long it takes to cut down the trees we need. All we have is one ax and those fancy flexible saws we brought along. I've never used one of those saws. I don't know how well they work."

"Actually," Cricket said, "I don't care."

"You don't care what, love?"

"How long it takes. Just so we make up our minds to stop running and begin building something we won't have to take down again a few hours later."

In tent number two, Lloyd Atkinson lay on his back with his hands clasped under his head, and said to Dan Frazier, "Have you given a thought to how it will be, Doc?"

Frazier, facing the tent wall, had been teetering on the edge of sleep. He opened one eye. Without turning his head, he said, "A thought to what?"

"How it will be for us and Prof, living alone for the rest of our lives. Without ever having a woman again."

"I don't give it a whole lot of thought, Lloyd. My memories of marriage don't exactly fill me with longings." But my memory of that night with Martha McNae does, Frazier thought, and suddenly felt a deep sympathy for his tentmate. Lloyd's Becky had been a true partner. The two had loved each other deeply.

"I keep wondering if I shouldn't go back," Lloyd said.

"Back? To what?"

"I know, I know. I'd have no money, no car, not even a place to live if the druggies have moved in. But the thought of living out my life here alone . . . God, Doc, I don't believe I could stand it."

"Prof evidently thinks he can."

"I wonder. I mean, I wonder what he'd say if I suggested he and I go back together."

Silence.

"I mean," Lloyd went on, "suppose Prof and I took one of the canoes and went back to Chetwood. We know the way and could get there; I'm sure we could. Then, if we couldn't get to the city—and why should we want to do that, anyway?—we could at least make some kind of a life for ourselves in Chetwood. If that didn't work, we could always come back here."

Silence.

"Doc? What do you think?"

"You're talking to the wrong man. You should be talking to Prof. But Lloyd, listen to me. Listen." Frazier was up on one elbow now, frowning down at the other's face. "If you and Prof do decide to go back, there's something you have to do for me."

"What do you mean?"

"You have to deliver a letter."

"A letter?"

"One I'll need some time to write. A lot of time to write. So if you talk to Prof and the two of you decide to go back, will you give me at least a day's warning?"

Lloyd looked up at him in silence. "Why

don't you write your letter and have it ready?" he said. "Just in case."

One of tent three's two occupants actually was writing at that moment. While Penny Bowen slept, Max Krist sat at the entrance, where moonlight shining in through the open flaps provided the necessary light.

"I think we have found our haven at last," Max wrote in his notebook. "This Lake Collier, as it is called on our map, seems to be large enough for our purpose—about a mile in length, I would say, and varying from a quarter to three quarters of a mile in width, with many interesting coves and bays. We can drink the water without fear. Fish appear to be plentiful. And I have no doubt the surrounding forest will keep us well supplied with food. I even saw some brain mushrooms when we were gathering balsam boughs for our beds today.

"We have problems, of course. I worry about the three men who have no women—Doc, Lloyd, and Prof—and about Cuyler, who already thinks Prof is trying to win *his* wife away from him. That isn't all that bothers me about Cuyler, of course. I was one of those who predicted he would mellow with the passing of time, but we seem to have substituted wishing for wisdom.

"What, I wonder, actually killed Becky and Sheila? A large hawk, a huge frog? If so, what caused the hawk and frog to grow so large, and are there other such horrors inhabiting this otherwise peaceful paradise? Penny thinks we should not settle here at Collier but go on for at least a few more days to be sure such aberrations are behind us. But *would* we be leaving them behind? Perhaps mutants are to be expected everywhere now. Penny, my love, if you vote against staying here I will of course vote with you, but the others will overrule us, I fear. From now on, this will be home. May God protect us from creations of his that have lost touch with him."

At tent number four Cuyler was not in the tent but behind it, urinating. Finished, he zipped his fly and wiped his hands on his pants. When he entered the tent, Rowena sat up in bed and said with a frown, "I wish you wouldn't do that, Cuyler. I mean, I wish you'd at least go far enough away so it won't smell up the place." Because the night was warm, she had stripped to bra and panties.

"It's dark out there, for Chrissake," Cuyler growled. "What am I supposed to do, fall over a boulder or something and break my neck?"

"You're supposed to be considerate, that's all. Especially if we're going to stay here. This is the second time you've gone to the bathroom right behind the tent. The more you do it, the worse the smell will be."

Cuyler was removing his boots and clothes. "If we stay here, we'll be digging a latrine," he said. "One latrine for all of us, at least until we get some cabins built. Then you can stop bitching every time I take a leak." Naked, he lay down and began to paw at his wife's panties. "So forget it for now, huh? Forget the professor, too. I'm the one you should be thinking about."

Sighing in surrender, Rowena pushed him away and took off her underthings. "I wasn't thinking about Prof," she said. "Why should I be?"

But Cuyler was in no mood for more talk. He was already on top of her, doing what he had always felt was his right as a husband. By the time he finished, some ten minutes later, Rowena's body was so sore that she lay in a fetal position for nearly an hour, waiting for sleep to bring relief.

Prof, she was sure, would have been more gentle. How nice it would be to be touched and stroked and whispered to, instead of being raped.

The camp slept. A nearly full moon climbed the sky and silvered with its light the tents, the fireplace rocks and bench logs, the grass of the campsite.

Here at Collier, no trees grew within two hundred feet of the camp. The grassy knoll on which it stood followed a broad curve of the shore, and from the bulge of the curve a long spit of land some fifty yards wide extended out into the lake.

From the forest at the back edge of the camp a small fawn stepped daintily into the open and looked around. Seemingly on tiptoe it advanced past the row of tents, past the fireplace, and descended the gentle slope to the spit. As it reached the outer end of the land finger, Cricket's little greyhound emerged from the Swensen-Neal tent and trotted toward it.

It had been Rambi's custom to bark shrilly at any forest creature that caught his attention. But he ran out onto the spit in silence. The fawn, drinking, did not even hear him until he was almost at its side.

When it did hear him—or catch the scent of him—the fawn leaped straight up, swung itself around to face him, and came down on stiff legs. Rambi skidded to a stop. Only a yard apart, the two studied each other.

Then the fawn advanced, one slow step at a time, and lowered its head to nuzzle the dog.

And Rambi, lifting *his* head, put out his tongue and licked the fawn's nose.

Chapter Twenty-one

To celebrate their finding a home, Don had shaved off his beard again. Now he sat with Cricket on a bench log they had dragged from the forest and placed in front of their tent. Across his knees was an alder stick some eight feet long. With his knife he was carefully peeling the bark from it.

At the other end of the log, Cricket worked with a fishhook, a spool of thread, and some feathers from a dead bluejay they had found. But her concentration did not match his. Every little while, with a smile on her face, she stopped work to glance over at him.

Blackflies or no, the beard would have to stay off, she decided, though how he would keep it off when he ran out of razor blades she had no idea. With his whiskers he had looked rather like a bear they had encountered one day on a portage—a big black one that lumbered off, snorting, at sight of them. Now, thank heaven, he was again the gentle schoolteacher she had fallen in love with—the man whose kids had adored him and worked so hard to make him proud of them.

New home, new man, she thought. Somehow all the apprehensions had fallen away.

The decision to remain at Lake Collier was not yet final, however. Over breakfast the group had agreed to wait a week, at least, before voting on it. By then, Professor Varga had argued, they would know a good deal more about the lake and whether their chosen campsite was as nearly perfect as it appeared to be. They might even have explored some of the surrounding forest and determined whether it held any dangers for them.

From a tent some ten yards away, Cuyler suddenly appeared with his automatic rifle. The activity in front of the Neal-Swensen tent caught his eye, and he strolled over. Don glanced up at him but went on working.

"You shaved, huh?" Cuyler said.

"Right."

"What the hell for? You know something I don't?"

Don was scraping the alder pole now, and the task required his full attention. "It's my birthday," he said without looking up again.

"Well, whaddaya know." Laughing, Cuyler

shifted his gaze to Cricket. "Is that right, or is he pulling my leg?"

Cricket airily waved a hand. "He's only kidding, Cuyler. Where are you going with that thing? Hunting again?"

"Before I vote on whether we stay here or not, I have to find out if there's any deer around."

Her face took on a frown. "We don't need meat, Cuyler. Dan got two rabbits a while ago."

"He what?"

"See them there?" She turned to point to the fireplace, where they had erected a poles-and-crossbar convenience on which to hang cooking utensils. From the crossbar hung a pair of large brown rabbits. "Dan is getting to be pretty good with the bow and arrows he made," Cricket could not resist adding.

Cuyler looked long and hard, then shrugged. "Okay," he said. "They're better'n nothing. But we're overdue for some venison." He returned his attention to what Don was doing with the alder pole. "You making something there?"

"I hope so."

"What's it supposed to be?"

"A fly rod, Cuyler—or a fishing pole, if you like—to replace the one I lost."

Cuyler's beard hid his expression, but a sneer came through in his voice. "That thing's a *fly*-rod? You got to be crazy." When the remark went unanswered, he added, "You and Prof lost your reels, too, you know. What'll you do for a reel?"

It was surprisingly easy, Don discovered, to

hold a conversation without looking at the one you were holding it with. "When I was a kid, Cuyler, I used to fish with a pole like this in a pond near my home. No reel, just an alder pole, some line, a hook, and a tin can of worms. I seem to remember catching a few fish."

"Sure, sure, but what kind?"

"Perch, bluegills, horned pout. It's possible I might have caught trout if there'd been any to catch."

"If you had all day to do it in," Cuyler sneered. With the rifle over his shoulder, he walked away. They watched him disappear into the forest.

"It's a good thing he didn't see what *I* was doing," Cricket said with a laugh. Getting up, she went over to Don and proudly held out to him what she had created. Don examined it, then admiringly looked up at her.

"But this is great, hon! It as good as the real thing!"

"I told you my dad used to make fishing flies and lures. Of course, he had a vise and other equipment that I don't have, but I watched him often enough to remember a few things. Can we try this out?" In her eagerness she was a little girl again.

"Just give me a few more minutes."

With Cricket watching, he finished shaping the pole and tied on a length of flyline. To the end of the line he attached a leader, and to that, the dry fly Cricket had made out of bluejay feathers. Then he handed the pole to Cricket.

"Me?" she said.

"You first, anyway. Let's go."

Side by side they made for the lake, Cricket proudly waving the rod at others of the group who were moving about the camp. Down the grassy slope they went to the spit, and out along that to a likely fishing spot near its tip. The shore there was sandy. Lily pads provided cover for fish to hide under.

Cricket lifted her face. "Wish me luck, huh?"

Don kissed her with feeling. "Just keep one thing in mind, love."

"What's that?"

"This could be important."

"I know." She stepped to the water's edge.

Cricket had not fished before—the men of the group had been the food providers—but it was soon apparent that her father had taught her more than how to tie flies. In a few moments, despite the crudity of the rod, she was casting with a fluid artistry that had Don wide-eyed with astonishment. Soon she was able to drop her homemade fly exactly where she wanted it to go, in the small pockets of quiet water among the lily pads where it would sit motionless until a twitch of the rod caused it to struggle like a thing alive.

Suddenly, after one such cast, the water boiled up under the fly and it disappeared.

"I've got one! I've got a big one!"

But with such a rod and no reel could she land it? Don felt his heart beating faster as he watched.

The fish showed itself by leaping into the air. "Looks like the ones Cuyler caught," Don said, striving to stay calm. "A laker or gray trout— whatever the right name is. But be careful. Don't let it—" The look Cricket flashed him cut him short, and he clapped a hand over his mouth, then removed the hand and said contritely, "Okay, I'll be good. I promise."

The fish was still fighting. As Cricket stepped backward, trying to coax it into shallow water, it leaped again and sent a long-stemmed lily pad flying.

"We should have brought a net," Don said with a groan.

But Cricket did not need a net. With a deft lift of the pole and a series of quick backward steps, she skittered the trout onto the sand. Don fell to his knees and subdued it. It weighed at least two pounds.

They looked at each other. Cricket dropped the homemade rod and thrust out both hands. Don clasped them in both of his. Laughing and shouting, they danced about on the sand until both were out of breath.

Don used the rod then, and soon caught a second trout as large as the first. "We can do it!" he shouted. "We don't ever have to worry about losing our gear again!"

"But we don't need any more fish than these," Cricket reminded him. "With these and the rabbit stew we'll have enough food for a while. So let's quit now, huh?"

Don knelt at the water's edge and cleaned the

Hugh B. Cave

fish. Cricket watched him. Suddenly frowning, she said, "Hon?"

He looked up at her. "Yes?"

"I know we have lots of extra line. Did we bring hooks, as well?"

"Uh-huh. Several kinds and sizes."

"And sewing thread—I know we have that. So I can be official fly maker for the colony, can't I? Now that we know they work, I mean."

He grinned at her. "That you can, love. And it'll drive Cuyler clean out of his macho mind."

Some of those working around the campsite had witnessed the triumph and called out the news to the others. Well aware of its underlying import, all members of the group—except Cuyler, who was still absent—excitedly gathered around the returning fishermen. The rod with its homemade fly was passed from hand to hand, to be examined and exclaimed over.

Most impressed of all was the professor. "Ever since you and I lost our rods, Don," he said, "I've wondered what we would do when all of them were gone—as one day they will be, without question. You and I learned how to make a fire without matches that day. Now you and Cricket have shown us how to replace lost fishing gear. And soon"—he looked at Dan Frazier, then at Max Krist—"we'll have bows and arrows, and snares, to take the place of guns for which we'll have run out of ammunition."

His little speech brought nods and murmurs of agreement.

An hour or so later, Cuyler returned empty-handed from the hunt. But by then the group had dispersed and the cleaned trout were back in the lake's cold water, being kept fresh. No one bothered to tell the hunter what had happened, and he, having failed again to bag a deer, was apparently too angry to ask about the fishing tool he had scorned.

If, indeed, he even thought about it.

"I'm not exactly sure how to use one of these things," Dan Frazier said.

Sliding the saw out of its tough plastic case, he grasped it by one of its two handles and let the weight of its other handle unroll a thin coil of metal. "Who bought it? You?"

Max Krist nodded. "I discovered them one day in a hardware store. Fellow who owned the store, a friend of mine, said he'd used one to cut down a tree in his yard, and it worked fine. When I saw they weighed little more than a hacksaw blade, I bought half a dozen for our expedition."

Frazier looked up at the tree on which they had decided to experiment. "And it's supposed to be a one-man tool?"

"That's what he said. Like this." Max took the saw from the doctor's hand and went to his knees with it. "It's made of some fancy new metal they developed for the space station before that project collapsed. Don't remember the name of it. What you do—" He passed the

243

blade around the tree as though it were a length of wire, which, in a sense, it was. Then, gripping the two handles, he worked it back and forth with apparently very little effort.

The spiny blade ate its way through bark and wood as though the tree were a giant candle.

"Hey, hey," Frazier said. "Let me try it!"

The pine on which they were testing the saw was so close to camp that they could see three of the tents from where they worked. Even better, there were many such trees in the vicinity, ensuring that logs for cabins would be conveniently near at hand if the group voted to remain at Collier.

But would they be staying? Frazier wondered. Would *he*, Dan Frazier, be staying? Earlier that morning Lloyd Atkinson had requested a meeting of the three men who had no partners. For an hour they had discussed their problems. Lloyd was for going back—no question of that—even if only as far back as the town from which their journey into the wilderness had begun. Professor Varga was equally determined to remain with the group.

"This is all I have in the world now," Varga had said. "There is absolutely nothing for me to go back to."

He, Frazier, had been unable to reach a decision then and was still torn by conflicting emotions. One voice in his head or heart kept urging him to go back to Martha McNae. Another kept telling him that his feelings for Martha were irrational—that if by some miracle she felt the same way about him, she would have come with him.

The way things stood at the moment, Lloyd would have to go back alone if, in the end, he decided that was what he wanted.

"What do you think?" Max said.

On his knees, Frazier had been sawing away at the tree with scarcely a thought about what he was doing. To his surprise, the blade had sliced halfway through its ten-inch trunk. Rising, he handed the tool to his companion. "What do I think? I'd say we owe your hardware friend a vote of thanks. Go ahead. Finish the job."

Max knelt and went to work. When the cut was as deep as he dared make it, he too stood up. "I'm no lumberjack," he said with a frown. "Do we have any idea which way it will fall?"

"Suppose we try pushing it."

"All right, but wait." Max walked away and laid the saw down where the tree could not fall on it. "Don't want to lose one of these, Doc. You realize how long it would have taken us to chop this tree down with an ax?"

"You bet I do."

"Ready?"

"Ready."

They pushed on the tree together. With a sound like that of firecrackers exploding, it yielded to pressure and began to fall. When it seemed likely to keep on falling without their help, both men stepped back.

The tree crashed with a thud that made the

forest floor tremble. From the top of a still-standing neighbor, a bluejay took wing and went spiraling skyward, screeching in protest.

Silence returned.

The doctor and the computer man faced each other and solemnly shook hands.

For six days the group had been camped at Collier Lake. Fish had been plentiful, and none of those caught had been mutants. Frazier had added small game to the larder with his bow, Max Krist with various kinds of snares, the building of which had become a hobby with him. Cuyler, though still failing to bag a deer, had varied the bill of fare with assorted game birds.

Tomorrow, after breakfast, they would vote on whether or not to stay.

It was dark now, or nearly so. With a nightcap cup of tea, Cricket Swensen sat on the bench log in front of her tent, gazing down at the lake. It was such a lovely place, she thought. At the moment, moonlight lay like a mist over lake and campsite, transforming the long spit of land into a silver finger. There would be a cabin on that spit of land one day, perhaps, and others along the shore here. Instead of a handful of Zylon tents there would be a small settlement as in the old days, when most of the feet treading this wilderness were shod with moccasins.

A rustling of the tent flaps interrupting her reverie, she glanced behind her to see Don coming out to join her. What a handsome guy he was with the moonlight shining on his clean-shaven face, she thought. What a lucky woman she was.

"What's up?" he asked with a smile.

"Nothing, darling. I was just sitting here."

He took his place beside her, and then Rambi followed him from the tent to sit at their feet. With the moonlight adding a sheen to Rambi's light-brown coat, the little greybound more than ever resembled a small deer.

Don reached for Cricket's hand. "Beautiful, isn't it?"

"M'm. I love it. What do you think will happen tomorrow?"

"The vote, you mean? I think Prof will want to go on, to be farther away from what happened to Sheila. Lloyd, instead of voting, will tell us he's decided to go back. The rest of us will want to stay here."

"Oh, I hope so. I really do."

"So do I."

Don put an arm around her and kissed her. Rambi turned his head to gaze at them with dark, shining eyes, his small ears laid back and folded as they always were when he was sleepily content.

Suddenly the ears flapped out at right angles to his head and the shiny black nose pointed to the woods beyond the tent.

"Uh-oh," Cricket whispered. "Here she comes!"

They knew just where the fawn would

appear and what it would do. For three consecutive nights that they knew about, and perhaps even before that, the young deer had emerged from the forest behind their tent and trotted down to the lake to drink. For three nights their little greyhound had followed the visitor down and romped along the shore with her. Now it was happening again.

Stepping into the open, the fawn turned her head right, then left. Apparently satisfied the coast was clear, she advanced one slow step at a time until abreast of the tent. There she stopped, looked toward the tent, and waited.

Without barking, Rambi left Don and Cricket and trotted over to her.

The fawn bent her head to the dog's upturned one. They rubbed noses. Side by side they walked down to the water's edge and drank together.

"They look like sister and brother," Cricket said.

"Don't they, though. Big sister, little brother."

The fawn and the dog finished drinking. They rubbed noses again. Suddenly the young deer went leaping along the lakeshore with Rambi in pursuit. In a moment a bend of the shore hid them from sight.

It might be some time, Cricket knew, before Rambi returned. The first time it had happened, Don and she had been afraid he might get lost and had been unable to sleep. But the manner in which he came back—bright-eyed, cocky, obviously full of joy at having found a friend—had taught them not to worry.

She stood up, turned to Don, and reached for his hands. "You know something, Mr. Neal?" she said. "I love those two. I love this place. I love you. Can we go to bed now and do something about it, please?"

Chapter Twenty-two

"So, then," said Professor Varga the next morning, "we all agree that the time has come for a vote on whether we pack up and move on or stay here and put down roots. And we all agree that the vote should be done by secret ballot, lest there be hard feelings afterward. Am I correct?"

It was like the time he had addressed them at his home, just before the start of what he still sometimes referred to as their hegira. This time, though, they sat not in a besieged city house but around a breakfast fire in a quiet wilderness camp, with a bright sun just rising into a clean blue sky above majestic forest trees.

"I'll get a sheet of paper from my notebook,"

Max Krist volunteered, rising. In a moment he returned with one and handed it to Varga.

"Thank you." The professor folded and tore the paper with care. He handed out the slips. He reached for a collapsible water bucket, an empty one, and snapped it open. "So let me just put this here as a ballot box," he said, placing the open bucket in front of the fire, "and after retiring to our tents to talk it over with some degree of privacy, we can come back out one at a time to cast our votes. Without, of course, looking to see how those already in it are marked." He smiled. "Has anyone a better idea?"

No one had.

"Perhaps, if I am permitted to vote first," the professor said, "I can remain here and call the rest of you out. Does that seem fair?"

It did, they agreed.

"Very well. I suggest that to avoid any misunderstandings we mark our ballots either 'stay' or 'go.' Are we agreed on that, also?"

"Wait, please," Lloyd Atkinson said.

All looked at him.

"I won't be voting. I've decided to go back."

There was a prolonged silence until Varga broke it at last by saying with compassion, "Are you certain that is how you feel, friend?"

"I'm sorry, but yes."

"Very well. I hope we can dissuade you, but for the time being we must accept your decision. So—" Shaking his head, the professor took a pencil from his shirt pocket, marked his ballot, and dropped it into the bucket. Then he moved away a few steps and stood with his hands in his pockets and a look of sadness on his face while the others, including Lloyd, went to their tents. Almost as an afterthought he called after them, "I'll summon you in alphabetical order, if no one has any objection."

He waited a full two minutes, then called out, "Penny Bowen!"

Penny came with her ballot, dropped it into the bucket, and retired.

"Eugene Cuyler!"

As he dropped his slip of paper, the gunshop man could not resist glancing into the bucket.

"Please," Varga protested. "We agreed—"

"What the hell," Cuyler flung over his shoulder as he slouched away. "You can't see what's in there anyhow."

"Rowena Cuyler!"

Dan Frazier was next, then Max Krist, Don Neal, and Cricket Swensen. With Lloyd leaving, there are only eight of us left, the professor thought sadly when the final vote had been cast. The others having returned to the fireplace, he took up the bucket and removed the slips of paper. After looking at them, he lifted his head and let his gaze travel from face to face before speaking.

"The count is seven to one in favor of our staying here." He paused. "The one 'go' vote was mine, I may as well confess, and in fact I am not unhappy to be overruled. Subconsciously I wished to put my personal loss a little farther behind me, I suppose. But if we stay here, I can at least hope to learn more about what happened that day."

Sighs of relief were followed by a buzz of excitement.

"So now that we are gathered here and have these slips of paper handy, should we not cast lots for our choice of cabin sites?" the professor said.

They looked at him. "Choice of cabin sites?" Cuyler said.

"Some spots would seem to be more desirable than others, don't you think? All of us, I imagine, would like to have that wide place there on the spit." Varga turned to point. "But obviously there is room for only one cabin there."

They talked about his proposal and decided they agreed with him.

"Then let me just number the blank sides of these bits of paper we've used for voting," the professor suggested, and began doing so but stopped. "Wait." He frowned. "Just how many cabins are we planning on?"

By their silence they forced him to answer the question himself. "One for the Cuylers," he said. "A second for Don and Cricket. A third for Max and Penny. A fourth for Dan Frazier." He turned to Frazier. "Do you suppose you and I might share a cabin, Dan? After Lloyd leaves, that is."

"I think we could stand each other," Frazier said with a smile.

"So, then, we are talking about four cabin sites, are we not?" He finished numbering four of the slips of paper, then crumpled them tightly and dropped them into the bucket. For all of two minutes he shook the bucket before placing it on the ground and quietly saying, "Let's do it alphabetically again. You, Penny, you first."

With a glance at Max Krist, Penny stepped forward. Straightening, she handed her piece of paper to Max and smiled at him.

Max opened it. "We're second."

"Cuyler?" Varga said.

Cuyler smoothed out his piece of paper and grinned. "Number one! That's right down there on the spit, by God, where you said! Prime waterfront property!"

Dan Frazier drew number four for the cabin he would share with the professor, leaving Don Neal number three for himself and Cricket Swensen.

Cuyler had been shamelessly smirking. "Like I said, I'm building down there on the spit. So where will the rest of you put up your cabins? Here where the tents are?"

"Are we talking about cabins close together?" Penny asked with a frown.

"Not *that* close," Don Neal said quickly.

Cuyler peered at them under lowered brows. "What's that supposed to mean? If we stay close, we can be one big family, like we are now."

"And when the children start coming, as they will if we survive—then what?" Cricket said.

"Huh?"

"Each of us—each couple—will want to bring up our children in our own way. That can't be a community thing."

"Good God," Cuyler said. "Who's thinking about kids at this stage of the game?"

"Children or no children," Don said, "Cricket and I are going to build our cabin where we can be alone when we want to be."

"Penny and I, too," Max said.

"Okay, okay," Cuyler flung back. "But if you're half a mile away from where I'm living, don't expect me to come running every time you need help." He turned to go to his tent, then stopped. "Hey, Lloyd."

"Yes?"

"While these others are deciding where they want to live, I'm going after a deer. You won't be picking out a cabin site. Why'n't you come with me?"

Lloyd hesitated.

"Come on, come on," Cuyler urged. "This is my lucky day. Didn't I just win the lottery?"

Still Lloyd remained silent.

"I'm gonna get us a deer today, I tell you," Cuyler persisted. "And I'll need help lugging it back, for God's sake. So let's go. I'll lend you a rifle."

"Well . . . if you say so."

They went into the forest a few minutes later,

Cuyler with his automatic weapon, Lloyd carrying a bolt-action rifle. Watching them as they disappeared, Don Neal said to Cricket Swensen with a frown, "Why do you suppose Lloyd agreed to go with him? He didn't want to. That was obvious."

"Perhaps he didn't want to be here while the rest of us are choosing homesites. Knowing he won't be a part of our life here, I mean. Perhaps he felt it would hurt too much."

"Then why is he going back?"

Cricket turned to face him. "If anything happened to either of *us*, what would the other do? Haven't you wondered sometimes?"

"Come on," Don said quickly. "Let's get started."

As both the professor and Cuyler had remarked, the best site was a wide portion of the land spit that extended out into the lake. The next most likely location was where the tents stood, they decided, but Max and Penny, having second choice, were already driving stakes into the ground there. The professor and Dan Frazier were talking together at the far end of the clearing.

"Just what are we looking for, exactly?" Cricket asked. "Don't you think we should sort of set some ground rules?"

"Well ... we want to be close to the lake, obviously. And not too far from the trees we'll need. Other than that—"

"Other than that, the main thing is that it has to feel right, no? It has to have some special appeal to both of us." Cricket glanced down at her Rambi, who faithfully trotted along with them, apparently wondering what they were up to. "And to him," she added with a laugh.

"That's about it, love. I think we'll know it when we see it."

"Why don't we look around that point," Cricket suggested. "There's a small clearing just the other side of it. I saw it one day when Penny and I were out in a canoe." She indicated an outcrop of land, some fifteen feet higher than the lake level, which with one of its trees leaning out over the water somewhat resembled a ship's prow with a bowsprit.

They walked in that direction. Pushing their way through a stand of pines on the point, with the dog romping on ahead, they came to an open, grassy plateau some two hundred feet in length and a hundred feet wide.

"All of us should have camped here in the first place," Don said. "Just look at that view!"

"We didn't see it in the first place," Cricket pointed out. "If you remember, when we paddled along here looking for openings, we were close in to shore. You can't see this clearing from below when you're that close."

They walked to the edge of the plateau. "If we build here, we'll have to make a flight of steps down to the lake, hon," Don warned. "Getting water up here won't be all that easy."

"Or all that hard, either."

"This is what you want, then?"

"Let's look it over."

They walked about. The clearing was large enough, they decided, and would be a little larger when they cut down the trees needed for a cabin. The soil—Don sharpened a branch to test it—was deep enough to support the garden they hoped to grow from seeds they had brought. The ship's prow point would afford them privacy, yet they would be close enough to the others to feel they had neighbors.

"If you ask me," Don said, "it's even better than Cuyler's spot. He and Rowena could be in trouble if heavy rains bring the lake level up. We're lucky he didn't see this first."

"This is it, then?"

"If you say so, love."

"Home," Cricket whispered. "Home at last, darling. Oh, I'm so glad!" Lifting her face for a kiss, she stepped into Don's waiting arms.

But the kiss was not forthcoming. A distant burst of gunfire interrupted it. Still embracing, she and Don turned their heads to look toward the forest.

"Cuyler must have found something to shoot at," Don said.

"Yes."

"Are you thinking what I'm thinking? That if he kills a deer, it may be—"

"Oh God, I hope not!" Cricket took her lower lip between her teeth and began to tremble.

As if in answer, a second sound of gunfire disturbed the peace of their newfound homesite. Not a burst this time. A single shot.

"Lloyd?" Cricket said.

"Maybe. But Cuyler's gun shoots singles too. And it doesn't have to mean they've killed anything. If you remember, Cuyler took off after a deer on the portage to Fletcher Lake, and we heard shots then, too. But he came back with nothing." Don reached for her hand. "Anyway, we've found what we wanted, love. So let's go back and tell the others."

The others, too, had heard the shots. But what Cuyler and Lloyd might bring back in the way of food was not of major importance to them. They talked about the homesites they had chosen and the cabins they would build, not about whether there might be venison for the evening meal.

Then, more than an hour later, the two hunters emerged from the woods not with a deer hanging from a pole between them but with the limp form of Lloyd Atkinson draped over Cuyler's shoulder, and Cuyler himself staggering from exhaustion. Rushing to help him with his burden, the others learned that Lloyd had been shot.

"It was an accident," Cuyler explained while Dan Frazier, on his knees, examined the hurt man's injuries. "I shot a deer. Lloyd ran up to see what I'd bagged—*ran*, for God's sake, with a loaded rifle in his hand—and tripped over a windfall. He fell, and his gun went off." Leaning over Frazier, Cuyler peered down at the unconscious man and shook his head. "Jesus. Is he hurt bad, Doc?"

"I'm afraid he is."

The head-shaking continued. "I got him back here as fast as I could. So help me, I did."

The remark went unanswered. The other members of the group stood around Frazier and his patient, tensely watching.

"He got hit in the chest, huh?" Cuyler persisted. From the bloodstain on Lloyd's shirt, that had to be obvious. And again, "Jesus. Is the slug still in there, you suppose?"

"No."

"You mean it went clean through."

Frazier looked up, not specifically at the man talking but at all of them. "Will one of you go for my first-aid kit? It's in my backpack."

Max Krist said, "I'll get it," and hurried away.

"He shouldn't have *run* like that," Cuyler said. "Nobody runs in the woods with a loaded gun."

No one responded.

Max returned with the kit.

While Frazier applied a bandage, he explained what he hoped to accomplish. "The bullet seems to have passed close to the heart and exited just under the left shoulder. An inch closer and he would be dead. He may still die. But if I can stop the bleeding and keep the wound sterile, he may make it." The bandaging finished, he looked up again at the circle of silent watchers. "We can carry him to his tent now, I think, but he should not be left alone. I'll stay with him for the first hour or two, in case he comes to. Then perhaps we can take turns."

"I better go for the deer I killed," Cuyler said.

"The guns, too—I left them there." Looking around, he targeted Don Neal. "You, Don, you want to give me a hand?"

"Will you be needing me here, Dan?" Don asked.

"No. Not yet, anyway."

"All right, Cuyler."

"It was a dumb thing to do," Cuyler repeated as he trudged through the forest with Don at his heels. "Running in the woods with a loaded gun—Jesus—he should have *known* it was dumb, even if he never did much hunting before."

Don chose not to comment.

Cuyler continued his monologue for a while, then it dissolved into an unintelligible muttering and died away altogether.

After a long silence, Don said, "How far do we have to go?"

"I dunno, for Chrissake. Half a mile, three-quarters maybe. It felt like five when I was carrying him, let me tell you."

"I'm sure it did." And I wonder what really did happen, Don thought.

"Anyway, I finally got me a deer, dammit. I said I would, and I did."

The deer, when they reached it at last, turned out to be a doe lying on a patch of soft earth in which the prints—and a second set of prints—were distinct enough to catch Don's attention. "There were *two* of them?" Don asked.

Cuyler was some distance away, cutting a carrying pole. "What?"

"Judging by the prints here, there were *two* deer. This doe and a fawn."

"Well, yeah, sure. I mean I shot the doe, see, and then Lloyd had his accident. While I was on my knees trying to help him, the little one come out of the trees. I could've nailed it, too, if I hadn't put my gun down when I ran to help Lloyd."

"I see."

"What the hell. Meat is meat, and we're gonna be living here from now on. If you have too much, you can always make jerky."

Don only gazed at him in silence as he came forward with the pole he had been cutting. On the way, he stopped to gather up the two guns, which lay on the ground only a few feet apart.

Cuyler had brought rope. With it he tied the dead animal to the pole in such a way that when the two men lifted the pole to their shoulders, the doe's weight was distributed more or less equally between them. Cuyler's burden was greater, though, because he insisted on carrying both weapons.

They stopped several times to rest on the way back to the lake. At the last of the stops they sat on a windfall, with the dead doe at their feet, and Cuyler leaned forward to stroke the animal's neck.

"Know what the Indians would've done with this hide?"

Don looked at him and waited.

"They'd've cured it and made things out of it. And that's what I'm gonna do. I read how in a book once." He blinked back at Don's stare. "What's the matter? You don't approve?"

"I haven't got that far with my thinking, Cuyler."

"Well, you better start. Because these clothes we're wearing won't last forever, buddy, and when they're gone, we won't be driving to any neighborhood shopping mall to buy replacements." Cuyler shifted his gaze to the doe. "If we live long enough, we'll be hunting these babies for more'n meat. We'll be wearing 'em for clothes and sleeping under 'em at night to keep warm, and even walking in moccasins made from their hides. You think about that."

"I will." Don was thinking, instead, of the second set of prints. "Shall we get on with this, Cuyler?"

They arrived in camp soon afterward, and the others came to look at the doe before Cuyler dressed it. Reactions were mixed, Don noted. Until now, rabbit, squirrel, and game birds had been the only alternatives to a diet of fish. Venison would be a welcome change. But several members of the group, after gazing down at the dead doe for a few minutes, walked away in silence.

Cricket was one of those. When he caught up with her in their tent a few minutes later and told her about the second set of prints, and how Cuyler would have killed the fawn too, she looked at him in horror.

"A baby?" she whispered. "Oh, my God, Don. You don't suppose that doe we're going to eat is the mother of . . ." Tears filled her eyes, and she could not say it.

Don took her in his arms. "Don't, darling. Please. There must be any number of deer in these woods. It isn't likely the fawn was Rambi's playmate."

"But he would have killed it! If he could have reached his gun in time, he would have *killed* it. Oh, my God!"

As he held and consoled her, Don tried again to form a mental picture from the fragments of information Cuyler had given him. The killing of the doe by Cuyler. Lloyd Atkinson's running to see what the shooting was about, and falling on his gun when he stumbled. The fawn's appearing out of nowhere to go to its fallen mother. Cuyler's being too far from his gun to do anything about it.

Again he asked himself what really had happened there. How much of Cuyler's story was true?

Chaper Twenty-three

From Max Krist's journal:

As I write this, we have been here at Collier three weeks.

Lloyd is still very ill. Dan was very pessimistic today about his chances. He has lost much weight and looks ghastly—more like a dead man lying in his coffin than a live one on a camp bed. He at times remembers at least a little of what happened, however. Which is an improvement, because until a few days ago he remembered nothing. "Cuyler shot a deer that day, didn't he?" Lloyd said when I sat with him this afternoon. "And there was a fawn. Yes, I remem-

ber there was a fawn." Dan says he may remember everything in time. But will he live that long?

Speaking of fawns, Don and Cricket have made a real pet of one that comes almost every evening to have a romp with their little dog. It's a female, and Penny and I saw her when we were visiting over there this evening. Out she came from the woods, quite unafraid, and trotted right over to their tent and actually pawed the ground at the tent entrance to call the dog out. We were sitting on a bench log only a few feet away, and our presence did not frighten her in the least. Meanwhile, Don and Cricket have been working harder on their cabin than any of us, and it is the one farthest along. I imagine they can't wait to begin living at the marvelous site they found. I know it would inspire me. I'm sure, too, that Cuyler wishes he had known about it before he so rashly claimed his site on the spit!

All of us are working on our cabins now, of course, and are making good progress despite the fact that we brought too few tools and must constantly share the few we have. At least the saws work well, and there are enough of those to go around. An unexpected problem has presented itself, however. With Lloyd determined to go back, we had planned on four cabins for the eight of us: Don and Cricket, the Cuylers, Penny and I, Prof and Doc. But Lloyd may feel he is not up to going

back, even if he recovers. This leaves Prof and
Doc in a bit of a quandary, because if he is to
live with them, they will have to build a larger
cabin than they had planned on.

Food has not been a problem here at Collier—at least, not yet. Fish are certainly
plentiful. Cricket, I should note, has been
making various flies and lures with great
success, and all of us, even Cuyler, use her
creations now in preference to the commer-
cial ones we brought along. Her "touch of
magic," we call it. Actually, she patterns her
flies after various insects found in the stom-
achs of the fish we catch, so I would call her
a scientist rather than a magician. And in
anticipation of a time when flying insects
may be "out of season," as she puts it, she
has been experimenting with lures that seek
to imitate helgramites, nymphs, grubs, and
other such wingless tidbits. At heart, I am
sure, our Cricket is a frustrated artist!

But fish have not been the only items on
our menu. No, indeed. Since providing us
with our first venison, Cuyler has killed a
small moose and a number of ducks, while
others have had success hunting smaller
game with our homemade bows-and-arrows
and snares. Don and Cricket, meanwhile,
have begun a garden, and though feeling it
is too late in the season to plant many of the
seeds we brought along, they hope that various greens planted now will mature before
cold weather sets in. If so, spinach, Swiss

chard, and mustard greens may provide a pleasant change from the berries, nuts, Indian turnips, rock tripe, and other wild things Prof Varga diligently finds for us. And—I feel this could be important—Prof came upon some brain mushrooms yesterday while hunting for berries. They were absolutely delicious and of course are safe to eat because none of the poisonous varieties even closely resembles them. Tomorrow, Penny and I hope to find out just how abundant they are.

At any rate, I feel I should repeat that our cupboard here has never been bare. Not once have we had to resort to Prof's food tablets, of which we still have a large supply in case of emergency. We do have one problem, however, for which I see no solution. Our supply of soap is nearly gone. Of course, we anticipated this, but soon we shall have to find some other way to keep ourselves and our clothes clean. I wonder what mankind did before soap was invented.

What else should be noted here? Ah, yes, the weather! Except for a few wet, cloudy days, it has been glorious. On those few days we had a serious problem for a time with mosquitoes and midges. (I think I prefer what Prof says is the Indian word for midges—"no-see-ums"—because the little hellers, though nearly as vicious as hornets, really are almost too small to see.) The rain brought the tiny pests out en masse, and our repellent seemed merely to whet their appetite. But Cuyler's Rowena, bless her, remembered a most effective defense against them, at least to keep them out of our tents and enable us to get some sleep at night. We built fires at the tent entrances, then gathered wet grass from the shallow water at the lake's edge and heaped it on the flames to make a smudge. Such smudge fires kept the little monsters at bay all night if enough wet grass was thrown on them. In passing, I might add that our life as a group has been like that from the start, more or less. A problem arises, and almost always one or another of us comes up with a solution to it. May it ever be thus!

"It happened again last night, Dan," Professor Varga said.

"What did, Prof?"

"The dream. But this time she came out of the water, not the woods. I was there alone by the fire and—" He paused, frowning. "Is that significant? It was there at the fire, remember, that I first heard what happened to her. I'd caught a cold from falling into the lake. You'd put me to bed. You'd given me something to make me sleep. But I heard the talk at the fire and went out to see what was going on."

"Yes, I remember."

"Strange. In the dream I was right there— alone—and I heard her calling me. 'Therry!

Therry!' She was the only one who ever called me that. And when I turned to look, there she was walking toward me. Not out of the water the way she did before. You remember I told you how she came out of the lake before? Not out of the water this time, but out of the woods. All in white, Ian. All in white, with her arms outstretched. And we clung to each other for the longest time. Dan, Dan, it was too real to be only a dream! I must go back there! Now, this morning, I must go back! Come with me, please!"

The two had felled a tree at the edge of the clearing, close to where they were constructing their cabin, and were sitting on it, resting, before confronting the more difficult task of dragging it to the cabin site. They had been at work since an early breakfast. It was now just after nine o'clock.

"Now?" Dan Frazier frowned. "You want to go now?"

"Yes, yes! Now! Dan, this is the second time I've had that exact same dream. Except that she came out of the lake before. It has to mean something!"

Well, yes, Dan thought. What it probably means is that you'll have to go back there to Hutchins Lake to convince yourself it means nothing. "Very well, Prof." He pushed himself to his feet. "Let me look in on Lloyd first. I'll meet you at the canoes."

Since that day when Cuyler had come from the forest with Lloyd unconscious over his shoulder, the injured man had been living in the doctor's tent. Professor Varga had moved out to make room. Frazier hurried to the tent now and found Lloyd awake.

"Well, hello." Fearful that his patient would not survive, Frazier had to make a real effort to seem cheerful. "Feel better this morning, do you?"

"About the same, Doc. Doc?"

Frazier hunkered down to make the talking easier. "Yes?"

"I've been thinking. Just what—just what did Cuyler say happened?"

"Do you really want to go over that again?"

Lloyd's hand came out, feebly reaching. "He said he—he said he shot a deer and I was running toward him and I tripped. That's what he said, isn't it?"

"And you fell on your gun and it went off. Right. But you shouldn't be dwelling on it the way you do. You've got to put it behind you and concentrate on getting better."

"It—didn't—happen—like—that." The words came slowly, in a whisper. "I don't remember everything yet, but it didn't happen that way, Doc. There was a deer, yes. But there was a fawn, too. What happened to me had something to do with the fawn. . . ." The effort was too much. With a heavy sigh, Lloyd stopped reaching and went limp again. "Oh God, oh God, I wish I could remember," he said in a voice barely audible.

"Lloyd, you will. Just give it time." Frazier

leaned closer. "Lloyd, listen. Prof wants to go back there to where Sheila disappeared, and I feel that for his peace of mind he ought to. He wants me to go with him. So I won't be here for a few hours. You understand?"

"I'll be all right, Doc."

"I'll ask the others to look in on you from time to time. You won't be alone."

"I'll be all right."

"I'm sure you will. But they'll keep an eye on you anyway. Prof and I will be back sometime this afternoon." Frazier touched the man's shoulder and left him.

Rowena and Cricket, with their men, were eating breakfast at the fire. Frazier walked over and talked to them.

"You're taking Prof back to Hutchins?" Cuyler said. "Jesus. Won't that make it worse for him? Like it happened yesterday?"

"Perhaps. But if I don't go with him, he'll go by himself. He's that determined."

Cricket said, "If you'd like Don and me to go along—"

"Thanks, but I'll be okay. Just look in on Lloyd every now and then, if you will."

"Of course," Don Neal said.

Frazier went down the grassy slope to the spit, and out along that to where the professor waited at the canoes. The Cuylers, he noticed, were nearly as far along with their cabin as Don and Cricket were with theirs. Rowena was responsible for that, of course. She was doing most of the work. Cuyler preferred hunting and fishing.

"Ready, Prof?"

The professor was not only ready but shaking with impatience. "Yes, yes! Of course!"

"Jump in, then." Frazier held the canoe steady while the older man stepped carefully to the bow and went to his knees there. Since the day of his accident, the professor had always paddled from a kneeling position. Now, with Frazier in the stern, they began the journey across Collier to the Hutchins Lake portage.

With no wind the lake was dead calm, the morning peaceful. It was possible to carry on a conversation without shouting.

"I had another talk with Lloyd, Prof," Frazier said.

"Yes?"

"He implied again that Cuyler hasn't told us the truth about what happened."

"But why should Cuyler be lying?"

"Yes, why should he be? Unless—well, Don had a theory when I talked to him yesterday. What if it was actually Cuyler, not Lloyd, who tripped over that windfall?"

"And shot Lloyd by accident, you mean?"

"Don thinks it significant that Cuyler insisted on carrying both weapons back to camp. Why didn't the fellow ask *him* to carry one? he wonders. Was it because he might have noticed that Lloyd's weapon hadn't been fired?"

"But if that's what happened, why hasn't

Cuyler admitted it?" the professor said. "We all know guns are dangerous and hunting accidents do sometimes happen."

"They're not supposed to happen to the Cuylers of this world, Prof. Only to people like—well, like Lloyd. Anyway, little by little his recollection of what took place that day is coming back. I think we may soon know the truth."

"If he lives. You said—"

"If he lives, yes. I wonder if he wants to live."

"You wonder if what?"

"I have a feeling he doesn't much care. If Becky were still alive, it would be a different story."

They had been talking in fits and starts, with long intervals of silence, while Frazier matched the bowman's paddle strokes and the canoe glided swiftly across the lake. On reaching the portage, Frazier lashed the paddles in place and swung the craft over his head, a procedure he could have performed now in his sleep. Conversation was difficult on the walk through the forest to Hutchins, with Varga plodding along in front and the canoe muffling the doctor's voice. For the most part they proceeded in silence. Then at Hutchins they returned the canoe to water and made for the campsite where the professor's wife had encountered the giant frog.

As they neared the weedy inlet where it had happened, Frazier fixed his gaze on the older man's back and watched for some sign, some

kind of body language, that might make him
privy to Varga's thoughts. What he saw was a
slowing down of the man's paddle strokes, a
rigidity of neck and head that gave way to
trembling as the distance to the inlet
decreased. As though—perhaps—the man
actually expected his wife to appear suddenly
from the water there, to welcome him.

When camped at Hutchins they had beached
the canoes at a point where the inlet met the
lake proper. With a hard stroke of his paddle
Frazier now turned the craft toward that spot.
The professor twisted around to look back at
him.

"I don't think we should do the inlet by canoe,
Prof," Frazier explained. "Too many weeds and
deadfalls in there. We'd better do it on foot."

"Oh. Very well."

"Anyway, didn't you say she came out of the
woods this last time? At the campsite itself?"

"Yes."

"Let's have a look around there first, then."

"Yes. Yes, of course."

The canoe whispered in through weeds and
lily pads, and Frazier held it steady with his
paddle while Varga disembarked. Frazier followed suit. Together they pulled the craft onto
dry land and walked on up to the campsite.

But as Varga went alone across the clearing
toward the forest, Frazier found himself thinking not of this site but the earlier one at
Fletcher Lake where they had left a grave and a

rock cairn—and, in a nearby forest pond, the remains of Martha McNae's husband. Walking over to the old camp fireplace, he sank onto a bench log and resigned himself to waiting. A glance at the timepiece on his wrist told him the morning was over, the day twenty minutes into afternoon.

For nearly an hour Professor Varga walked back and forth, back and forth, along the edge of the forest where, in his dream, his red-haired Irish wife had appeared and called his name. When he gave up at last and directed his steps toward the inlet where Sheila had last been seen alive, Frazier rose to follow him. Except in Varga's imagination there might not have been a ghostly figure at the forest's edge, the doctor thought, but there *had* been a very large, three-eyed, predatory frog in the dark, weedy waters of the inlet, and the frog might still be there.

"Wait, Prof," he called.

Varga obediently stopped.

"Let me do this with you. I never did like this place."

They walked the inlet shore together, back and forth, with Frazier's hand on the other's arm to steady him. He needed steadying. At every slightest movement in or on the water, every scurrying minnow or leaping small frog or darting dragonfly, Varga froze in his tracks. At every bird cry or flutter of wings in the trees at the inlet's edge, he caught his breath and

spun himself about as though expecting the
worst. Yet, despite an obvious fear bordering
on terror, he insisted on trudging the water's
edge not once, not twice, but three times
before he would admit defeat.

"She was here, Dan. In my first dream she
was here. And it was more than a dream! It had
to be a message of some kind!"

"Prof, it's getting late and we ought to go. We
can come back another time."

"You will?" Like a small child pleading for
understanding, Varga faced him. "You'll come
with me again?"

"Of course. But for now let's call it a day,
shall we?"

With a hand on the professor's arm, Frazier
led him back along the shore to the canoe and
helped him into it. "You must be tired, Prof.
Why not let me do the paddling?"

"Yes . . . thank you."

"I'm sorry."

"Yes." Varga was almost in tears. "I thought
we would find something, Dan. Not a living
Sheila, perhaps—I'm sure she can't be alive—
but something to tell us what really happened
to her. Or why it happened. Yes, *why* it happened. I thought when she came to me in the
dreams she was trying to tell me something. . . ." After a long, sobbing sigh he fell
silent.

In no great hurry, Frazier paddled to the
portage, where he again held the canoe steady

while his companion stiffly clambered out of it. Then, for no good reason—even wondering why he felt it important to do so—he turned his head, while still seated, for a last look at the old campsite.

"What—?"

Beyond the campsite a canoe had appeared. If the person paddling it had not been wearing a light-colored jacket, he might not have noticed it against the background of forest, for like their own canoes it was green. With a hand over his eyes to block out the sun's glare, Frazier sat motionless, watching it.

Suddenly he whispered, "My God!" and began to tremble. Then, lurching to his feet in such haste that he nearly upset the canoe he was in, he flung up his arms and began shouting at the top of his lungs, "Martha! Martha!"

On a windy day she probably would not have heard him, unless the breeze happened to be blowing in her direction. She heard him now, though, and stopped paddling. Later she was to confess that all she could see of him against the forest background was a dim figure waving its arms. "But all at once I knew, darling. I knew it was you!"

All at once she stopped being a statue and went into swift action. Her paddle shattered the lake's calm and tossed showers of shining water into the sunlight. At triple its former speed, the craft sped toward the two men.

Frazier, with a yell, waded knee-deep into the

lake to welcome it, then walked it ashore and turned with his arms outstretched.

Martha McNae leaped from the canoe to dry land and, laughing like a child, ran pell-mell into his embrace.

Chapter Twenty-four

"I found your letter at Fletcher," Martha said. "And the one asking whoever came upon it to deliver it to me. And the grave there. 'Becky,' it said on the cross. Who was Becky?"

"Lloyd's wife."

"What happened to her?"

Frazier had not told her about the deaths. Had not wanted to introduce talk of that kind into their euphoria. He had, of course, introduced her to the other members of the group, all of whom remembered her as one of the two waitresses who had served them at the little hotel in Chetwood. Now Martha and he were putting her things away in the tent they would share.

Her coming had presented a minor problem

in that department—one that would be intensi-
fied, he realized, when the time came to move
from tents to cabins. In the beginning he had
been the odd man out, having a tent to himself.
After Becky's death he had taken Lloyd in for a
time, and after Sheila's death, the professor.

What next? He and Prof had begun building
a cabin together on the assumption that Lloyd
would be going back. Then they had agreed
that if Lloyd lived, they would make room for
him. But Martha's coming had changed all
that. An extra cabin now seemed in order, to
accommodate Prof and Lloyd.

Yet to begin a fifth cabin at this time would
be reckless, would it not? Lloyd might not pull
through. *Probably* would not pull through.
Then, surely, either Cricket and Don would
invite Prof to live with them, or Martha and he
would. Only time would provide the answer.
Meanwhile the two men still without women,
Lloyd and Prof, were sharing a tent.

"It was a beautiful letter," Martha went on. "I
needed it, too, because about that time I was
beginning to ask myself what I would do if you
didn't want me."

"You *what*?"

"Hey," she said softly. "It's a long way from
Chetwood to Fletcher Lake. Paddling a canoe
day after day, lying there in my sleeping bag
night after night, I had lots of time to wonder if
I was making a mistake. Then I read your letter
and everything was all right again."

"More than once *I* thought about going back

for another try at persuading you," Frazier said. "More than once I almost did. But I kept asking myself what right I had to hope—"

"I read all that in your letter." Martha faced him on her knees, across the bed she had been reshaping—she was much better at making a bough bed than he was. "Like I said, it was a wonderful letter. No one else ever said those things to me. Not even my husband." She paused, and the smile faded from her face. "And—yes—the belt buckle was his, Dan."

"I'm sorry."

"You found him in a pond?"

Filling in details of what he had briefly told her earlier, Frazier described the unnamed little body of water near Fletcher Lake and his finding the skeleton and bits of clothing there. And the belt with the buckle on it.

"What do you think happened?" she asked.

He told of the bear he had encountered near the pond, and his belief that her husband might have been attacked while standing at the pond's edge and knocked unconscious into the water. "I'm sorry," he repeated.

"He was a good man. I never did believe he just walked out on me." Martha stopped what she was doing and simply sat there, silently watching him rearrange his gear on what would be his side of the bed.

Sensing she wanted to talk, Frazier stopped, too, and turned to face her.

"That's why I didn't come with you when you

asked me," she said quietly. "You understand, don't you? I knew you and I had something very special, something that doesn't happen to most people. But he was a good man, and I kept asking myself what if he wanted to come back but wasn't able to because he was hurt or something. What if one day he did come back and I wasn't there."

"I understand," Frazier said.

"Then I couldn't stand it anymore. I thought, it's been over a year since he disappeared, and I could wait the rest of my life, all the time knowing there was a man I loved who wanted me. By the way"—she leaned toward him—"I just might be pregnant. And you're the only man I've ever slept with except my husband."

Frazier felt as though he had swallowed something all bright and shiny that played a music-box kind of tune inside him. Ellen, the wife who had left him to go to her sister in Florida, had been unable to have children. "Pregnant?" he echoed in awe.

"You don't mind? That isn't why I came. I swear it isn't."

"Mind?" On hands and knees he went across the bed to her. *"Mind?* What are you saying? Martha—Martha—I couldn't be happier! But you're not sure? You said you *might* be . . ."

"I tried to be sure. When I missed my period and couldn't get one of those home pregnancy tests in Chetwood, I went all the way to Thessalon. I didn't find one there either, though, or even a doctor to check me out. But I *feel* pregnant, Dan. I do, I really do. And you're glad? Are you sure?"

Frazier pulled her into his arms and they fell back on the bed together.

They slept after making love. When they awoke, night had fallen and the tent was dark. Flickers of light from the usual campfire danced on the walls of the tent.

Dressed again, they went out hand in hand to join the others. To their surprise, the fire was not a cookfire. It had been fed with brush to send up a tower of brightness.

"Max and Penny haven't come back," Don Neal explained.

Since Martha's arrival, Frazier had been too busy to know or even care what any of the others might be doing. "Back from where?" he asked, puzzled.

"They went to gather some mushrooms. We're afraid they may be lost."

"Or lost track of the time and can't find their way back in the dark," said Cricket.

"We're hoping they'll see the light from the fire," Professor Varga said.

"I'd fire a shot," said Cuyler, "but I hate like hell to waste ammunition. They probably wouldn't be able to tell where it came from, anyway."

At Frazier's side, Martha McNae had listened in silence. Now, in the composed tone of voice she had probably used when helping her husband guide sports into the wilderness, she said, "Which way did they go? Do you know?"

"That way." Don pointed.

Turning in that direction, with all of them staring at her, Martha formed a megaphone with her hands. "Whooo-eee! Whooo-eee!" Without question the sound would carry far and would not be mistaken for the cry of any animal or bird.

Lowering her hands, Martha waited. There was no answer. "They must be a good way off," she said in the same matter-of-fact voice, and repeated the call, this time with a change of direction.

Again there was no response.

"I wouldn't think there is anything to worry about," Martha said then. "It's going to be warm tonight, with no rain or wind likely. They'll be a little scared, maybe, but safe enough unless they do something foolish. As soon as it's light, we can look for them."

"You don't think they might see the light of our fire?" Professor Varga asked.

"Not if they're so far off they haven't heard me yelling. But then"—Martha made a face—"maybe they did hear me but can't yell loud enough back for us to hear *them*. So I'll just keep at it."

For a while she did just that, splitting the forest stillness every few minutes with her "Whooo-eee!" Then: "They mustn't be hearing me," she said, "or they'd be close enough now for us to hear their answer."

The fire, untended, had burned down to embers. Rowena and Cricket had begun to prepare the evening meal. Martha stepped forward to help. "Do they have a knife?" Martha asked, turning to look at Frazier.

"Max does, I'm sure."

"And matches?"

"We all carry matches now."

"They should be all right, then. They can rig up a shelter and light a fire if they need one. We'll find them in the morning."

Martha McNae was talked about that night.

In the Neal-Swensen tent Don lay in bed, waiting for Cricket to join him. Every night, before retiring, she brushed the reddish-brown hair, now grown long, that he so much admired. Brushing it now in the dark, she said cheerfully, "Isn't it wonderful that Martha came? Have you noticed what a difference it has already made in Dan?"

"Such as?"

"Well, for some time now he's acted as though he wasn't sure he ought to have come with us. Now all at once—"

"He's full of enthusiasm again. Right. What I can't figure out is how he got that way about her in such a short time. They spent only a few hours together."

"It happens with some people. Didn't it happen with us?"

"The first time we made love, you mean? Or the first time we met?"

"Well—"

As she finished the hair-brushing and settled down beside him, Don reached for her. "If you remember, young lady, on our first date you had a dog with you. When I bought you an ice-cream cone at a drive-up, you fed him the biggest part of it."

Cricket laughed. "That was Blackie. He loved ice cream, poor little guy. But you didn't mind. You fed him some of yours, too."

"It wasn't a lifetime commitment on a first date, though. We may have touched hands and tiptoed in, you might say; we didn't grab each other and dive in off a hundred-foot cliff, the way Doc and Martha apparently did that night."

"Well, anyway, I like her," Cricket said. "Don't you?"

"I do. Yes."

"And weren't you impressed, the way she sort of took charge about Max and Penny when none of the rest of us—not even Cuyler—knew what to do?"

Don frowned. "But she didn't know what to do either, actually."

"She calmed us all down, though. It will be warm tonight, she said. With a knife and matches they can make a shelter and have a fire. And that call of hers, that was really something. We all ought to learn how to do that, just in case."

"Her husband was a guide. She used to go on trips with him."

"So having her here will be like having a guide with us, won't it?" Cricket said. "And for Dan, the start of a whole new life."

In the tent occupied by Lloyd Atkinson and Professor Varga, the professor had to explain the "Whooo-eee" to his tentmate. Too weak to leave his bed, Lloyd had not been present during the performance at the fire. He had met Martha McNae only once, when Frazier had taken her to his tent and introduced them.

"I don't understand." Lloyd's voice was little more than a whisper now; Varga had to lean close to hear him. "She—this Martha—is one of the two women who waited on us at the hotel, isn't she? The homely one."

"The older one, yes. 'Homely' is in the eye of the beholder, friend."

"I thought it was beauty that—"

"It's both. Ask Cuyler, who sees nothing to like in our lovely Penny because she had a black ancestor somewhere down the line. But what is your problem? That Dan hasn't known her long enough?"

"I guess so, Prof. It just doesn't seem—natural. I mean, for a woman to come all this way—alone—to spend the rest of her life with a man she only had a one-night stand with."

"It was more than a one-night stand, Lloyd," Varga said with conviction. "You have only to talk to Dan for five minutes to know it was very much more than that. I would call it a rare meeting of two compatible souls. Perhaps not by chance, either, but by some guiding hand."

"The Lord giveth and the Lord taketh away." Bitterness gave Lloyd's voice the strength to rise above its usual weak whisper. "Only, with you and me he did the taking away first, didn't he?"

"Now, Lloyd."

"Well, it's true, isn't it? He took away my Becky and your Sheila. Now he turns his other face and sends Dan this—this call girl."

"I don't believe Martha is a prostitute, Lloyd."

"He'd never seen her before he spent the night with her, had he?"

It was time to change the subject, Varga thought. "Tell me," he said, "have you remembered any more of what happened the day you were shot?"

It was not easy, apparently, for Lloyd to switch his train of thought so abruptly. At least, not onto that track. For a while he lay there silent, with his eyes closed. Then: "Only the fawn," he said. "And I'm absolutely sure I didn't stumble over anything. If Cuyler says I stumbled, he's lying."

"Your gun didn't go off?"

"My gun didn't go off."

"Well then, did *he* stumble over something?" Varga persisted. "Was it *his* gun that accidentally went off and shot you?"

"I don't—I just can't remember, Prof. I only know I didn't shoot myself."

* * *

"What do you think of Martha?" Rowena Cuyler asked her husband.

"What do I think? She's okay, I guess. Homely, God knows, but that's Doc's problem."

"You really think she's homely?"

"She'll never win any beauty contest. That's for sure." Cuyler got up on one elbow and began pounding the blanket to subdue a balsam bough under it that was bruising his hip. "Christ, I wish you'd learn to make a bed right," he said.

"I told you yesterday we need some fresh boughs."

"Then why the hell don't you go cut some?"

"Because I think you ought to do a few things around here besides hunt and fish all the time."

"At least she's not a nigger," Cuyler said.

"What?"

"A nigger, like Bowen. She may he homely as a moose, but she's white."

"I hope you don't ever say anything like that in front of Max," Rowena said.

"Huh?"

"Unless, of course, you've got a gun in your hand."

"What the hell's that supposed to mean?"

"What it sounded like." Rowena turned over on her back. "If you're going to demand your rights, as you always put it, will you get it over with now, please, so I can go to sleep? I'm tired, and we have to be up at the crack of dawn to go look for Max and Penny."

"Forget it," Cuyler said.

With a sigh of relief, Rowena turned her back on him and closed her eyes.

In the morning, Martha McNae and Frazier rose early and had coffee ready by the time the others came from their tents. "We can eat after we find them," Martha said in her take-charge way. "The coffee's just to get the kinks out."

They ought to search in pairs, she suggested, and go in different directions, with the professor remaining in camp in case Lloyd took a turn for the worse. "That way we'll cover more ground. And we're going to get pretty tired of yelling, not to mention sore throats, so I suggest we take along some things to make a noise with. Like this." Reaching for a cook pot, she whacked it with a stick of kindling from the firewood pile. "That kind of racket will carry a long way in the woods. Will you be all right here, Prof?"

Professor Varga smiled at her concern. "I'm sure I will be."

"Then if we're ready, gang . . ."

Varga watched them separate into pairs—Martha and Frazier, Cricket and Don, the Cuylers—and disappear into the forest in different directions. He returned to his tent with a mug of coffee for Lloyd, who lay there in bed.

"Did you hear any of what was said out there?" the professor asked with a chuckle.

"Some of it. She's really taking over the concertmaster job, isn't she? Cuyler must hate being second fiddle."

"You should have seen the look on his face. It would have curdled milk if we had any to curdle." Even through his bushy beard Varga's grin made its presence known. "And speaking of food, why don't I fix us some breakfast before the fire goes out? What would you like?"

"What do we have?"

"Fish, of course. And there's still some flour left for pancakes or bannock. Still some of the moosemeat, too, but it's been dried in the sun and I'm not quite sure how to proceed with it. Suppose I whip us up a fish chowder. I've watched the women do that."

"But not too much, Prof," Lloyd said. "I'm not really hungry."

"You feeling all right?"

"Well, yes, but I haven't had much of an appetite lately, as you know."

"I'll be back in a bit, then. Call if you need me."

While busy at the fire, Varga was conscious of the sounds made by the searchers in the forest. Martha had been right in saying that the pounding of pots and pans would create a far-ranging racket, and her own eerie yodeling, if that was the word for it, was even more attention-getting. But as the searchers moved farther away, the sounds faded. Presently he was much more aware that time was passing without the hoped-for results.

Breakfast ready, he sat with Lloyd to eat it, then for something to do carried the cooking utensils and dishes down to the lake and washed them. Cricket's little dog, who had been left in his care, romped along with him and then, perhaps in response to a command from its greyhound genes, went racing at top speed to the end of the spit and back. At another time Varga might have smiled. This morning he did not.

The hours dragged by. A bright sun traveled across a sky so blue it seemed unreal, and the day was almost too warm. Noon came and went. Lloyd slept. In the afternoon Varga busied himself with small tasks at the cabin he and Frazier had started—the cabin in which, with Martha's coming, he would be less a true partner, he realized, than a kind of tolerated guest.

Through it all, the dog kept him company and was there to be talked to.

By midafternoon he began to be anxious, and as the day wore on his anxiety deepened. He spent the last hour of daylight preparing a meal for people he knew would be hungry. Then, with daylight fading, the searchers began to return.

The Cuylers came first. Ten minutes later Don and Cricket appeared. Finally, in darkness, guided by the light of the fire, came Frazier and his Martha. All were bone-weary, dragging their feet. None had found a trace of the missing couple.

"They must have gotten completely turned around somehow," Martha McNae said with a shake of her head. "They're nowhere near here, that's for sure, or they'd have heard us."

Varga served them. When they had eaten, they sat around the fire for a while, exchanging stories of their day's adventures. Don and Cricket had seen a bear that ignored them. The Cuylers had seen a moose. "Wouldn't you know it would happen when I didn't have a gun along?" Cuyler said in disgust. Martha and Frazier had heard what they thought might be a response to her "Whooo-eee!" but had been unable to locate its source. "We think it must have been a bird of some kind," Frazier said. "An owl, perhaps." He used the word "we," Varga thought, as though it lay on his tongue like some special delight he had never hoped to taste again.

But soon the talk died down and the talkers, exhausted, went to their tents.

At daybreak they dragged themselves from bed, drank coffee, and went doggedly into the forest again.

And just before noon of that second day, Don Neal and Cricket Swensen found what they were looking for.

Chapter Twenty-five

Mushrooms.

Max and Penny had been looking for them, and had carried a collapsible bucket in which to collect them.

Cricket found the bucket lying on its side, next to a small heap of mushrooms that had apparently spilled out of it, on a patch of soft, damp earth in a glade where the fungi grew in profusion.

"Don!" she yelled. "Over here!"

Then as Don came running she found herself gagging on a strong stench of skunk and saw animal footprints among the bootprints of the mushroom hunters. Animal prints as large as those of a bear, but different in shape.

Lurching to a stop beside her, Don too saw

the bucket and spilled mushrooms. He too gagged on the stench and stared wide-eyed at the mix of prints in the damp earth. Then he continued forward, past a clump of bushes, and gasped out, "Oh, my God."

The stench was so strong there that it seared his lungs and made his eyes water. It was too strong to be what it seemed to be, he told himself. No mere skunk could have done what had been done to the two bodies at which he was staring.

They were scarcely recognizable. Only something big and powerful, something very angry, could possibly have torn its victims so savagely.

Stumbling to his side, Cricket caught her breath as he had done, and clutched his hand.

Whatever the creature had been, it must have caught Max and Penny by surprise, they agreed. Must have leaped upon the two before they had time to flee, for both of them lay facedown as though they had been gathering mushrooms side by side and had been knocked forward from a kneeling position. Slammed forward and then brutally savaged by something with claws or teeth capable of tearing flesh from bone.

Did skunks have claws? Neither of them knew. Neither had ever been that close to one. Skunks had teeth, of course. No doubt about that. But all this had happened hours ago. The blood on the bodies had dried. There was nothing to be done now.

Don stopped staring and drew Cricket away. "We have to tell the others. Come on."

She could only nod.

Only Lloyd and Varga were in camp when they reached it. The pharmacist was in his tent, the professor puttering about his cabin-in-progress. When told what they had found, Varga sank onto a log and stared at them.

"A skunk? A huge *skunk*?"

"We think so. It was a skunk smell, no question of that."

"But a skunk big enough to—to—"

"It was a larger-than-life hawk that killed Becky," Don reminded him, "and a big frog that—"

"Yes, yes, I know."

"Please," Cricket protested. "The important thing now is, what are we to do about Max and Penny?"

"We can only wait until the others come back," Varga said. Suddenly the full significance of what they were telling him seemed to strike home, and he lowered his face into his hands. "Oh God, why?" he sobbed. "Why are these terrible things happening to us? What have we done to deserve them?"

It was Cricket's idea that they fire one of Cuyler's guns as a message to the others. Don did so, and soon afterward Cuyler and Rowena appeared, followed in half an hour by Frazier and Martha. Martha insisted on going with the three men to bring in the bodies. At the death scene, wincing at the odor, she examined the prints of the creature that had done the killing.

"It was a skunk, all right." Down on one knee, she looked up at the men and shook her head, obviously perplexed. "But skunks don't grow big enough to leave prints like these. Not ever."

Don glanced at Cuyler and saw a look of bewilderment on the face of the gunshop man, too. Or was it something more? Was Cuyler perhaps remembering the day he had wantonly killed a baby skunk in a rage at not finding a deer to shoot?

Rejecting an offer by Martha to make stretchers, the men took turns carrying the two bodies back to camp. There a gravesite was selected in a small glade some distance from the cabins, and graves were dug. With a brief remembered ceremony the bodies of philosopher Max Krist and his girlfriend Penny Bowen were laid to rest.

An evening meal was prepared then and indifferently eaten. With darkness creeping in from lake and forest, the group gathered around a built-up fire to talk. As usual, Professor Varga assumed the role of moderator.

With the firelight again transforming his face into a portrait from an old-style Bible, he said brokenly, "I believe the question before us now is—is whether we should remain here at Collier or go on in search of—of some place where these things are less likely to happen. I should like your thoughts, please." He directed his gaze at Frazier. "Dan?"

"Was it a mutant of some sort that killed them?"

"I think we have to say yes to that. It must have been."

"Have we any guarantee there won't be other such mutants waiting for us if we go on?"

"Only that the farther we are from where we came from, the more likely—"

"Which is no guarantee at all, is it?" Frazier said with a shrug. "And if we move on, we leave our unfinished cabins behind and must start all over again. I vote for staying here."

"Martha?"

"I don't think I should vote," Martha McNae protested. "I've only just joined you and don't have the right."

"You are one of us now, Martha. We should all take part in this."

"Well, I agree with Dan, then. I think we ought to stay here and tough it out. You've been here quite a while now. There can't be many of those mutant things around or you'd have seen them."

"Don?"

Don had been watching Cuyler, fascinated by the intensity of the man's gaze as he in turn stared at the professor. The fire seemed to be doing something to Cuyler's eyes, as though it were lighting them from behind, inside his head, rather than from the front. Or was it simply that he stared without blinking?

"Don?" Varga repeated.

"Oh. I—ah—can't see much point in going on, Prof, when we don't know what we might get into. Or, for that matter, what we're actually running *from*."

One by one the votes were for staying, until at last the professor turned to Cuyler.

"And you, Cuyler?"

"I say we ought to get the hell out of here, and fast!" Cuyler shook a fist to add emphasis. "This place gives me the unholy creeps!"

"Are you saying you are afraid?"

"Of course I'm afraid! And if the rest of you had any sense, you would be, too."

"But what guarantee do we have, Cuyler, that the next lake, or the next, will be any safer? We could be running from our fears forever."

"All I know is, me and Rowena are leaving!"

"What about your cabin on the spit?"

"To hell with it. We'll build another."

Varga gazed thoughtfully into the fire. "Will you take a little time to think about it, Cuyler?" he said then. "For that matter"—his gaze touched other faces—"why don't we all take a little more time to think about this, and agree to vote on it again in, say, a week? By then we may know more than we do now."

They talked it over, with Cuyler taking part in the discussion and becoming less belligerent. In the end he voted with the others to meet again a week later for a final decision.

"Thank you," Varga said, obviously relieved. "And now, before we adjourn, there is one more item on the agenda. What are we to do with Penny's and Max's belongings?"

No one, it seemed, had thought about that. He had to answer the question himself.

"May I suggest, then, that we establish a pool? And that Becky's and Sheila's things go into it as well, along with any excess items such as backpacks and blankets? All such items will then be available to anyone in need."

They talked about it and voted unanimously to follow his suggestion, after which Cricket Swensen said quietly, "Would anyone mind if I took over Max's journal? I don't think we should let it die with Max. The time may come when someone—perhaps our children or grandchildren—will want to know how all this began."

She should have the journal, they agreed.

"One week from tonight, then," Professor Varga said, rising. "Meanwhile, let us try not to be depressed or fearful. We knew from the beginning, didn't we, that this venture would present certain risks? But we also knew that staying in the city meant having no chance at all for a life worth living." He turned to the fire. "Now, would anyone like to have a cup of tea with me before we turn in? We still have a little left."

"What do you think of Cuyler?" Cricket Swensen asked Don Neal as they prepared for bed. "He's afraid, isn't he?"

"Of something. That's for sure. And he's the last one I'd have expected to *be* afraid."

"He's been sort of—furtive, if that's the word I'm after—ever since Lloyd was hurt. I wonder. Has he told us the truth about what happened that day?"

"Somehow I don't think so," Don said. "But until Lloyd remembers—if he ever does—we'll probably never know."

Chapter Twenty-six

Five of the seven days had passed. With a final vote pending, no one had done any work on the cabins for fear the decision would be to move on. When he awoke on the morning of day six, Cuyler nudged Rowena and said, "Hey, wake up. It's time we got started."

"Time we got started on what?" she said sleepily. Then: "Oh. I remember. You want to check out Nadeau today." On the map Cuyler had been studying, Nadeau was the next lake to the north.

"And maybe the one after that, too. Kelsa, or whatever it's called. Depends on how rough the portages are."

Sitting up, Rowena began to pull on her

jeans. "And you still don't want to tell the others?"

"To hell with the others. What they don't know won't hurt 'em. I just know I'm not voting tomorrow till I find out what we'll be getting into if we move."

The camp slept when they emerged from their tent and made their way down to the spit, where the canoes were. With work suspended on the cabins, it had been a lazy week for all except Frazier, Rowena thought. He, poor man, had been struggling to keep Lloyd Atkinson alive, in what looked like a lost cause. Every day now, Lloyd seemed less likely to make it.

Cuyler impatiently motioned her into the canoe. She put a foot in and turned to frown at him. God, she thought, he looked like one of those hairy monsters that were supposed to live in the mountains of the Pacific northwest. A Bigfoot. Why couldn't he shave once in a while, like the other men did? "Aren't you even going to leave a note or something?" she demanded. "So they'll know where we went?"

"I told Prof we'd be going fishing early this morning."

"But they'll see we're not on the lake."

"You can't see the whole lake from camp, for God's sake. Come on, come on!" When Cuyler wanted to do a thing, it had to be done right now, this minute, and don't hold him up. Like when he was hungry—where's my food? Like when he wanted sex—come on, get your clothes off.

Taking up a paddle, she went forward to her place in the bow and sat down in silence.

It was a nice morning, though, she observed. Nice and warm, not a cloud in the sky, the lake like glass. As Cuyler gave the canoe a shove and swung himself into it without even getting his boots wet—you had to give him credit, he could handle a canoe—she looked back at the camp and thought what a peaceful, pretty place it was, and what a shame it would be if they had to move. The cabin on the spit, the others up on the level ground above it, the one Cricket and Don were building around the point—you couldn't see that from here, but she knew what a neat job they were doing on it . . . No, she didn't want to move.

Cuyler might insist on moving, though, because he was afraid of something. He'd been afraid of something ever since they'd found Max and Penny dead, and the skunk tracks. Twice since they'd buried Max and Penny she had seen him take the big hawk feather from his backpack and look at it for minutes on end.

"Hey," Cuyler said. "You daydreaming or something? Let's have some action."

Better quit thinking about things and concentrate on here and now, Rowena told herself. With a wave of one hand to let him know she had heard, she put her shoulders into paddling. Ten minutes of silent effort later, when she turned her head to look back, the camp was out of sight.

"Over there." Her husband pointed. "That little cove where the fish just jumped. See it?"

"I see it. What about it?"

"Head for it. That's where the trail starts."

He was right, of course. In a moment they were off the lake and trudging along an overgrown footpath through a big-tree forest, Cuyler leading with the canoe, she carrying a lunch bag that contained among other things some strips of moose meat cut thin and dried in the sun. Martha had made this particular jerky. It was better than Cuyler's. If you didn't mind chewing till your jaws ached, it actually tasted pretty good.

A big brown bird—a grouse of some kind, she guessed—darted out of some underbrush, looked at them, then turned and took off like a plane, using the trail for a runway.

"Damn!" she heard Cuyler say, his voice muffled by the canoe. "Why didn't I bring a gun?"

"Because we're going to look at a lake," she told him. "And right now we don't need any food. We have more than enough in camp."

"You can't have more than enough food. Not when it's all around you."

"And how long will it be all around us if you keep killing it off?" she said. "Anyway, you *don't* have more than enough ammunition. One of these days it'll be gone."

"What the hell," he threw back. "When that day comes, I'll go with snares and a bow, like the others. But you won't eat so good, believe me."

The portage was a long one; Rowena trudged on, wondering when he would admit he was tired and stop to rest. He did eventually, but only for a few minutes. Then, a quarter mile farther on, they reached their destination.

Nadeau was a long lake and, she thought, every bit as interesting as Collier. Not a hundred yards from where they stood at the end of the portage, a doe and her fawn were drinking at the water's edge. "Jesus!" Cuyler said in a hoarse whisper. "Look at that, will you!"

Startled, the two deer lifted their heads in unison, looked at him, and went bounding into the forest.

Rowena glanced at her husband. He was trembling. "Jesus!" he said again, this time under his breath as he lowered the canoe into the water. "Two deer the first minute! This could really be the place! And look there!" He jerked up an arm to point.

Rowena looked and saw a pair of mallards swimming out from a weedy inlet on their right—an inlet much like the one in which the frog had seized Sheila Varga. Cuyler had a hunter's reflexes, she decided. Like a preying mantis, he saw everything that moved.

But as they began a tour of the lake, so Cuyler could make up his mind about it, she too was intrigued by things that moved. Not for the same reason, but enchanted all the same. A beaver, a family of mergansers, a pair of loons, a long-legged wading bird fishing for minnows, and suddenly, as they rounded a heavily wooded point of land, two men in a canoe . . .

Two men in a canoe? Here? She squeezed her eyes shut in disbelief and opened them again. There was nothing wrong with her eyesight. And beyond the canoe, down the shore a little way, a shaft of gray smoke rose from a kind of shed with a tent pitched beside it. Astonished, she stopped paddling.

Cuyler stopped, too. "What the hell," he said.

The two men appeared to be fishing, but with handlines, not rods. They hadn't seen Cuyler and her, yet, Rowena thought. Suddenly one did, and spoke to the other, and both stopped what they were doing to stare across the water. One was bigger than Cuyler, the other about the same size. Both had long black hair that glistened in the sun. Both wore dark pants and white shirts. They did not wave.

"Who the hell are they?" Cuyler said. "What are they here for?" Plainly he was disappointed. Bitterly so. The lake and all its wildlife belonged to him.

"What kind of shed is that?" Rowena asked.

"How the hell do I know?"

"A kitchen of some kind, do you suppose? They've got a fire going."

"Suppose we ask 'em." Cuyler dipped his paddle again, but not with any enthusiasm.

As the distance between the two canoes shortened, the two men in the other one remained motionless, watching. They were clean-shaven, Rowena noticed when the two craft were close enough. Sunburned, too. The face of the smaller man was almost red.

Cuyler stopped paddling. "Hi, fellas." Not being too friendly. Not exactly challenging them, either. "We didn't know there was anyone else here. Name's Cuyler. This here's my wife."

The two men looked them over before answering. Then the big one said, "James Luck and Harry Spring. Hello."

Cuyler lifted a hand in salute. "Glad to know you. Where you from? Chetwood?"

"Chetwood?" James Luck said.

"I guess not. So where?"

"We are from Moosonee."

"That's up north, no? On Hudson Bay?"

"Hudson's Bay, yes."

"Is that your camp over there?"

"You ask many questions," James Luck said.

Cuyler hunched his shoulders up around his ears in an exaggerated shrug. "Well, shit, we're camped down on Collier, a whole bunch of us, and we like to know who our neighbors are. *Is* it yours?" He pointed.

"We are from the next lake to the north. Kelsa."

"Then whose camp is that?"

"It is not a camp. Only a smokehouse."

"I get it. You're smoking fish, huh? You catch 'em here, smoke 'em, and take 'em back to your place on Kelsa."

"Yes."

"How many of you living there on Kelsa? Just you two?"

It was James Luck's turn to shrug. But, unlike Cuyler, he did so with a small smile. "More than two, Mr. Cuyler."

"Well—Jesus—how many? It's not an international secret, is it?"

"At present, five men and five women."

"That many, huh? And you're all from Hudson Bay?"

"From James Bay, actually. But that is part of Hudson's Bay."

"Yeah. Say, isn't there a railroad spur runs north to Moosonee from the Trans-Canada?"

"There was."

"It's finished now, huh?"

"Both lines have been abandoned, yes."

"So ten of you are living on Kelsa, and you two are here at Nadeau for the fish. And you smoke 'em when you catch 'em." Cuyler looked at Rowena. "How about that, huh? That's real neat. We should've been doing that when we had extra fish."

James Luck said, "If you would like to see our smokehouse, we can show it to you."

"Well, hey, sure. Sure we would."

"Come, then."

Cuyler spoke only once while Rowena and he were following the other canoe. In a voice not loud enough to reach James Luck and Harry Spring he said, "You know what these guys are, don't you?"

"What they are?"

"They're Indians, for Chrissake."

"So?" Rowena said.

"So watch yourself."

Puzzled, Rowena turned to look at him, but he gestured impatiently for her to resume paddling. Then, when they reached shore and were out of the canoe, he gave her a warning nudge as they pulled the craft onto a ribbon of shale beach. "Watch yourself," he repeated under his breath. "I'll do the talking."

James Luck and Harry Spring led them up a short path to the shedlike structure, and James Luck opened the door. With her vision blurred by smoke-induced tears, Rowena could not at first see what the place contained. After a while, though, she made out rows of lake trout hanging on wires. Under them a smoldering fire produced the smoke that was making her throat hurt.

"You would like one?" James Luck asked.

Cuyler hesitated. Before he could make up his mind, Rowena said, "Yes, please!"

James Luck stepped in, removed a fish from a wire, and backed out again. He handed the fish to Rowena.

"Thank you. Thank you very much," Rowena said. "How do you cook them? Do you soak them first?"

"Sometimes, sometimes not, depending on what they are to be used for. Or you can eat them just like this." Drawing a knife from a sheath at his belt, he stepped into the smoke again and reappeared with a chunk of fish, which he cut into two pieces. He put one piece into his mouth and offered the other to Rowena. She offered it to Cuyler, who shook his head. When she tried the fish herself, she found it was chewy and had a strong flavor of smoke, but tasted surprisingly good.

"I like it," she said.

"What kind of wood do you use for the fire?" Cuyler asked.

"Nothing special. Whatever you have."

"You just get the fire going good and throw wet stuff on it?"

"That is all."

"How long do you smoke the fish?"

James Luck looked at Harry Spring and shrugged. "Until they are done."

"Well, how long is that? A day? Two days?"

"When you are sure they will not become soft and spoil, you take them out. You will know."

"Well, thanks." After a brief, somewhat awkward silence in which the two men stared at him, Cuyler shrugged again. "I guess we better go now. They're expecting us back at Collier."

"Thank you for showing us how you do this," Rowena said. "It will be a big help to us, I'm sure."

The two men nodded.

Carrying the smoked trout, she followed Cuyler to their canoe and got in. Neither spoke until they were well away from the shale beach, where the two men stood watching them. Then Rowena said, "We could learn a lot from those people, Cuyler. Maybe we should try to get to know them. The rest of them, I mean. Five men and five women—isn't that what he said?"

Cuyler was heading straight down the lake toward the portage, and putting muscle into his paddling. "Are you crazy?" he said. "They're Indians, I told you."

"So?"

"*Indians,* for Chrissake. We stay on our lake, they stay on theirs."

Rowena turned her head to look at him. "Is there something wrong with being an Indian, Cuyler?"

Cuyler only shook his head in a gesture of disbelief. But a moment later, when she had given up waiting for an answer, he said under his breath, "Is there something wrong with being an Indian? Jesus Christ."

From the journal begun by Max Krist and continued by Cricket Swensen:

> We voted again this afternoon, and this time the vote was unanimous. We are to stay here at Collier. The strange thing is that Cuyler, who was so determined to move on before, was dead set against moving on this time, and all because he and Rowena went exploring and met some Indians at Lake Nadeau, the next lake to the north of us. Evidently Cuyler feels about Indians the way he felt about poor Penny. Anyway, we are staying. Hooray!
>
> When Cuyler revealed that he and Rowena

*had gone to Nadeau without telling us, Prof
was really angry with him. Cuyler, of course,
can't stand any kind of criticism, and for a
moment I thought they might come to
blows. Perhaps they would have, if Cuyler
hadn't known he would have to take on all
of us.*

*Prof pointed out that if anything had hap-
pened to the two of them there at Nadeau,
we might have spent days searching for
them in vain. Rowena said she agreed with
him. She said she had wanted to tell us but
Cuyler would not let her. They brought back
a smoked fish that the Indians had given
them. Now we have decided to build a
smokehouse here, so we can preserve fish
when we have more than we need. We can
smoke other food too, like moose meat and
venison. The trout tasted pretty good—
rather like some smoked salmon a friend
sent me from Seattle years ago, before all the
trouble started. I can't imagine what
smoked meat might taste like, but Prof says
the Indians have always preserved it that
way. He says the Indians Cuyler and
Rowena met at Nadeau were probably
Crees, if in fact they did come from up
around Hudson's Bay. All of us—except
Cuyler, of course—agreed that we ought to
try to make friends of them. It would be silly
for us not to be friendly, with us living here
at Collier and them such a short distance*

away. We could help one another in all kinds of ways.

Don and I have been talking almost every night about the deaths of Becky, Sheila, Max, and Penny. No doubt I will be writing more about this in the days to come. Meanwhile, we are keeping our thoughts to ourselves.

Poor Lloyd Atkinson. He is still in bed and seems to get weaker every day. If we could have taken him to a hospital when he was shot, Dan Frazier said today, he probably would be entirely over it by now, but without surgery there was never any real hope. But, Dan said, he would not have survived the journey to a hospital in any case, and by keeping him here we have at least saved him a lot of needless suffering.

Chapter Twenty-seven

Nearly three weeks had passed since the decision to remain at Collier. All in the group, with the exception of the dying Lloyd Atkinson, had spent most of that time working on their cabins.

At breakfast one morning Cuyler said, "Hey, listen. We're damned near out of food, in case you guys don't know it. I'm going fishing this morning. How about it, Don? You want to come with me?"

Don glanced at Cricket. He and she had planned to work on the roof of their new home today—in fact, had lain awake in their tent until after midnight discussing some problems that had arisen. But Cuyler was right, he knew. The food supply was dangerously low.

"Come on, come on," Cuyler urged. "Or nobody eats tonight."

Cricket shrugged. "I can keep busy, Don."

"Okay, Cuyler. I'll get my gear. Meet you at the canoes."

The morning was overcast, with a breeze that kept the surface of the lake in constant motion. On reaching a little bay not far from camp, where the fishing was usually good, Don was not surprised when Cuyler said, "They won't be feeding on top today," and produced a container of worms. Nor was he surprised when the gunshop man began fishing without offering him any.

He *was* surprised a moment later when Cuyler produced an almost full liter of bourbon from his gear bag.

"Where'd you get that?" Don asked.

Cuyler grinned through his beard. "Been saving it to celebrate with. Rowena and I move into our cabin today. You want a drink?" He held the bottle out, then drew it back. "I forgot. You don't drink."

"Not anymore. But thanks."

With Cuyler in the stern, Don in the bow, they began fishing. The far-from-smooth water reflected a steady darkening of the clouds overhead. Half an hour passed with no action—an unusally long time on this lake. Then Don had a strike and boated a good-sized lake trout.

Cuyler silently watched him go through the routine of disgorging the hook, killing the fish, and hanging it overside in a plastic bag to keep it fresh.

Ten minutes later Don caught another.

Twenty minutes later, a third.

"What the hell you using?" Cuyler demanded then. The bottle was half empty at this point. His voice was noticeably thick.

"One of Cricket's bottom lures. An imitation of something she found in a fish Dan caught a while back." Don took from his jacket pocket a small plastic box containing an assortment of Cricket's latest creations. "Here." He tossed the box to Cuyler. "Help yourself."

Cuyler selected one and tossed the box back without comment. After a swig at the bottle he reeled in his line, removed the live-bait hook from his leader, and tied on the lure.

Don't thank me, Don thought.

Cuyler didn't. But soon he too was catching fish.

Don waited until the bottle was nearly empty. "While we're out here alone, do you mind answering a question?" he said then, carefully keeping it casual.

Cuyler looked at him. After downing that much liquor in such a short time, the man was no longer sober.

"It's a thing I've wondered about ever since it happened," Don said. "You remember the time, on the portage to Fletcher, you saw a deer and went after it?"

Cuyler took his time about answering, but at

last did answer. "Yeah, I remember. What about it?"

"You were pretty intent on bagging a deer at that point. I guess you'd expected it to be easy and it wasn't. But we know you blazed away at something that day, because we all heard you."

"So I shot at something," Cuyler said. "So what's the big—" Suddenly the tip of his rod went down and he was fighting another fish, but was no longer sober enough to do so with his usual skill. The talking had to wait all of ten minutes while the fish, a big laker, put up the best fight of the morning before allowing itself to be netted.

With the trout hanging overside and his lure back in the water, Cuyler emptied his bottle in triumph and turned again to Don. "So you want to know what I shot at that day, huh? Why?"

"No special reason. Sometimes a thing just bugs a fellow. Like when you're trying to put a name to a tune that keeps running through your head, and can't seem to do it."

"I didn't shoot at anything. I just got an itchy finger."

"Oh, come on. You never waste ammo. Not you."

"Well, I did that day. I was so goddam fucking mad at that deer, I couldn't help myself. I kept getting a glimpse of him, see? He was like a fucking ghost, always there but just out of reach behind some trees or a stand of brush. Like he was leading me on and laughing at me."

"So you fired that shot at the deer?" Don said. If so, the theory he and Cricket had arrived at after so many hours of talk would have to be discarded. And all this morning's careful probing would have led to nothing.

"So I what?"

"The shot we heard? You were firing at the deer?"

"Christ no," Cuyler said. "I said I *followed* the stupid deer and tried for a shot but never got one. It was on my way back I finally fired at something. At a hawk. Hey, you got a strike!"

It was not a strike. It was only Don's hand trembling so hard that the rod tip twitched. Nevertheless, Don went through the motions of jerking the rod to set the hook, then pretending he had lost the fish. "Guess I should pay attention to what's important here," he said in a voice meant to be sheepish. "But go ahead, finish your story first. You shot at a hawk?"

"Yeah. And it was dumb of me to waste ammo like that. I know it. But Jesus, I'd walked a hundred miles after that dumb deer and never got a clean crack at it. So when this stupid hawk lit on a branch right in front of my face, I blew it away." Cuyler shook his head and laughed at what he was saying. "You never done much hunting. I guess you wouldn't understand."

"Have we got enough fish, do you suppose?"

"Huh?"

"I've got five. You've caught that many too, haven't you? Don't we have enough?" It was important, Don thought, to tell Cricket what he had just learned. Because Cuyler had just supplied the last piece of the puzzle. The very last piece.

Suddenly Cuyler, still using the lure Cricket had made, hooked another fish and landed it. "That puts me one up on you," he said. "Yeah, we have enough now, I guess." He was grinning again. "I'm ready if you are."

With the fish in the canoe they paddled back to camp, beaching the canoe some distance from the other craft so they could clean the catch without fouling the sand there. But when they had stepped out of the canoe and drawn it up on the sand—even before they had lifted the sacks of fish out of it—Cuyler spread his feet apart, unzipped his fly, and began to urinate.

Don watched in dismay until he was finished, then said, "Cuyler, we *drink* this water!"

Evidently the bourbon-induced good nature was beginning to wear off. "Oh, for Chrissake," Cuyler retorted, "all kinds of animals piss in it. Some of them even crap in it."

Don gave up. But in tossing the fish ashore he was careful not to throw them on the patch of sand darkened by the other's urine. And on the way to the fireplace where the women still did the cooking for all, he ventured one last comment.

"Cuyler . . ."

"Yeah?"

"We did build a latrine, you know. We did

agree not to relieve ourselves anywhere but there."

Cuyler stopped walking and turned to face him. "For Chrissake, will you knock it off? I *had* to. Right there and then, I *had* to. It wouldn't wait. So stop making such a lousy fuss about it, will you?"

With a sigh of surrender, Don walked on in silence.

"So there you have it," Don said to Cricket ten minutes later, at the cabin they were building. "The truth is, I think we knew all along that there was something more than mutations involved."

Seated on a log, shaping an end of it with a hatchet, Cricket stopped work and frowned up at him. "Something *more* than mutations? What are you saying?"

"He killed a hawk without any reason for doing so, and a huge hawk killed Becky. He destroyed a harmless little three-eyed frog—a mutant, yes, but harmless all the same—and a giant frog with three eyes took Sheila away. In a fit of anger he shot up a baby skunk, and—"

"Are you saying the deaths were some kind of revenge?"

He nodded.

"I don't understand, Don. It was Cuyler who killed those poor creatures, not the ones who died."

"When we're angry, do we always save our anger for the real culprit? Don't we sometimes

turn on the first thing that presents itself?" Don
reached for the high-tech saw with which for
the past three days he had been slicing logs
into boards for the roof—a tedious job even
with that most modern of tools. "But let's talk
about this later, shall we?" He glanced at his
watch. "It's five after three, love. We've a lot to
do here before dark."

At twenty past four that afternoon Lloyd Atkinson opened his eyes after a restless hour of
sleep and groped for the hand of the man sitting beside him.

"Doc?"

"Yes, Lloyd," Dan Frazier said. "I'm here."

"I think—I think I remember what happened, Doc."

"What happened when?"

"The day I was shot. I didn't trip over any
tree and fall on my gun."

Dan Frazier had been in and out of the tent
all day, checking on his patient. The end was
near, he felt. In the tent's dim light, the face he
now stared at was that of a cadaver; the hand
that clung to his, a claw. How much, he wondered, did Lloyd weigh now? There was no way
to be sure, of course, but he would be surprised
if it were more than a hundred pounds.

Lloyd's eyes, though, were abnormally bright
at this moment. Bright, perhaps, with a desperate eagerness to tell what he remembered
while there was still time.

"I didn't trip, Doc. I wasn't running toward

him at all. When he shot the doe, I was standing right there beside him. You hear? I was right there at his side. Then—then a little fawn came out of the trees—a pretty little thing—so small—looking for its mother, I suppose. And he—Cuyler—he drew a bead on it. We already had more than enough meat, but he was going to kill the fawn too and—and—I let out a yell to warn it and knocked up his gun. Are you hearing me, Doc? Are you?"

"I hear you, Lloyd." Leaning over his patient, Frazier gently stroked the man's forehead. "He was going to shoot the fawn you've been telling us about, and you knocked up his gun. What happened then?"

"He got—he got ang— He was furious with me, Doc. He cursed me and called me names. I think he went a little—went a little berserk."

"And?"

"Suddenly in his rage he spun around and pointed the gun at me and pulled the trigger."

Frazier felt himself trembling. "My God, Lloyd, are you sure? Do you realize what you're saying?"

"You don't—you mean you don't believe me?"

"Tell me again. Cuyler deliberately shot you?"

"Well, I can't be sure it was deliberate." Lloyd's voice was growing weaker now. To hear it, Frazier had to lean so close that the man's trembling lips brushed his cheek. "He just—just lost his temper, I suppose. Lost control of himself. But he—he shot me from two feet away, Doc. It wasn't any acci—"

Sensing the word, the sentence, would not be completed, Frazier pulled back and saw that the speaker's eyes, though still wide open, were staring into space. He laid a finger against Lloyd's neck, seeking a pulse, and felt nothing. When he was sure, really sure, he got stiffly to his feet and walked out to the fireplace, where Martha—his Martha—was preparing to light a fire for the evening meal.

"He's gone, Martha." There was a sob in Frazier's voice. It had been such a long, long fight, and so very difficult because from the beginning he had not really believed he had a chance of winning it.

Martha McNae looked at his face and read his feelings there. She stepped close and put her arms around him. Not until she had held him that way for more than a minute, in silence, did she step back. "Sit down, Dan," she said then. "I'll go tell the others."

As before, the men dug the grave, and words from a remembered funeral service were recited. At the evening meal, which consisted of fish caught by Don and Cuyler that morning, no one talked much. Frazier said nothing—absolutely nothing—of what Lloyd Atkinson had told him just before the end.

Soon after dark, the Cuylers went to their cabin on the spit and the others to their tents.

Don Neal and Cricket Swensen had only just settled into bed, and were about to resume the conversation begun earlier at their cabin, when a low growl from Rambi warned of someone outside.

In through the flaps came Dr. Dan. Frazier, to quiet the dog with a gentle pat and seat himself on the floor. "I'm sorry," he said. "We have to talk."

He told them what Lloyd had told him.

They were too stunned to speak.

"So," said Frazier, "we have a murderer in our midst."

"My God," Don said faintly.

"The question is, what are we to do about it?"

"Have you told the others?" Cricket asked.

"I came to you first. Martha knows, of course. Now I'll go talk to Prof. But we need to hold a meeting very soon—all of us but Cuyler and Rowena—and decide what to do. Any suggestions?"

"Why don't we meet in Prof's tent right now?" Don suggested. "The Cuylers have moved into their cabin. Down there on the spit, they won't know that anything's going on up here."

"Very well. But better bring this little guy, too." Frazier reached out to pat the dog, who had settled down next to him. "If you leave him alone and he starts barking . . ."

"Yes," Cricket said.

"Prof's tent, then," Frazier said, and was gone.

Chapter Twenty-eight

With five persons present the professor's tent was crowded, but after a brief flurry of confusion in the darkness all had found places and silence took over.

Into the silence came the voice of Dan Frazier, repeating the last words of the man they had buried that day.

"Are we agreed that he must be told to go?" the speaker asked in conclusion. "Remember, he was not drinking when he shot Lloyd. He was only angry because Lloyd had stopped him from killing the fawn."

"Another senseless killing," Don Neal said. "When he and I were out fishing today—and this time he *was* drinking—he admitted he killed a harmless hawk the time he went after that deer on the portage to Fletcher. Cricket and I have been talking about it. Tell them, Cricket, will you?"

"We think he may be responsible for *all* the deaths," Cricket said. "We think nature—or something—has been avenging the harmless creatures he killed not for food or in self-defense but simply for the sake of killing. How else can you explain such bizarre deaths?"

The voice of Theron Varga said, "How, then, do you explain the fact that Cuyler himself is still alive?"

"I asked that same question this afternoon. Don had an answer. One that satisfied me, at least. Don?"

"I only pointed out that when we're angry about something, we sometimes strike out at innocent people. A man may be up tight about a thing that happened at work, for instance, and take it out on his wife."

There were murmurs of assent.

"All right," Dan Frazier said. "But let's get back on track now, shall we? We're here to decide what to do about Cuyler. I say there's no place for a murderer in the new life we're trying to build here. Let's have a vote on it. Prof, how do you feel?"

"I agree. Absolutely," Varga said.

"You, Don?"

"Cuyler has to go."

"Cricket?"

"Of course."

"Martha?"

"Should I be voting?" Martha McNae said. "I mean, the Cuylers have been with you people from the start, and I've only just—"

Frazier interrupted. "The rest of you—should she vote?"

Without hesitation they said she should.

"Then yes," Martha said, "I think any man who goes crazy with a gun is a bomb just waiting to explode. He should be told to leave."

"Which brings us to our second problem," Frazier said. "What if he refuses to go? How do we persuade a man who has a violent temper and an arsenal of weapons?"

Seated there in the dark, able to judge one another's feelings only by tone of voice, the five of them discussed the problem and reached an agreement. They would wait until both Cuylers were absent from their cabin and Cuyler did not have a weapon with him. Then one of the group—whoever happened to be nearest the cabin at the time—would slip in and remove Cuyler's guns. Only then would they order the man to leave, giving him a canoe, a tent, and whatever else he would need to return to civilization or establish himself elsewhere in the wilderness.

"Are we saying Rowena, too, must go?" Professor Varga's voice conveyed an unmistakable note of melancholy.

"Will she have any choice?" asked Martha.

"I suppose not, unless she is prepared to defy him. But she has done nothing to deserve being sent away. Actually, she has been one of *us*, doing her very best at all times to make a more—more temperate person of him." The professor sighed. "Of course, no woman could ever effect a change in that man. Why she ever married him I will never understand."

"She told us why," Cricket reminded him. "At least, she told me. She grew up on a farm next to one his folks owned. They went to school together. Cuyler was a high-school football hero and she—"

"Ah yes," Varga said. "A high-school star who once had a chance to attend our university on a football scholarship. I remember. I asked him once, when we were out fishing, why he never followed through on it. 'I went over there and talked to some creep named Raffer,' he told me. Those were his exact words: 'Some creep named Raffer.' Jack Raffer was our coach at the time—a fine man, a wonderful man who hated violence, even violent language, with a great passion. He is dead now—killed in his home by robbers. And when I asked Cuyler what had happened when he talked with Jack, he said, 'Hell, I dunno. The creep never told me nothing, only sat there nodding his head. All I know is, I never heard from them again.'" Again Varga sighed. "Poor Rowena. But she will go with him, you'll see. She will consider it her duty."

"So, then," Dan Frazier said, "we keep an eye on them from now on, and the first time they're both away from their cabin—"

"And he doesn't have a gun with him," Don said.

"And one of us is close enough—"

"And let us hope," Professor Varga said, "that when he is gone, the dying will end and we can stop being afraid."

Two mornings later, soon after daybreak, Cuyler emerged from his cabin, fishing rod in hand, and walked along the spit to where the canoes were kept. Martha McNae, building a fire at the camp fireplace, watched him turn one of the canoes over, launch it, and paddle out to go fishing.

A few minutes later his craft disappeared from sight around a bend of the shore.

Hurrying to the tent she shared with Dan Frazier, Martha excitedly told Dan what she had seen. "Why don't I tell Rowena I'm going to pick some berries and ask her to go with me?" she suggested.

"Good idea," Frazier said.

He watched her go down to the cabin on the spit, and saw her talking with Rowena in the doorway. He saw the two of them walk up to the fireplace together, take two of the folding buckets from a rack there, and disappear into the woods. He looked at his watch.

After waiting five minutes to be sure they were out of hearing, he went to the professor's tent, then to the one occupied by Don and Cricket, and told them what had happened. The four then hurried to the spit.

Don and Frazier searched the cabin for weapons and ammunition. They unloaded all but a twelve-gauge shotgun and a lever-action rifle, which they took outside and left leaning against the cabin to defend themselves with, if necessary, when Cuyler returned. The ammunition from the others, and all the extra ammunition in the cabin, they carried up to the camp and hid in Frazier's tent.

On their way back down they carried a folded tent, some cooking utensils, tools, and a measured share of what food supplies remained. Then, at the cabin again, with the help of Cricket and the professor, they assembled the Cuylers' personal belongings and heaped everything alongside two empty backpacks just inside the cabin doorway.

After that, with Don and Cuyler holding the two still-loaded weapons, the four of them nervously stood about in front of the cabin, awaiting the expected confrontation.

"Rowena, there's something I have to tell you."

For more than an hour Martha McNae had sought some way to tell her companion what would happen when they returned to camp. No way could she simply walk her back there without some kind of warning to soften the shock. She *liked* Rowena. The woman was honest and decent, and didn't deserve the terrible thing that was about to happen to her.

Busy at a nearby berry bush, Rowena turned her head and said, "Yes?"

"Let's sit a minute, shall we? That log over there?"

"Of course," Rowena looked at her watch. "It will feel good to sit awhile. You know we've been at this over an hour?"

They walked to the fallen tree and sat on it.

"Something you want to tell me?" Rowena said then, with a little frown.

"No, not something I want to tell you. Something I *have* to."

"Okay."

"First, let me ask you a question," Martha said. "Has your husband ever told you what really happened the day Lloyd was shot?"

"What do you mean?"

Martha tried to keep her voice free of anything that might seem to be a threat. "Rowena . . . before Lloyd died, he finally remembered and told Dan. Lloyd didn't stumble and shoot himself that day, like Cuyler said he did. That wasn't what happened."

Rowena let her breath out only when she had to. "It was Cuyler who stumbled. Wasn't it?"

"Uh-uh. Nobody stumbled."

"What?"

Quietly, in the same nonthreatening voice, Martha told her what Lloyd had told Frazier.

"Oh, my God." It came out as a kind of moan. "Are you *sure*? Couldn't Lloyd have been . . . You said he was dying when he said it? Couldn't he have been out of his mind?"

"He was never out of his mind, Rowena. He just didn't remember until the end. Maybe it's true that when you're dying, your whole life comes back to you."

Sobbing a little, Rowena closed her eyes and moved her head slowly up and down. "It's the kind of thing Cuyler would do. I know it. That awful temper of his."

"That isn't all I have to tell you," Martha said. The eyes opened. "I think I know."

"Last night, when you two were in your cabin, the rest of us held a meeting in Prof's tent to talk about it. To decide what we ought to do about him. Rowena, I don't know how to tell you this, but I have to. I can't let you go back there not knowing."

"They want us to leave," Rowena said. "That's it, isn't it? We have to leave."

"Not you. Just him."

"They're going to tell him when he comes back from fishing?"

Martha nodded.

"And you wanted me out of the way when they told him. That's why you asked me to come berrying with you, isn't it? To get me out of the way."

"They had to get the guns out of your cabin— unload them, at least—in case he became violent again. It seemed best for you not to be there." Martha reached for the other's hand. "I wasn't supposed to talk to you like this. It was my own idea. We never discussed what *I* would do—only what they would do at the cabin."

The sobbing had stopped. Rowena gazed at her in silence.

"You don't have to go with him," Martha said. "We don't want you to. We love you."

"He's my husband."

"That's not good enough. Not the way he treats you. You don't have to throw your life away just because you married Cuyler." Wanting desperately to help, Martha moved closer with her arms outstretched.

All at once Rowena was in those arms, sobbing against her breast as though they had known and loved each other since the beginning of time.

Twenty minutes later they arrived at the cabin and found the others still waiting there for Cuyler. Like a sleepwalker, with her gaze on the ground, Rowena went past them in silence and disappeared inside.

Half an hour later, Cuyler returned.

With fish to clean, he beached his canoe not in front of the cabin but farther down the shore, close to where Don and he had nearly come to blows about his urinating at the water's edge. Apparently puzzled by the presence of the others in front of his new home, he left the fish on the sand and walked toward the cabin with a scowl twisting his face.

"What's going on?" he demanded when close enough.

They had decided to let Professor Varga, the father figure among them, do the talking. With folded arms and an unblinking stare, the professor said without preamble, "Before he died, Cuyler, Lloyd Atkinson told us how he was shot."

"He told you what?"

"Let's not drag this out with a pointless discussion, Cuyler. Lloyd told us what really happened. We have held a meeting and put the problem to a vote. We want you to leave."

Cuyler put his hands on his hips. Had he been the western gunslinger he so often apparently imagined himself to be, one hand would undoubtedly have hovered near a holstered revolver. "It was an accident, for Chrissake. Anybody can have an accident."

"No, Cuyler. You shot him in anger, and it was murder. Pack up now and go, please."

"*Now*? Just like that?"

"Now."

Cuyler let his gaze travel from the professor to the others and then to Rowena, who had suddenly appeared in the cabin doorway. "Well, I'll be damned," he said. "So now you stupid bastards think you can get along without me. After I've taught you everything you know."

No one responded. No one moved.

"Okay." He took his hands from his hips and spread them in a gesture of mock helplessness. "You want me out of here, I'm gone." With an exaggerated swagger—the cowboy's gesture of contempt when ordered out of the saloon—he took his time walking to the cabin. Rowena stepped aside to let him enter.

In a moment he reappeared in the doorway with his favorite weapon, the automatic rifle.

"So you unloaded the guns and took my ammo, huh?"

"Merely as a precaution," Professor Varga replied. "When you are ready to leave, all but the ammunition for these two weapons will be returned to you."

"You mean you're keeping those?" For the first time, Cuyler's sneer was obviously meant to convey a threat.

"Until we have learned to feed ourselves without such weapons, I'm afraid we shall need them."

"They belong to me, goddammit!"

"Without question. But perhaps you will mark them down as a form of payment, so to speak, for the life of our dear friend. As you see, we are allowing you and Rowena to depart with a full share of everything else—a tent, supplies, and of course a canoe. Kindly load your canoe now, Cuyler."

From the doorway Cuyler once more let his gaze travel from face to face. "You bastards," he said then. But having said it, he turned back into the cabin, and a moment later reappeared with a backpack and his collection of firearms.

Rowena, too, had her arms full as she followed him in silence to the canoe.

They made several trips to the water's edge in the next fifteen minutes. Each time they returned to the cabin, Cuyler glared at those who stood silently watching. Especially at the two with the guns.

In contrast, Rowena looked at no one, but walked back and forth with her head down.

When the canoe was ready for departure, Cuyler walked halfway back to the others and faced them again with his hands on his hips. "Consider yourselves lucky I don't have some gasoline," he said in a voice of cold fury. "If I did, I'd burn this fucking cabin to the ground before I'd let you bastards have it. Now, where's my ammo?"

Frazier said quietly, "I'll get it," and handed his weapon to Martha. Turning, he walked up the slope to the camp and circled the fireplace to his tent. In the few moments he was gone, no one spoke. When he returned, he handed the bag of ammunition to Cuyler, who accepted it in silence and walked with it to the canoe, where Rowena stood waiting.

"Cuyler?" Professor Varga unexpectedly called after him.

He turned. "Whatever you want, you can go to hell. All of you. Go to hell!"

"I was only going to ask where *you* plan on going."

"Why should you care, for Chrissake?"

"We care because of Rowena. We would like to know whether you plan on returning to civilization or—"

" 'We care because of Rowena!' " Cuyler mimicked, the sneer back in his voice. Or was it a snarl now? "You bet your ass you care about Rowena, you bastard. You think I haven't known all along how you'd like to get it into her? You think I'm blind, for Chrissake?"

"I merely asked—" Varga began, but the sob in his voice choked him.

"Well, go ahead and ask. Eat your heart out. Because from now on you won't *ever* know where she is!" Shaking with rage, Cuyler lurched about and strode to the canoe, where Rowena stood waiting. "All right," he growled at her. "Get in!"

Staring at him, with her hands clenched at her sides, Rowena stood her ground.

"Get in, goddammit!"

Rowena backed away from him.

That was enough. The gunslinger image fell from Cuyler like a discarded cloak, and the curtain came down with a crash on his slouch and sneer. When he spoke again, his voice was a scream. "Get in, I said! What the hell are you waiting for? A farewell party?"

For three seconds Rowena stood there frozen, staring back at him. Then with a cry of "No! I'm not going with you!" she spun herself around and began to run.

Not to the cabin. Not to the two men with loaded weapons. But blindly, unthinkingly, up the slope toward the tents on the bluff. As though pursued by something monstrous that she knew would destroy her if it overtook her.

"You bitch!" Cuyler yelled, and started up the slope after her.

But abruptly he stopped.

If he tried to follow her up the slope she would outrun him, he must have decided. But there was a better way. By going along the beach and up a steeper but shorter stretch of slope, he could head her off. Suddenly he would appear in front of her, and she, thinking him behind her, would run blindly into his waiting arms.

At full speed he raced along the sand.

They all saw it. Later, both Don and Frazier, who had the guns, confessed they had considered shooting him, or at least shooting at his legs to stop him, so that Rowena might escape. But the other happened first.

He was running. And suddenly he stopped.

The sand, or something in the sand, or something under the sand, had seized his feet. He was a fly who had stepped on flypaper. Momentum almost sent him sprawling forward on his face, but with his feet ankle-deep in the first fraction of a second he could not fall. He could only throw himself from side to side in a frantic struggle to break the sand's grip.

But the grip only tightened. The flypaper was all at once a black circle some four or five feet in diameter that began boiling like a hot spring. It sucked him down so swiftly that even before the first shriek of terror tore from his throat his legs had been swallowed and his writhing, twisting body was disappearing at the rate of an inch a second.

He shrieked. He flung his arms about in a desperate, futile attempt to grab at something.

He was not, after all, a fly trapped on flypaper but a helplessly struggling insect being devoured whole by something alive and ravenous. His earsplitting shrieks supplied a wild accompaniment to the unfolding drama as he sank to his waist, his chest, to the wide-open mouth still howling for help. All about him the sand, now black as night, convulsed like boiling lava and made unearthly gulping sounds.

Those watching were too stricken to move, even had they dared to approach. They could only stand and stare as the man's screaming mouth filled with blackness and was silent—as his bulging eyes disappeared in the tarry whirlpool—as the boiling upheaval swallowed his head. Then the last visible part of him, a solitary upthrust hand with twitching fingers, vanished from sight.

The patch of black sand convulsed one last time. Then a deathlike silence settled over the spit.

The whole horror had taken no more than a minute. Varga and the others had scarcely moved. Rowena had frozen in her tracks halfway up the slope. Even time, it seemed, had momentarily stood still.

Like zombies Varga and the others, including Rowena, slowly approached the still-black circular stain that marked Cuyler's grave. But before they could reach it, Don Neal stopped them with a warning.

They turned to look at him.

"Don't," he said, holding up a hand. "There's

nothing anyone can do for him, so leave it alone." Groping for words to explain what he thought had happened, he paused, then had to settle for a shrug. After another brief pause he added simply, "This is where he did it. The circle here. This exact spot."

"Where he did what?" Dan Frazier asked with a frown.

"Urinated on the sand. And cursed me when I told him he shouldn't foul the water we drink."

Chapter Twenty-nine

Three days had passed. There had been another meeting. In the morning they would abandon the camp on Collier, leaving behind the cabins on which they had worked so long and hard.

Perhaps, eventually, they would find some lake to the north where they could live in peace, without fear.

There had been arguments. The discussion had gone on for hours. But all had known, even before a word was spoken, how the meeting would end.

How could they stay where they were, knowing that a certain patch of shore—and perhaps other such horrors of which they were not yet aware—lay in wait for them?

Fraizer and Martha talked about it that night as they lay naked on their sweet-smelling bed of balsam boughs. They had just made love, and for both of them it had been like that night at her home in Chetwood. In truth it was always that way for them—a repetition of the wonder and magic of that astonishing first time.

"Do you suppose Cuyler's relieving himself there actually had anything to do with what happened?" Martha asked.

"God knows. I threw a stick onto the place yesterday and it just lay there. But what does that prove? How do we know the thing wasn't just—well—sleeping? Maybe if we were to go down there now and throw something, what happened to Cuyler would happen again."

"Well, then, do you suppose the Halleluja had something to do with it?" After Cuyler's death, Rowena had found a supply of that powerful drug in a pocket of her husband's backpack. But obviously he had not used it often, or they would have suspected.

"Who knows about that, either?" Frazier said. "Though his having it probably does explain some of his behavior."

Martha turned and pressed herself against him, with one arm across his chest. "Rowena's been telling me more about the two Indians she and Cuyler talked to," she said. "It seems they were from a small colony at Lake Kelsa. What do you suppose would happen if we asked to join them?"

Frazier's laugh was mirthless. "I think if they knew the history of this expedition, they'd probably run us off. What I'm wondering—are there Indians on *every* lake north of here? Because if there are—if every lake has already been taken over—we may have to come back here to Collier whether we want to or not."

Rowena and Professor Varga were in bed together, too, though Varga had not planned it that way.

In the beginning he had thought only of consoling her, because even though she had lived in constant fear of her husband, watching him die in such a terrible way had been traumatic in the extreme. She had refused to sleep in her cabin that night. Had begged to be allowed to sleep in one of the tents, so she would not be so close to where it had happened. "Stay with me," Varga had urged her. "I too am alone. I know how it feels."

He had not slept much that night. Rowena had kept him awake by constantly talking in her sleep. Once she had sat bolt upright with a scream so shrill it aroused the rest of the camp and brought one of them, Don Neal, running to see if help was needed. Thank God there had been moonlight. A dark night would have been unbearable.

In the morning he had talked to Dan Frazier, saying, "I don't think she should return to the spit, Dan. Not even for the few days we are likely to remain here. Do you agree?"

"I agree. Keep her with you."

"Will you talk to her?"

"About moving in with you? For keeps? Yes, of course. It's what she ought to do."

"Thank you," Varga said. "Coming from me it would seem less—less—"

"That's what doctors are for," Frazier said with a smile. "And Cuyler was right about one thing, you know. You and Rowena will be good for each other."

The day after Cuyler's death the professor had spent most of his time with her. Had persuaded her to talk about her life before her marriage to Cuyler—as a child growing up on a farm and going to a small-town school. He had given her an almost classic classroom lecture on the subject of people with dual personalities, in hope of helping her understand the man she had married and even why she had made the mistake of marrying him. It would be a kind of purification, he hoped. A driving out of ghosts. Actually, toward the end of that day, she was smiling again—as she was smiling now in his arms on the third night of their being together.

"You know, I don't feel my age when I am with you," he said. "Though I ought to, I suppose."

She said with a laugh. "You don't look any older. Or act it. You never have."

"In any case, there isn't much we can do about it, is there?" He was surprised to hear himself laughing along with her. Since Sheila's

passing there had been very little in his life to
make him feel lighthearted.

Rowena had turned to face him. Both were
ready for sleep, their outer garments off, Varga
in undershirt and shorts, she in bra and
panties. "And you know something else, Prof?"
she said. "When I'm with you I feel—well, not
older exactly, but more—more—"

He knew the words she was groping for.
"More mature" was what she wanted to say.
But if they were to have the kind of relationship he hoped for, he must never set himself up
as a teacher instructing a student. She would
always be conscious of his being older if he did
that. They must be equals. Equals in everything. "I know what you mean," he said.

"You do?"

"But if you feel older, I feel younger, and that
means we meet somewhere in the middle,
wouldn't you say? Rowena?" He spoke her
name very softly while turning to face her.

"Yes?"

He reached for her, but gently, very gently.
"May I? Or is it too soon for anyone to—to
touch you? If it is too soon, tell me. If you
would rather I never touched you, tell me that.
It will make no difference in our friendship, I
promise."

She answered him without any hesitation.
Without even speaking. One moment they were
lying face-to-face with a space between them.
Next moment they were naked and her body
was warm and soft under his, her arms were

around him, her mouth was moist and sweet against his own.

Even as he made love to her, he sensed that she had never been loved that way before. Her ecstasy told him so. Cuyler must have indulged in sex with her—one couldn't call it making love—the way he did everything else, taking what he wanted with no concern for her needs and feelings. She was a woman who yearned for affection and desperately wanted to love someone.

When it was over, she slept like a child in his arms.

"No," Cricket said. "I don't think I could bear to. Not after all the work we've done on it."

The question had been, "Shall we get up at daybreak, love, for a last look at our cabin before we start packing?" Don had asked it as they lay together in their tent.

"And all the dreams we built into it," she added with a tremor in her voice. "Oh God, Don, I was so sure we'd found the right place here."

"So was I."

She lifted her head to look at him, a movement made plausible because the tent walls were awash with moonlight and everything in the tent seemed to have absorbed some of the glow. "But you haven't made the same commitment," she said.

"Hey, young lady, I resent that." *Make her laugh*, he told himself. *If we can laugh at it, we'll both feel better.* "What do you mean, I haven't made the same commitment? I worked every bit as hard on that cabin as you did!"

"I mean you're not pregnant."

With a gasp, he hiked himself up on one elbow to look down at her. "You mean you are?"

"I stopped using the control the day we began to put the roof on the cabin. I thought with Martha being pregnant, it would be wonderful if we could have a baby about the same time." Her wide eyes gazed up at him without blinking. "You're not angry, are you?"

"Angry!" His cry was a mix of joy and awe. "Darling, darling—haven't I always told you I wanted a child as soon as you felt right about having one?" In fact, from the very start of their life together he had wanted her to give him a child. But with everything of value collapsing around them, both had agreed it would be unfair.

"I don't know yet, of course," she said, smiling now as she looked up at him. "I won't know until next week. But so long as you're glad . . ."

He lay beside her again and took her into his arms, and though they had made love earlier they would have done so again, without question, but for an interruption. The interruption was provided by their little Italian greyhound, who suddenly stirred at the foot of the bed, leaped to his feet, and ran out of the tent.

"Uh-oh," Cricket said in a whisper. "What's out there?"

Don was off the bed instantly. With Cricket close behind him, he scrambled on hands and knees to the flaps and looked out. The relief in his voice was almost comical. "Well, what do you know? Look who's here again!"

Cricket followed him from the tent and got to her feet beside him. In the moonlight they had no trouble following Rambi's movements as he ran to join his friend from the forest. The fawn spread her forelegs and lowered her head as she always did. Dog and deer nuzzled each other, then turned and trotted side by side past the fireplace and down the slope to the spit.

"No!" Cricket cried. "No, don't!"

"Rambi, come back!" Don shouted. "Rambi!"

The two paid no attention. Perhaps on a night so bright with moonlight, human voices could not penetrate some private world of magic reserved for those with special senses. Even as Don again yelled the dog's name and began racing after them, frantically waving his arms, the two reached the spit and went trotting toward the water's edge.

In doing so, they ran onto the spot where the sand had sucked Cuyler to his death.

Don skidded to a stop. Reaching his side, Cricket clasped his hand. Together they stood there rigid, waiting with held breath for the horror to repeat itself.

But dog and deer continued unchallenged to the water's edge and began to drink. They drank their fill. Then they turned, trotted back across the sand, and climbed the slope to the camp.

There, breaking into a run, they disappeared together into the forest.

Don Neal turned to the woman at his side. "Did we just see what I think we saw? Or was I dreaming?"

"They crossed it *twice*," Cricket said. "And nothing happened!"

He turned to look around. His shouting at the dog had not aroused the camp, it seemed. He reached for Cricket's hand again. "Come on, love. We need to talk about this."

Back in their tent they sat on the bed, facing each other in the filtered moonlight.

"It happened, didn't it?" Don said in the low, quiet voice he used when grappling with a problem. "We both saw it happen. They walked, ran, trotted—whatever—right across the patch of sand that came alive under Cuyler and sucked him down. They did it twice."

Cricket nodded. "Yes. It happened."

"There is something I was going to do tomorrow that I haven't told you about. A sort of last gasp or last hope, I guess you'd call it. When daylight came, I was going to go down there and throw a log onto that spot to see what would happen."

"Dan has already done that," Cricket said. "I saw him do it yesterday."

"Then maybe he had the same idea I've had—that what happened there wasn't just a random shot but something aimed specifically at Cuyler."

"Because?"

"Because of what he was, or what he represented. Look." Don paused to get his thoughts in order, then leaned toward her, reaching for her hands. "What are we talking about here, do you suppose? Nature?"

"Well, yes. I think so."

"Then what do we mean by 'nature'? The earth? The planet? God? Are God and Nature—with a capital *N*—one and the same?"

"I've never thought that much about it," Cricket said.

"Well, I haven't either, until now. But think of what's happened to us. Being the kind of man he was—uncaring, insensitive, given to fouling even the language for no reason except that he liked the sound of ugly words—Cuyler killed a harmless frog because he enjoyed killing things, and then a frog killed Sheila. He shot a hawk in anger, and a hawk killed Becky. He destroyed a harmless baby skunk, and some kind of skunk killed Max and Penny. Then, after murdering Lloyd in a fit of temper, he urinated on the sand there at the water's edge, fouling the water we and all the forest creatures drink, and the sand opened up like an angry mouth and devoured him." Don took in a deep breath. "What if Nature is determined to save this wilderness from people like Cuyler? What if she has given up on the cities but is determined to keep corruption out of certain selected places where she is encouraging new beginnings? If we can accept that as a premise, why can't we accept that when Cuyler introduced his brand of corruption here, she became angry? Am I making any sense?"

"I think so." Cricket sat there staring at him and nodding. "You're saying—I think—that when Sheila and Max and Penny were struck down, Nature was really trying to eliminate Cuyler—to stop the intrusion of evil—but didn't succeed until the sand caught him. You're saying—or hoping—that with Cuyler gone now, we have nothing more to fear. Is that what you're saying?"

"Maybe in the morning we can find out."

The sun was up. The six survivors had met at the campfire for what would be their last meal at Collier. "Before we eat," Don quietly announced, "there is something I want to do."

They looked at him. "Wait, please," he said, and went to his tent.

While the camp was still asleep, Cricket and he had put together a length of Zylon rope, lightweight but strong, from tent-ropes no longer in use. He returned to the fire with it over his shoulder. To the others' questions his response was a simple "Trust me, please. Cricket and I talked about this half the night."

They looked at Cricket, who stood beside him. "He's right," she said. "Please. It's important for all of us that we do this. It may be the most important thing we've done since leaving the city."

Side by side, she and Don walked down the slope to the spit. To the place on the spit where Cuyler had disappeared. Where the fawn and the dog had drunk together last night in the moonlight. The others followed in silence.

Ten feet from the circle of sand that had sucked Cuyler to his death, they stopped. Don lifted his arms. Cricket passed one end of the rope around his body, and together they made it fast. Walking back to the others, she uncoiled the rope as she went.

"We are going to hold this," she said, "so we can pull him back to safety if anything happens. Does everyone—?"

"No, no!" Professor Varga protested. "It would be too dangerous!"

"We don't think it will be dangerous," Cricket said. "Last night our Rambi and the little fawn he plays with walked across the sand here and nothing happened to them. We think—" She turned to Don. "Tell them, hon."

"We think the fawn may have been sent as a messenger," Don said calmly. "Anyway, with five of you on the rope ready to haul me out at the first sign of trouble, I'll be safe enough."

"Well . . ." The professor yielded, but continued to shake his head. "We must agree on a signal, though. If you feel the least movement under your feet, you—"

"Don't worry, Prof. I'll yell loud enough." Don

watched them take up their positions, then looked across the lake at the rising sun. It was a glorious dawning. He took in a breath. On guard against any slightest movement of the sand, he slowly paced forward.

The sand stayed firm.

He reached the water's edge, turned, and slowly walked back.

The sand remained quiet.

He repeated the whole procedure.

The sand did not stir.

He took off the rope, let it fall, and walked to the water's edge and back without it. Nothing happened.

Then he strolled to the others and said quietly, "You see? We don't have to leave. That's what the fawn came to tell us."

Epilogue

From Cricket Swensen's journal:

Exactly one year has passed since Don and I moved into our cabin here on Lake Collier, so perhaps a brief summing-up is now in order.

First, the baby. Dawn is an absolute darling, and has to be the happiest child in all creation. The only time she ever really cried was the one I wrote about a while back, when she got a splinter in her hand from the crib we made for her. And speaking of cribs, the person who invented those saws we are using would be astonished, I'm sure, at the number of ways we have found to use them. We've been able to build all sorts of things with them.

The Crees, with whom we visit back at forth all the time now, have shown us many helpful things. When they stay overnight they use the empty cabin on the spit. For a time Prof rather fancied that for himself and Rowena, I believe—to have what Cuyler used to call "waterfront property"—but Rowena put her foot down. We keep it up, though, and one of these days will find a use for it, I'm sure. Meanwhile, as I say, the Crees use it when they visit.

The Crees are good neighbors. While it was Martha who showed us how to put chimneys on our cabins so we could heat them and cook indoors—I've already mentioned that—the Crees have passed along all sorts of valuable knowledge that must have come down to them from their ancestors. The first thing they taught us, of course, was how to smoke fish and meat. We don't eat much meat anymore, however. Feeling as we all do that the fawn was sent to us as a messenger, and having made a pet of her since that day, all of us are now more or less vegetarians. And there again the Crees have helped us. We had some seeds, but they gave us others for vegetables that grow better here, and even taught us to use inedible fish parts for fertilizer. And from Martha we have learned how to preserve certain veggies in root cellars. We never go hungry. Having been the wife of a guide and at times his helper, Martha actually knows more about surviving in a wilderness than Cuyler ever did.

So, as I say, the winter was not at all the ordeal we expected. We caught fish through the ice without any trouble. The Crees taught us how to make warm, comfortable clothing from the hides of the few animals we killed. And, in fact, it was never so cold as we had anticipated.

Prof thinks that may be because of a sudden acceleration in the rate of the global warming that has been going on for years now. He thinks that with the druggies taking over the cities and responsible people being unable to function, an increase in the various pollutants causing the global warming was inevitable. Here at Collier, though, we haven't noticed any change in the air we breathe or the water we drink. Perhaps the planet will one day cleanse itself after those who are fouling it have passed on. Surely, by now, there can't be that many smokestacks left to contaminate the air, or that many industries left to poison the earth itself with their waste products.

The truly surprising thing is our health. All of us, without exception, are in much better shape than when we left the city. Prof, especially, looks years younger. Of course, he gives Rowena credit for that, and perhaps she deserves it. They certainly are happy together, and now that Martha and I have had babies here without any trouble—after all, we have a doctor in our midst!—Rowena too is talking about having one. Another child was born last week in the Cree colony at Lake Kelsa. They now have two infants and four other children ranging from three to thirteen years old. I wonder if, in time, some of their children or grandchildren will mate with some of ours. The Kelsa tribe merging with the Colliers, so to speak. That would rewrite history in an interesting way, wouldn't it? The whites intermarrying with native North Americans instead of killing them off. And I wonder if there are not little pockets of survivors elsewhere on earth, living much as we do, intended by Nature to be the nucleus of a new civilization that will take the place of the one presently destroying itself. If that is Nature's intention, we certainly won't let her down by making the same stupid mistakes. I am sure of that.

And so—what else? As I write this on a bright, sunny afternoon in a wilderness cabin that is more home to me than any other I have ever lived in, with my baby in a handsome crib at my side and my man building a chest of drawers outside in the sunshine, I am grateful and happy. I hope, of course, that there are others like us alive and well on Planet Earth, and that in time a new and better civilization will arise from the ashes of the one now dying. But if we and the Crees are the only ones left, so be it. We'll start our own new world.

Quenched

MARY ANN MITCHELL

An evil stalks the clubs and seedy hotels of San Francisco's shadowy underworld. It preys on the unfortunate, the outcasts, the misfits. It is an evil born of the eternal bloodlust of one of the undead, the infamous nobleman known to the ages as . . . the Marquis de Sade. He and his unholy offspring feed upon those who won't be missed, giving full vent to their dark desires and a thirst for blood that can never be sated. Yet while the Marquis amuses himself with the lives of his victims, with their pain and their torture, other vampires—of Sade's own creation—are struggling to adapt to their new lives of eternal night. And as the Marquis will soon learn, hatred and vengeance can be eternal as well—and can lead to terrors even the undead can barely imagine.

___4717-9 $5.50 US/$6.50 CAN

Dorchester Publishing Co., Inc.
P.O. Box 6640
Wayne, PA 19087-8640

DRAWN TO THE GRAVE
MARY ANN MITCHELL

"A tight, taut dark fantasy with surprising plot twists and a lot of spooky atmosphere."
—Ed Gorman

Beverly thinks that she has found something special with Carl, until she realizes that he has stolen from her. But he doesn't just steal her money and her property—he steals her very life. Suddenly she is helpless and alone, able only to watch in growing despair as her flesh begins to decay and each day transforms her more and more into a corpse—a corpse without the release of death.

But Beverly is not truly alone, for Carl is always nearby, watching her and waiting. He knows that soon he will need another unknowing victim, another beautiful woman he can seduce...and destroy. And when lovely young Megan walks into his web, he knows he has found his next lover. For what can possibly go wrong with his plan, a plan he has practiced to perfection so many times before?

___4290-8 $4.99 US/$5.99 CAN

NAILED BY THE HEART
SIMON CLARK

"One of the year's most gripping horror novels . . . Truly terrifying." —*Today* (UK)

The Stainforth family—Chris, Ruth and their young son, David—move into the ancient sea-fort in a nice little coastal town to begin a new life, to start fresh. At the time it seems like the perfect place to do it, so quiet, so secluded. But they have no way of knowing that they've moved into what was once a sacred site of an old religion. And that the old god is not dead—only waiting. Already the god's dark power has begun to spread, changing and polluting all that it touches. A hideous evil pervades the small town. Soon the dead no longer stay dead. When the power awakens the rotting crew of a ship that sank decades earlier, a nightmare of bloodshed and violence begins for the Stainforths, a nightmare that can end only with the ultimate sacrifice—death.

___4713-6 $5.99 US/$6.99 CAN

NIGHT FREIGHT
BILL PRONZINI

"Pronzini makes people and events so real that you are living those explosive days of terror."

—Robert Ludlum

An empty train yard at midnight . . . a small cabin bathed in the light of a full moon . . . a seedy Skid Row hotel in San Francisco . . . These are the places where fear lives, where the chill in the air has nothing to do with the temperature, and where Death can be someone you've already met. Collected here for the first time are twenty-six terrifying stories by Bill Pronzini, a master of dark suspense and horror. These chilling stories span nearly three decades in his award-winning career, and most have never been published before in book form. Prepare yourself now for an unforgettable gift, a very special delivery of . . . night freight.

___4706-3 $5.50 US/$6.50 CAN

Dorchester Publishing Co., Inc.
P.O. Box 6640
Wayne, PA 19087-8640

Please add $1.75 for shipping and handling for the first book and $.50 for each book thereafter. NY, NYC, and PA residents, please add appropriate sales tax. No cash, stamps, or C.O.D.s. All orders shipped within 6 weeks via postal service book rate. Canadian orders require $2.00 extra postage and must be paid in U.S. dollars through a U.S. banking facility.

Name_____

Address_____

City_____State_____Zip_____

I have enclosed $_____ in payment for the checked book(s).

Payment <u>must</u> accompany all orders. ❑ Please send a free catalog.

Cold Blue Midnight

Ed Gorman

In Indiana the condemned die at midnight—killers like Peter Tapley, a twisted man who lives in his mother's shadow and takes his hatred out on trusting young women. Six years after Tapley's execution, his ex-wife Jill is trying to live down his crimes. But somewhere in the chilly nights someone won't let her forget. Someone who still blames her for her husband's hideous deeds. Someone who plans to make her pay . . . in blood.

___4417-X $4.99 US/$5.99 CAN

BARRY HOFFMAN
EYES OF PREY

Lysette has seen it all. As a child, she witnessed her parents' gruesome murder, and as an adult, she sees men leering at her as she works the strip clubs. But that night in the subway, the night she shoots the mugger, she sees something else. She sees the mugger, dying and bleeding, at her feet. And she sees her mission in life. That night, the Nightwatcher is born.

Barry Hoffman burst onto the scene with *Hungry Eyes,* a stunning debut that was nominated for both a Bram Stoker Award and an International Horror Guild Award. Now he takes us even deeper into the world of horror—a world of vengeance and of pity, of the natural and of the supernatural. A world in which the predator can be seen most clearly through the eyes of prey.

___4567-2 $5.50 US/$6.50 CAN